D0129799

At seventeen, Luke Sawyer seems to have just about everything a boy could want—a happy family life, good friends, a budding romance with the most popular girl in town. Sometimes Luke even feels guilty about his good fortune. Yet he has ambiguous fears and uncertainties in his life, much like the capricious fog that so often envelops the small Southern town of Mill Gate. Then, that autumn, everything begins to fall apart. The clubhouse burns down, injuring two friends; he loses his girlfriend and his father dies suddenly. Miserable, worried about his mother and castigating himself for his aimlessness, Luke gropes about for something to hold on to. His emotional fog seems interminable until he begins to realize that he must leave much of his youthful self behind if he is to take on manhood.

MILDRED LEE was born in Alabama and now lives in St. Petersburg, Florida, with her husband and daughter. She is the author of the highly acclaimed novel *The Skating Rink*, also available in a Laurel-Leaf edition.

THE LAUREL-LEAF LIBRARY brings together under a single imprint outstanding works of fiction and non-fiction particularly suitable for young adult readers, both in and out of the classroom. This series is under the editorship of Charles F. Reasoner, Professor of Elementary Education, New York University.

ALSO AVAILABLE IN LAUREL-LEAF BOOKS:

THE SKATING RINK *by Mildred Lee*
PISTOL *by Adrienne Richard*
THE DOLLAR MAN *by Harry Mazer*
GUY LENNY *by Harry Mazer*
SNOW BOUND *by Harry Mazer*
THE WAR ON VILLA STREET *by Harry Mazer*
GARDEN OF BROKEN GLASS *by Emily Cheney Neville*
WONDER WHEELS *by Lee Bennett Hopkins*
A FATHER EVERY FEW YEARS *by Alice Bach*
THE GLAD MAN *by Gloria Gonzalez*

FOG

Mildred Lee

FOR ELEANOR

Published by
Dell Publishing Co., Inc.
1 Dag Hammarskjold Plaza
New York, New York 10017

Text copyright © 1972 by Mildred Lee

All rights reserved. No part of this book may be reproduced in any form, except for brief extracts in reviews, without the written permission of The Seabury Press, Inc., New York, New York 10017.

Laurel-Leaf Library ® TM 766734, Dell Publishing Co., Inc.

ISBN: 0-440-93133-9

Reprinted by arrangement with The Seabury Press, Inc.

Printed in the United States of America

First Laurel printing—January 1974
Second Laurel printing—December 1974
Third Laurel printing—May 1976
Fourth Laurel printing—August 1977
Fifth Laurel printing—August 1979

ONE

The other three were there when Luke and Sim arrived at the hut. Dim yellow light flickered against the two windows, throwing a huge shadow against the wall. Luke knew the shadow had to be Butch's. He scratched softly on the door and Butch's voice rumbled, "Mice or men?"

"Men," Luke answered and Sim echoed, "Men."

The door creaked open and they went in. Warm air, high with the scent of kerosene from the old portable heater in the middle of the room, welcomed them. Luke closed the door behind him and the candle flames jittered, then settled to a normal flickering.

Butch jerked his shaggy red head in greeting, Chuck raised a hand, and Rollo smiled. Luke set the brown paper bag he was carrying on the table.

"How come you guys are late?" Butch demanded as little Sim spread thin hands above the perforations in the rusty top of the heater.

"Couldn't make it sooner," Luke said. He saw no reason to explain that he had been detained by one of his father's rare lectures, though he knew Butch or Chuck would not have hesitated to do so. He folded his lanky height into a corner of the ratty old sofa. Broken springs jangled as the end of the sofa settled on its artificial leg of three cinder bricks.

Chuck padded over the chilly floor on bare feet to peer into the brown bag.

"Store cookies. Jeez, no brownies even?"

"Fresh out," Luke said, kicking his scuffed loafers off and wriggling his toes. He would have been more comfortable with his shoes on but no one wore shoes in the clubhouse. It was past the middle of November and nights were cold, especially down here by the river with the fog pressing at the hut windows and creeping in at the cracks of walls and floor. Luke saw little Sim fumbling with the laces of his sneakers, his fingers clumsy with the cold.

"What's on the agenda?" Rollo asked, his face the color of fine mahogany in the candlelight. Luke thought, startled, that it was beautiful. He wondered how a mug like Rollo's could look beautiful at a certain angle, in a certain light. Could all of them—not just Chuck who was beautiful because God made him that way—appear so, given the right lights and shadows?

"Cookies don't go so good with beer," Rollo observed mildly. "Huh, Butch?" And Luke said, "Brownies wouldn't either," adding in Rollo's voice, "Huh, Butch?"

"Well, it don't make a helluva lot of difference," Butch drawled, "seeing we haven't got any beer. My old man beat me to the refrigerator. As usual."

Chuck groaned, Rollo slapped his leg bound by tight jeans, Sim giggled.

Luke puckered his face, pulling his lips across his teeth so that not one showed, wagged his chin, and bent forward to blink and peer painfully so that even his eyes looked filmy with age. The boys howled, Butch louder than any of them.

"Do some more," Sim pleaded when the laughter had subsided. "Come on, Luke. Do Mr. Penson. Like when he caught Butch with the chew of tobacco in his jaw!"

"Yeh yeh yeh," Chuck urged in a sort of chant. "Do Penson, Luke," and Butch shrugged benignly, as one granting permission.

Luke relaxed the muscles of his face, passed his hand across it like a magician and the old man vanished. He leaned back and closed his eyes, a furrow gathering between his sandy brows under the ragged thatch of his sandy hair.

"Come on, Luke," Rollo prodded, but Sim hissed him to silence. "He's got to *call him up,* see," he whispered, his eyes brilliant behind the thick lenses of his glasses.

They sat quiet, their expectant gaze on Luke. The marvel of it gripped them as if it were the first time they had seen it—the subtle shifting and transformation of plain old Luke Sawyer into someone else. They could see the pointed beard his bony hand caressed, though actually Luke managed only a shave or two a week. They watched as he rose and began to pace the floor with a measured, heavy tread that jostled the candles and caused the kerosene heater to sputter in protest.

The pacing figure wheeled, pointed, shouted, "You! Boyle!" and Butch actually jumped. "You will relieve yourself of that disgusting impediment to your speech. *Imm*-ediately!" Only the slight break in Luke's voice on the last word betrayed it as Luke Sawyer's and not that of Mr. Penson, their physics teacher.

Next, they demanded Reverend Winterbligh, the old preacher who appeared in Mill Gate every summer and called himself the "man of God." He was very old and approaching senility, but the women of Mill Gate saw to it that he had enough to eat during the two weeks of his brush arbor revival. He would not accept shelter, claiming he could not sleep under a house roof, preferring God's sky. People said he must move into the arbor when one of the violent thunderstorms of August came up in the night, but no one knew for sure. It was a popular pastime of the young to drive out to the brush arbor beyond the old mill and listen from their cars to the singing and shouting and talking in tongues.

Luke clawed his thick hair into a semblance of the mad old preacher's scanty white strands, managed to give the illusion of dark hollows under his eyes, and faithfully reproduced the sepulchral whispers into which the cracked old voice would fall after each bellowing threat of eternal damnation. Not for the world would he have had his flattering audience suspect that he always experienced a nibble of guilt when he imitated Reverend Winterbligh. He did admit to Sim once that his dad would "skin him alive" if he caught him mocking an old coot half off his rocker, and showing disrespect for anybody's religion into the bargain. The clubhouse was a place where you could do what you couldn't get away with at home.

"Man, oh man," Rollo said. "You oughta be on the stage somewheres, Luke, or on TV raking in the dough."

Luke wouldn't do any more, though they clamored like a bunch of kids at a puppet show.

"I'm pooped," he said, throwing himself on the sofa. "Let somebody else make an ass out of himself for a change."

Chuck went back to the earlier grievance. "Too bad we haven't got any beer. Couldn't anybody swipe any? I brought it the last two times."

Butch began, "I told you my old man—" and Chuck finished for him, "beat you to the fridge. Yeh yeh yeh, too bad. You, Luke?"

Luke shrugged. "It was like the brownies. Fresh out. Else they hid it on me."

"My mama don't indulge in any kind of alcoholic beverage," Rollo said, pursing his mouth. "And my daddy can't on account of his job. Make a helluva fine night watchman half-stoned, wouldn't he?"

Sim giggled and Chuck turned to him, half teasing, half sly. "How 'bout you, Sim?"

"Yeh, how about that, Simmons?" Butch thrust his wide shoulders forward belligerently.

Sim started to stammer, his pinched face reddening, "I-I-"

Luke felt himself starting to get tense. He didn't want to take the kid's part all the time; to tell the truth he was sick and tired of it, sick of Craig himself sometimes. But it bugged him like crazy for Butch to pick on Sim. Butch was twice the kid's size and three years older; Sim was only fifteen and looked about twelve.

"Who needs beer?" Luke said, looking dreamily at the wall. "I'd just as soon have a Coke. Sim brought two six-packs last time."

Butch groaned, stretched his long legs in front of him and took a sad-looking pack of cigarettes from his pocket. He passed it around the circle and only Chuck (whose father was a doctor and had laid the law down too grimly about cancer) took one.

Sim scuttled over to the cupboard and brought the Cokes out eagerly, his fingers clutched around the necks of the bottles. His feet looked blue-white under the fringed bottoms of his jeans.

"If you'd of brought cans," Butch grumbled, "we could of at least pretended like it was something else, huh, Rollo?"

"How about we shoot some crap?" Rollo said, his Afro shadowed large on the wall behind him.

"That's all we ever shoot around here, you ask me," Chuck said mildly, his usual sunny disposition apparently restored by one long swig of Coca-Cola.

Butch breathed a four-letter word but without venom. Nobody was in a hurry to begin the game and they continued to sit, relaxed and peaceful, in the kerosene-tainted warmth of the hut.

The hut had been Sim's discovery. His secret place. He had found it on one of his solitary walks in those first solitary weeks after his mother brought him "home" to his grandparents' house next door to the Sawyers' on River Street. He was twelve then, with a mind that forced him into an age group at school his frail, undersized body could not cope with. All that first year the Mill Gate kids called him a "loner" and a "brain," and any hope he'd ever entertained of getting "in" died almost as soon as it was born. Then Luke Sawyer, unable to get around his mother's insistence any longer, began to tolerate the kid out of school hours and Craig gave up his walking in the woods alone, told Luke about the hut and took him to see it.

By that time Craig Simmons was thirteen and Luke fifteen. Craig had grown scarcely at all in the year he'd lived in Mill Gate, while Luke had run up like a string bean, growing out of his clothes almost as fast as his mother could buy them.

"Gosh almighty," Luke breathed, following Craig through the narrow tunnel in the blackberry and wild plum thicket leading to the door of the hidden shack. "All the times I've fooled around in these woods and never even knew it was here! And you smelled it out in no time. I better get *me* some glasses!"

Craig glowed with happiness. Not only from Luke's

admiration but from being called "Sim"; Craig was a sissy name and he'd hated it a long time. On the way home, scuffing along the path beside the river that day, Luke had said, "Look, Sim. You know those guys I hang around with, Chuck Holland and Rollo Prince and Butch Boyle?"

Sim nodded.

"Well. We been chewing on an idea—it's Butch's idea actually—of getting up a sort of a club. Like calling ourselves something-or-other, getting together, yacking, playing a little poker, stuff like that. Well, we never got off the ground with it on account of having no place to meet. Nothing like private. You know?"

Luke sidled a glance at Craig and kicked a stone in the path, his thin shoulders far above Craig's pale head. "I wouldn't want to horn in on anything special of yours, but if you wanted to share your hut for a clubhouse . . . Naturally," he added quickly, talking fast to cover the faint tinge of shame at his opportunism, "you'd be a member of the club. I could fix it with Butch. Clarence is his real name. Never think it, would you, a guy like him? Clarence Boyle, Junior!"

Luke stooped and picked up the stone, rubbing his fingers over it to free it from sand. He could feel Craig looking as he dropped it into his pocket. Craig had showed Luke his rock collection in a plastic shoe box he kept under his bed.

"How about it, Sim? Don't get me wrong. I'm not twisting your arm. It's up to you."

"Sure, Luke," Craig answered, not needing to give the matter any consideration. "Sure I'd be willing." His adoration was embarrassing. Luke was ashamed to look at him. I'd like to share it, Luke, only—"

"Only what?"

"Well, Butch—Clarence Boyle." Craig's nervous giggle always irritated Luke. "I—I don't think he likes me very much."

Luke swaggered a little. "If that's all you're worried about, forget it. I can handle Butch. Besides, he's O.K. when you get to know him. Will it be all right if—if we bring the other guys to have a look?"

"Oh, sure, Luke." Craig's voice positively trembled.

Luke's father, getting wind of the plans, told Luke he was not to be any part of a gang of boys using the shack for meetings without permission from its owner. Henry Sawyer was the mildest of men but there was a firm note in his voice that Luke knew there'd be no getting around.

"Aw heck, Dad. I bet nobody knows who owns it. It's just a crummy old shack. Sooner or later, come a storm, it'll blow into the river or just cave in and fall down all by itself, you wait and see."

But Henry Sawyer, as Luke had known he would, held firm. It was this quiet, usually justified determination of his father's that most infuriated Luke. You always knew he was going to turn out to be right. Luke had sunk into sulky frustration to which Henry appeared to pay no attention when he startled Luke by speaking.

"Seems to me," he said thoughtfully between puffs on his pipe, "all that land round there belongs to old man Ben Tandy. I know it did one time. I'll see him soon's I can, Son, and find out."

Luke had felt compelled to adjust his father's ultimatum a little so the gang wouldn't see how square his dad could be.

"We got to have it legal," he had pointed out, looking sharp as if it were his own idea. "Otherwise we're liable to get thrown out on our cans soon as some old busy-

12

body finds out we're having a little fun. You know how it is." Looking at Luke with something like respect, the boys had agreed that they did. "My dad says he'll ask around."

They hadn't long to wait. Henry Sawyer came home from the hardware store where he had clerked since his high school days and reported to Luke that the property did belong to Mr. Ben Tandy.

"He says some poor devil slung the hut together during the Depression. Old Ben never had the heart to make him move out—just let him squat there. He says you boys are welcome to use it for your meetings, long as you're careful and behave yourselves." Henry gave Luke a level blue glance, serious but trusting. "I don't know about that old stove in the garage your mother said you could have. Be sure you give it a thorough testing before you take it over there."

So the boys had hauled their spoils in Chuck Holland's secondhand car—an eight-year-old Chevy—to the hut and moved in. They were jubilant over all they had collected. Martha Sawyer added a bookcase with a crack across one of its glass doors to the kerosene heater. Sim's grandmother donated three lumpy cushions and two straight chairs. ("You shouldn't have to bring anything," Luke had protested to Sim, "because actually the hut's yours.") Butch Boyle's contribution of a sofa with only one missing leg (broken springs hardly counted as the boys were not overparticular about details) wouldn't go into the trunk of Chuck's car, and Luke's father hauled it over in the hardware store's pickup along with a delivery out River Street. Rollo's mother brought herself to part with a metal table she put her ferns on when the weather turned cold and she had to bring them in the house (Rollo had persuaded her they'd look better lined up against the

13

wall in the dining room anyway). Chuck brought a couple of good-as-new braided rugs his mother had taken out of his sister Esme's room when she had it done over and newly carpeted. At the last minute, Luke and Sim brought an armload each of dog-eared soft-cover books—science fiction, mysteries, and even a stray classic or two Sim had added "just to fill up space" on the bookshelves.

Butch eyed the books coldly. "All this reading matter must be for Simmons in case we run out of couth and culture, huh?"

"O.K., Clarence." Luke used the name deliberately and with malice aforethought, yet not without apprehension. He was nearly as tall as Butch but not nearly as well-fleshed. "Whose place was it to start with? We wouldn't have a clubhouse yet if Sim hadn't found the hut and said we could use it. What's wrong with a few books around the joint?" Having got this far, Luke thought he might as well finish the job. "Matter of fact, I'm the one thought of it." He pulled a grease-spotted edition of *Tom Sawyer* from the shelf and flipped the pages with a flourish. "What's a bookcase without books in it?"

Butch mumbled something about using the shelves for groceries, then never referred to the bookcase or its contents again. He had been bitterly opposed to including Craig Simmons ("that little white-headed, bug-eyed punk") in the Mice-or-Men Club. Rollo had partially pacified him by pointing out—not in Sim's presence—that maybe there ought to be one mouse to give meaning to the name Luke had suggested as a joke to begin with.

It was almost eleven when the meeting broke up. Luke squatted beside the heater to watch its last feeble tongue of flame flutter round the wick. They pinched out the candle flames and put the padlock (to which each of the five boys carried a key) on the door. It was a rule that any member was entitled to come to the clubhouse at any time so long as he brought no outsider with him.

Fog swirled in thick, yellowish clouds just above the ground and the splash and gurgle of water was all that told them where the river was. Luke had the feeling —exciting and spooky—of walking through clouds. As if he'd stepped out of an airplane. They groped their way along the path, their flashlights making pale smears of weak light in the thick mist. Butch stumbled over a root and released an impressive stream of obscenities. Sim sneezed and Luke whistled, softly and steadily, under his breath, letting his feet serve for eyes.

They left the path and came out into River Street where the sidewalk, such as it was, began.

"Who-all wants to ride?" Chuck offered, his teeth chattering. "Jesus, it's cold! Bet it's gonna freeze before morning."

"Nah." Rollo was scornful in spite of his own shivering. "It just feels like that down here on account of the river. Haven't you noticed when you break outa the fog it's a heap warmer?"

"Y'all wanta ride?" Chuck asked again.

"Whereabouts you leave your car?" Rollo asked.

"Up the street a step or two."

"Well, I reckon I could be home about as quick as you'd get her started," Rollo teased.

Luke said he'd keep Rollo company. "Wouldn't get settled before I'd have to climb out," and Sim chattered, "M-me, too, Ch-Chuck, thanks just the same."

"I'll ride with you, Chucky," Butch conceded. He had the farthest to go but made it sound like a preference for Chuck's company.

Rollo's laugh emerged from the turtle-necked sweater drawn up to his chin. "You gonna push if he can't get 'er started?"

Butch's reply was brief and typical. Chuck began beating his pockets for his always elusive key. The car squatted at the curb under an ancient and mighty oak tree, barely to be made out through the veil of mist. Street lights had rings of vapor about them, but farther up the slope the scattered houses stood almost clear of the fog.

Luke and Rollo called, "See ya, men," and Sim sneezed again.

"What'd I tell you?" Rollo crowed as sounds of the laboring starter struggled from the old car. "Hope old Butch is in good shape to push him off. You catching a cold, Simmy?"

"Nah," Sim sniffed. "It's just my allergy."

"Who you allergic to, Luke or me?"

"Fog, I guess. I hate it," and another sneeze racked Sim.

Behind them the car wheezed to an uncertain start, followed by a mighty roaring as Chuck revved the motor for all he was worth.

"Aw hell," Rollo breathed sadly, "Butch ain't going to have to push."

"When it takes a notion to run it's not such a bad car," Luke defended the old Chevy. "Anyhow, Chuck doesn't have to ask for it. That's something I purely hate to do. You know?" Old resentment flared in his memory; his father had grounded him for a solid week because he'd flunked a physics test earlier in the school year. Maybe that had been the beginning of the thing between them, the distance neither of them seemed to know how to bridge.

"Aw, I just get a kick out of bugging Butch," Rollo said, amiably. "Give him some of his own medicine once in a while, right?"

Luke said, "Right," and Sim blew his nose loudly.

Chuck's car roared past, spitting and coughing, horn beeping and Butch adding a raucous "Yoweeee." Fumes from the exhaust rolled back to mingle with the fog and Luke said, "When it comes to doing its bit for pollution that vehicle's no piker."

At the Prince house Rollo said, "I sure hope my mama is asleep. She's taken to asking me too damn many questions lately."

"Yeah," Luke sighed. "I know what you mean. You get a break, though, your dad not being home to help ask 'em." Rollo's father's job of watchman at the sheeting factory across the river kept him away five nights a week.

"Why would they ask questions about just a club meeting?" Sim wondered aloud. It was that dumb innocent way he had that annoyed all the boys.

Rollo fumbled at the latch on the latticed gate. From the street they could see the dimly lighted hall of the Princes' little house. Rollo would not turn it out; it burned all night because Aletha Prince was afraid. The Princes had lived on River Street three years, but Aletha could not get over her fear of being molested by Mill Gate whites.

As the gate whined open, Rollo said in a loud, hoarse whisper, "See you guys round if you don't turn square."

The big house next to the Princes' was vacant. It had belonged to Mr. P. G. Conway, a retired banker who, according to Henry Sawyer, "didn't know the war between the states was over." Mr. Conway had taken it as a personal insult that the properties adjoining his had been sold to blacks. He had moved to Florida where he would doubtless live out his days in bitterness toward the changing world.

River Street, just across the river from the all-black section in Sandy Hollow, marked the timid beginning of open housing in Mill Gate. Some whites, like Mr. Conway, had pulled up stakes and left but most had stayed on. Luke had heard Mrs. Mountjoy, Sim's grandmother, worrying to Martha Sawyer that the neighborhood was "going down."

"Oh, I don't think so," Luke's mother had answered. "Seems to me it's the other way round. The Hollow's moving up. About time, too."

It wasn't long after that that the Mountjoys' daughter Linda got her divorce and came back to Mill Gate with her son Craig. Martha said at supper, "Hilda says it's a blessing she and Karl changed their minds about selling and going into one of those new apartments across town. They wouldn't have had room for Linda and Craig."

Henry Sawyer had cocked an eyebrow and said, "What makes you look like a cat that's been at the cream pitcher, Marty?" Luke had laughed, remembering the overheard conversation between his mother and Mrs. Mountjoy.

"Spooky old place," Sim remarked of the Conway house, set in a dark grove of sycamore trees. He hunched his spare shoulders. "I don't blame Rollo's mother for being scared."

But the vacant house was behind them now and they looked at the big square of window where light filtered softly through rose-colored draperies in the Weavers' living room. Mr. Weaver was principal of Bailey Junior High which had been an all-Negro school before en-

18

forced busing. His serious-minded daughter Arlene was in Luke's class.

"Old Rollo's trying to work up the nerve to ask Arlene to go steady," Luke said, laughing a little. "I don't blame him for being nervous. He's lucky to get a date with her, she's so independent."

Sim wasn't one to give out much on the subject of girls, Luke knew. He'd been the same at Sim's age. Now that he and Milo Tarrant were going steady, though, it was all different.

At the Mountjoy house one upstairs window glowed against the night. Sim said, "My mother's still reading. Says she can't go to sleep till I'm in. Don't they ever want their kids to grow up?"

"Guess not," Luke said. " 'Night, Sim. See you round."

"See you round, Luke."

Watch, the Sawyers' ten-year-old sheep dog waddled down the brick walk to greet Luke. Little whines of pleasure escaped him as Luke stooped to fondle his rough head.

"Hello, old boy. Hi, you old dog, you." Then, "Down, Watch. Down, boy," as ecstatic paws pushed against his legs.

The living room window curtains had not been drawn and Luke stopped on the porch to look in at his parents. Watch sat beside him, thumping his tail against the floor boards. Luke's father was raking the wooden squares of the scrabble game from the card table into a box. His profile sagged. If he was a fat man, Luke thought, he'd have a double chin. Funny to think of his parents getting old. But they would; the time wasn't that far away either, considering they'd been pretty old when they'd had him.

Luke wondered what sort of entry he should make. Should he ignore the way he slammed out of the house a few hours ago, every nerve bristling at his father's wrapping up of the heated discussion that had been going on over the poor record Luke was making at school.

"I want the best for you, Son."

Why did he have to say *Son* in that reasonable, *fatherly* kind of way? Why couldn't he call Luke a big dumb ox or a blithering jackass? Why couldn't he yell when he was mad! Like Dr. Bob Holland, Chuck's dad, or even Clarence Boyle, Senior, who was always getting drunk and threatening to belt his kids—except Butch who had got too big and jeered right back at the old man, or so he said.

Luke scratched behind Watch's ear, stalling a little longer, then opened the door and called, as if he were in a very good mood, "I'm home, you lucky people."

He hung his jacket in the coat closet and ambled into the living room as if nothing had happened. He wasn't going to sulk; Henry never did. "Who won?"

Henry Sawyer snapped the rubber band around the beat-up old box that held the game, his blue eyes twinkling. "Modesty forbids," he murmured, pretending humility.

Luke went over to the fireplace and Watch padded after him, settling near the hearth where bits of wood were graying to ash.

"Why don't you beat the stuffing out of him, Ma?"

"I can't," Martha grumbled. "He's too lucky—and then calls it skill!"

"Yeh yeh yeh, I know." He grinned at his father and Henry looked pleased. "Well. Guess I'll sack in. Night, Ma, Dad."

Watch groaned softly, struggling up to follow. Luke

had to help him a little, going up the narrow stairs to his room in the upper half story of the house. Old Watch's fat body was almost too much for his skinny, rheumatic legs. "You're gonna have to start sleeping downstairs, old fella," he told the dog. "I'm not about to lug you up like a puppy for goshsakes."

He had meant to think about Milo tonight. But when he'd put his light out and clasped his hands behind his head it was his father who occupied his thoughts. Why had he started bugging Luke about making good at school? Oh sure, it was next to his last year and his father had always taken it for granted Luke would go to college. But Luke wasn't that sure he wanted to.

Henry Sawyer himself hadn't been able to manage more than a high school education and Luke couldn't believe he'd ever regretted marrying Martha Clement right after graduation, even though it meant working for that old skinflint Thad Wilson forevermore. As a matter of fact, Henry didn't seem to mind that at all, took a sort of crazy pride in the business, as if it were his own! Who was he to plan Luke's life for him? Surely he couldn't think Luke would do worse—slaving away at a piddling little wage, saving against the rainy day he always feared, always cautious because he had to be, not because it was his nature.

Luke turned restlessly. He knew how lucky he was compared with Butch and Sim—knew it as well as they did. It was only since he'd got to Mill Gate High that his dad had started stewing about Luke's "applying himself," "realizing his potential"—stuff like that. You'd think he was one of the cotton-picking teachers when he got going—which wasn't often, Luke had to admit. But he didn't want anybody on his back. Not any time. Especially his father. He thought sourly, I guess I'm a disappointment to him. Too bad I came along so late.

The girls never gave him anything to worry about, not in school anyhow.

What did his father expect anyway? A brain like old Sim? A lawyer like Anita's husband, that stuffed shirt Euclid? A doctor? Teacher? Somebody with a string of degrees a yard long? Forget it. Luke wondered what Henry Sawyer's face would look like if he were to come right out with the truth—tell him he'd like to do impersonations. Professionally. Well, he'd never told anyone. Not his mother or his sister Anita or his girl Milo —and he certainly wasn't about to tell his father.

The quarrel—if you could call it that—tonight had been different, though, and Luke knew why. It was that look in his father's eyes—a look he might have seen but had never to his knowledge caused before. A hurt that seemed to leap from the kind blue depths of Henry Sawyer's eyes straight at Luke. All the words, his father's and his own, came back to Luke now as from a tape recorder.

"I can't figure you out," Henry had said, pushing both hands over his face, as if he were trying to wipe his puzzlement away. "You've got good sense—I think! Why won't you use it? I may not always be here to keep a roof over your head and food in your belly. You used to do all right in grade school. Now you're old enough to buckle down and start making something out of yourself, all you care about's playing around with that gang of yours. I'm not talking about your girl friend. Milo Tarrant's a nice, pretty, sweet little girl and you're lucky to have her. But that Boyle kid—I don't know. I worry about him. One thing's for sure: he's nobody to model after."

Luke had flared at that.

"I don't listen to anybody cutting my friends down.

22

Butch talks rough—who doesn't?—and he may not be exactly out of the top drawer. But he's my friend just the same. Like Rollo and Chuck and Sim."

Henry said, patiently, "I don't mean the boy's language—not that I go for it or mean to listen to it in this house. It's his attitude, I guess. I want the best for you, Son."

"Why?"

Luke knew he'd blown it the moment the insolent word was out. That was when the pain had leapt from Henry's eyes to Luke. The little word was so loaded. With Henry's own failures and insecurities.

Luke would have taken it back if he could; he didn't mean it, didn't mean to cut his father down. He couldn't even say he was sorry, burned by anger and wounded dignity as he was. Leave it. Forget it. He had slammed out of the house and walked round the block to cool down before stopping for Sim and going on to the clubhouse.

If it had been his mother, Luke thought, there'd have been no problem. He'd have told her he was sorry, given her a quick hug, and everything would be O.K. Fathers were different somehow. Luke didn't understand the awkwardness that built up between a man and his son. There were so many things he didn't understand and they had a way of appearing lately, to hang him up. What the hell? It was the same with all of his friends, worse with most.

He propped himself on an elbow to look out the window. The fog was more dense than when they'd left the hut. Street lights glimmered dully through it, the windowsill was beaded with moisture along the inch-wide opening. Tomorrow it would burn off, the sun would come out, and everything would be better. He would

23

take Milo out and maybe do some little thing for his dad—like go by the store on his lunch break and come home to eat with him instead of having a hamburger at Syd's. That would look pretty obvious, though. Better to let it go. Kinder to both of them just to forget it.

TWO

Luke didn't know exactly when he had stopped looking forward with pleasure to the family gathering at Thanksgiving. It had slipped up on him somewhere along with his teens and now seemed long ago. He loved his sisters, of course. (When had he started tacking the "of course" on?) He loved them. Period. Especially Anita, the older one. She'd been a second mother to him when he was a kid. He guessed it was only natural with the difference in their ages. Eighteen years. He could have been her kid! And there were thirteen years between him and Edith.

Anita was the one he rushed to for comfort when he skinned his knees or his mother spanked him. He always got the greater part of the chocolates Anita's boy friends gave her and when she married Euclid Pierce, Luke bore the rings on a sissy satin pillow down the church aisle—though he had balked flatly ten minutes before. He was three and a half at the time, with a mop of sandy curls and a string of freckles across the bridge of his nose that was already shaping up like Henry Sawyer's beak. It made Luke blush to recall that procession or glance by accident at the picture in Anita's elegant living room in Baysboro.

His sister Edith's elopement two years later with Mike Donaldson now seemed to Luke a much more sensible arrangement, in spite of his mother's frantic tears at the time and his father's floor pacing. Luke preferred Mike to Euclid by a long shot. Mike had been a high school dropout but was now a skilled mechanic with a half interest in Jones and Donaldson's Garage in East Mill Gate.

This year, Luke could see that his father shared his reluctance to face the family reunion.

"It's your mother," Henry said. "Year after year she takes on this big deal. To tell the truth, they'd probably rather go out and eat at a fancy restaurant. It's just a habit we've got into, that's all."

"Why don't you tell Mom to skip it then?" Luke said. "She would if you said so."

"Maybe that's why I don't," Henry sighed. "It's dear to her, all that nonsense. She's sentimental about all of you kids, or thinks she ought to be."

"I guess women are like that," Luke said.

Henry flashed him a quick look, then looked down at the pipe he was filling. "It's good to see the grandchildren. And good to see them go." He shook with brief, soundless laughter, then sobered. "Your mother and I are getting on. No sense trying to dodge facts. Older and set in our ways. Used to just the three of us here in the old house."

Luke was beginning to feel uneasy; he hoped his old man wasn't going to launch into a heart-to-heart. But Henry added with his crooked smile, "That shake you up a little?"

"Heck no, Dad. Those kids take *me* apart in about thirty minutes."

There was a little silence, then Henry said, "Not Sylvy. Never Sylvy."

Sylvy was Anita and Euclid's ten-year-old daughter. She was gentle and beautiful and doomed to wander in her strange little private world. For a while Anita had watched her ride away in the orange bus to the school for "Exceptional Children," but it hadn't worked out as they had hoped and they had kept her at home.

"She is so much company," Anita told Martha Sawyer. "I am—bereft without her."

Sometimes, right out of the blue, those words of his sister's came to Luke. When he wasn't thinking of Anita or Sylvy or anything in particular they just popped into his head. He would see his sister's face, with the flawless complexion other girls—especially Edith—used to envy, drawn tight over the cheekbones and her brown eyes too bright with tears she wouldn't let fall. *I am bereft without her.* Then Luke would feel a sort of helpless rage boil up in him. It was crazy, one of those crazy, screwed-up things. Look at Anita, look at old Euclid for that matter. He was a smart guy even if he was sort of a pompous ass. And for Anita everything had to be just so, just right. So their first kid wasn't right in her head. God must have had a good laugh at that one.

Martha Sawyer cooked for three days before Thanksgiving.

"Enough for an army," Henry grumbled, eating his grilled cheese sandwich at the kitchen table while the scent of roast turkey, creamed onions, and boiling cranberries filled the house. Luke thought he could taste it, seeping through his pores. His sandwich was two thick slices of home-baked bread with a round of Spanish onion, lettuce, and green tomato pickle between.

"I hope you're not taking Milo out after *that,*" his mother said.

"Milo's no sissy," Henry said. "She can take 'em nitty-gritty. Right, Luke?" Maybe he imagined it, but it seemed to Luke his father was bending over backward lately in a sort of man-to-man attitude.

Luke mumbled, "Right," over a mouthful and slid his cup toward the percolator in Martha's hand. He had only this year begun to drink coffee and didn't like it very much yet, but thought it was time to cultivate a taste for it.

Anita, Euclid, and the three children came from Baysboro on Wednesday. The early dusk was falling and fog had begun to creep up from the river. Euclid's big car crunched the gravel of the driveway under its tires, came to rest under the oak whose branches nearly touched the roof of the house on one side and extended over the garage roof on the other.

"You're not to think about supper for us, Mother," Anita had said over the phone the day before. "The children will want to stop for hamburgers."

The little boys, Clement and John, spilled out of the car and Euclid led Sylvy forward. Luke saw his mother stoop and clasp the child tightly to her. It had never seemed strange to him that Sylvy was their favorite grandchild—as if their love could make up for what she had been denied. Now his father was hugging her, stroking her pale hair back from her brow and temples where threadlike blue veins showed through the delicate skin. He could hear her humming one of the little tunes she composed, thin and minor and sweet. Luke shivered, suddenly aware of the damp chill sneaking up from the river. He heard his father saying over the silky top of the little girl's head, "Come in out of the cold, come in."

In the too-warm house sweaters and jackets were peeled off, Anita ordering the boys to put theirs where they belonged. "Daddy will hang them up if you can't reach the hooks."

"I can," Clement piped indignantly. "I can reach."

Luke, thinking back to eight, understood Clem's wounded pride. Anita was wailing, "Oh, Johnny, look

28

at the mud you've tracked onto Gram's rug! Everything's so *spotless,* Mother. I'm afraid you've worn yourself out—"

On and on it went. Luke was relieved when his mother asked him to call and tell Edith the Pierces were here. "They're coming over, too, of course."

Luke eased the door of the little closet under the stairs to, shutting himself in with the telephone. Like a public booth. The closed door muted the sounds in the living room, though the light winked at the vibration of the boys' feet thumping en route to the bathroom.

"They're here," Luke said when Edith's harassed voice answered. "Sounds like a thousand of 'em."

Edith giggled. "Luke, you're terrible. We'll be over just as soon as I can finish the dishes. Is Nita still gaining weight?" Luke remembered people used to say, "Anita has the pretty face but Edith's figure is lovely."

"I didn't notice," Luke said.

"Oh, you wouldn't! O.K. Thanks for calling."

Luke hung up and sat a moment, wondering if he should maybe call Milo. Just to hear her voice . . . The stairs began to shake under the pounding of feet; those kids going up to meddle in his room? He sighed and emerged.

Anita looked as slim as ever to him. Must be Edie's wishful thinking that she was gaining weight. Old Euclid was starting a slight paunch, though, and his hair was thinning fast. Luke could see a small area of pink scalp where the light shone through the carefully arranged locks. Euclid was leaning forward, talking to Henry Sawyer.

"This case coming up would interest you, Henry—" He fitted the tips of his fingers together, making like a lawyer.

". . . something to do with the way they teach reading now," Anita was saying to Martha. "And *arithmetic,* Mother! I don't understand this new math at all. I don't believe I could even do Clem's homework."

Sylvy stood beside the clumsy, old-fashioned combination radio-and-record player Martha had refused to junk when they bought the television set. Luke's father had given her the radio phonograph the Christmas before Anita was born and Martha was sentimental about it. Sylvy stroked the satiny wood, touched a knob uncertainly.

"She wants some music," Martha said, looking from Anita's earnest face to her granddaughter's.

"Oh, not now, Mama. Not in here where we're talking. You know we try not to spoil her. We really do try."

"I'll take her up to my room," Luke offered, surprising himself. "There's a player up there." He heard the boys stomping down and hoped they hadn't wrecked anything.

Anita laughed. "Heavens, Luke! *Your* kind of music? My daughter's taste may be influenced beyond repair. It's sweet of you, though, darling."

"Now, Nita, Luke has very good taste himself," Martha protested. "He's got some lovely symphony records. Some nice folk music, too, that I really enjoy. He doesn't play just rock all the time." She gave Luke a warm smile as he crossed the room and took Sylvy's hand.

"Mom, me and Johnny want to go outside. I can reach down our jackets." Leading Sylvy toward the stairs, Luke heard Anita's "No, Clem. It's dark and cold out there" backed up by Euclid's "You heard your mother" and Henry's mild "Seems to me there ought to be some games in the den, boys, way back in my desk."

30

Sylvy's passive little hand lay cool and soft in Luke's big one, her fingers so tiny-boned he would have been afraid to close his hand tightly. He looked down at her smiling face tilted to his. His eyes searched her gaze, halting at the great dark pupils ringed with deep blue.

She's all scrambled up in her head, Luke thought, and for the first time he was sure he felt his parents' and Anita's and Euclid's sorrow. He had always accepted her difference; after all, he'd been no older than Johnny when Sylvy was born. Now, sharp and sudden, the pain of it hit him. He remembered something he had heard his mother say to his father a long time ago: "What people don't realize is that even a thing like this has compensations. Anita will keep this child. She'll always be needed by her." Then she had begun to weep, and the child Luke had listened to his father trying to comfort her until he couldn't bear it anymore and had run outdoors and shut it out of his mind till now.

He dug some old records from the bottom shelf of his cabinet, childhood ones, badly scratched and worn. He allowed Sylvy to manipulate the player herself, pleased but not surprised at how well she did it. Anita had always said, "She's awfully good with her hands. Her coordination's awfully good." He began to feel peaceful and happy, closeted in his little room under the sloping roof with the little girl who would never grow up. With only the edge of his mind he knew when Edith's family arrived.

After a long or a little while, he didn't know which, Anita tapped at the door and thrust her golden head in.

"We're going to have coffee and cake. Don't you want to come down? Sylvy, Aunt Edie wants to see you." She turned again to Luke. "Thanks, Luke dear. I know she's had a wonderful time."

"Me, too," Luke said. He winked at Sylvy but she wasn't looking at him. Anita moved her head toward Luke's chest of drawers.

"Is that Milo Tarrant?"

"Yep." Luke fiddled with the arm of the record player as if something was wrong with it.

"Imagine," Anita breathed. "I don't believe I've seen her for years. She's grown into a pretty young lady, little Milo Tarrant."

"She's still little," Luke said, flinging his hair out of his eyes.

"And you're so tall. I can't believe my little brother's actually courting a girl!"

Little brother! Courting! Wouldn't you know she'd have to go and crap it up with something like that? But he closed the record player and followed Anita down the stairs.

It was noisier than before. Edith's two sons, Steve and Michael, seemed determined to outshout Clem and John in disagreement over the game. The shrill voices pierced the wall dividing the living room and den. Suddenly there was a crash, followed by silence more shattering than the noise.

"Now what was that?" Martha gasped, setting her tray of cups on the table beside the brass-bowled lamp with the beaded shade. It had burned kerosene in Martha's grandmother's day and Henry had wired it for electricity.

"Ceiling coming down, I imagine," Luke murmured. Silence still reigned in the other room.

"Mike, you go and see," Edith begged, taking her arms from around Sylvy. "I don't dare. It *sounded* exactly like Steve. I think little Mike's old enough not to—"

"Wanta bet?" Mike got up, and Euclid followed.

32

Martha said, "Never mind, girls. There's nothing valuable in there except Henry's papers. And I expect they're all locked up in the drawer." Luke's mouth twitched. Mom knew damn well they were locked up; she always locked them up herself before the invasion of the four grandsons.

Martha fussed over the coffee pouring as if nothing had happened and Edith helped, keeping a worried eye on the door. Luke took a sugar cookie, then passed the plate. He'd got about halfway around when his brothers-in-law appeared, each with a son gripped by the arm. Euclid marched Clem to Martha, Mike planted a squirming Michael in front of Henry. The two younger boys hovered at a safe distance, looking pious and uninvolved.

"Say you're sorry you broke grandpa's reading lamp," Mike ordered. "Apologize to your grandmother for fighting in her home," Euclid commanded.

Luke crammed a cookie into his mouth to stifle laughter. Anita wailed, "They *didn't* fight, not already—"

"We dint fight," Michael quavered. "We just pushed some."

"An' I bumped the stupid table and it went over," Clem continued in a rush.

"And the lamp busted," Steve finished, unable to keep out of the scene any longer.

Martha turned placatingly toward the grim fathers. "It's just an old lamp Henry reads by in there. A cheap old thing I picked up at—" Then, alarmed, "Is glass all over the place, Mike? Did anyone get hurt?"

Luke saw his father set his cup on the coffee table and reach for Sylvy. He gathered her into his arms and her blonde head settled against his shoulder.

"Mike and I will take care of the broken glass. Also a new lamp for Henry," Euclid said, making a thing of it. "You boys just make your apologies now. At once."

The little boys mumbled; Henry smiled his crooked smile and stroked Sylvy's hair. Martha said, "Give them a cookie, Luke. They didn't mean any harm."

Luke set the plate with the fluted edges carefully on the coffee table. His sisters were talking at the same time. Little Steve began a howl that was quickly muffled by the cookie Martha put into his mouth. Luke slid past them all and through the arch. He got his jacket from the closet in the hall and went out the front door.

Night air struck pleasantly chill on his boredom and disgust. There comes a time, he thought, when the last thing a guy needs is his family. He stood for a moment, pleased at how simply he had escaped. Nothing to it. Just walk out.

Now that he was free, what was he going to do? The Mountjoys' house was dark from top to bottom—they'd all gone away for the holiday. He could go down and see if Rollo was home—but he didn't stir. He glanced over his shoulder at the windows of his own house and grinned. Had they missed him? Down the street toward the river ragged scarves of mist rose and he fastened the collar of his jacket. Bought in September, its sleeves were already a bit short, letting his big, raw wrists protrude. Reckon I'm just a growing boy, he thought, slogging off in the opposite direction from Princes' and the river.

He had wanted to go this way all the time, of course. Wanted to so much he had distrusted the wanting and had had to fiddle around, pretending he couldn't make up his mind. It still gave him the jitters to appear unexpectedly at Milo's house.

THREE

This time last year Milo Tarrant had been Forrest Mac-Lane's girl. Quite a set-up that was, all the girls envying Milo and most of the boys envying F. MacLane. Milo wore his gold ring on the same chain as her little gold cross, the two slipping just out of sight between her breasts.

Before he had ever dreamed she could be his girl Luke had more than once caught himself staring at the spot on Milo's chest where the chain ended, his mind guiltily picturing the heavy gold ring and the frail, gold cross lying side by side between the twin hillocks of her breasts (Luke didn't know where he'd got that but it had a fine Biblical sound).

Whenever this happened, something great and a little frightening took place inside Luke Sawyer who had never dated or even thought much about any other girl. His heart galloped, his breathing became so rapid it threatened to choke him, and he was certain his temperature soared. All in the space of seconds.

He was always terrified these changes would show on the outside and he would get busy at once with something—any stupid old thing—and keep at it till his inner man simmered down and he recovered his calm.

Afterwards, it seemed extraordinarily dumb to Luke that this could have gone on an entire school year without his catching onto what it was that was happening. Not that it would have done him any good if he had wised up; you didn't barge in on a couple going steady, even if you knew how. Not even if you were as good-looking as Chuck Holland or as nervy as Butch Boyle or as good a dancer as Rollo Prince. Or if you were all those things rolled into one—which Luke reluctantly admitted Forrest MacLane was.

As for other girls, they just didn't turn Luke on. Some of them worked at it; he wasn't so dumb he couldn't catch onto that. Holly Mason and Judy Hayes were so obvious sometimes it made them look stupid, and Chuck's younger sister Esme was worse than Holly and Judy. Luke just about quit going to Chuck's house because of her.

Then, right at the end of school, during exams, the truth exploded like a bomb. About Forrest MacLane and Eva Covington. Talk started buzzing all over school, all over Mill Gate, but Luke Sawyer never opened his mouth. When the guys started to chew it over at the club Luke just sat there, uptight and careful, smoking Chuck's cigarettes. (He didn't really like to smoke but he felt he should now and then, along with the others.) While he smoked he hoped Butch would not make any cracks about Milo because if he did Luke knew he would have to fight him, and if they fought, Butch would probably beat Luke to a pulp.

He didn't have to fight Butch, but something happened that stuck like a burr in Luke's mind. One day, while the talk about Forrest and Eva was going strong, Luke joined some of the girls in a booth at Syd's in time to hear Esme Holland say in the show-off way she had, no matter who was around, "Isn't it just like old Eva Covington to be so dumb? Hasn't she ever heard of the pill?"

The others, Judy and Joy, had looked at Luke side-wise and Joy Dekle had giggled in a shrill, excited way. Luke hadn't known whether he'd felt more disgust at Esme's remark or at the blush that flamed up his throat into his face.

Forrest MacLane's parents bundled him off to his uncle's until the talk died down and Eva Covington, too, was gone all summer. People said the MacLanes took care of all the expense, but nobody seemed to know what became of the baby. Chuck had said to Luke, "They usually put 'em in a foster home till somebody adopts them. Not that I know anything about this one, see? It wasn't my old man's case and even if it had been he never talks cases at home. It'd be unethical."

All through June and part of July Milo Tarrant had a fragile, sad look. Most of the time she wore her big dark glasses. When she ran into any of the school crowd —at Syd's Sundries or the swimming pool down where the old mill used to be—she kept her chin up but didn't fool around with anyone. They were all a little afraid of her, afraid of saying the wrong thing.

Not only the kids noticed. Luke heard his mother say to his father one night, "I saw the Tarrant girl downtown today. Why, she's like a little widow! That's one of the troubles with this going steady. They're children, playing at marriage."

It was a day early in August that changed Luke Saw-yer's life. Milo came into the hardware store to buy an insect bomb. She said their house was full of ticks. Luke was helping at the store that day because Ed Baines was at the hospital waiting for his wife to have a baby. Luke had been sitting in a lawn chair in the front of the store reading a mystery story when he saw Milo come in. He jumped up and was reaching for the can of fogger before his father could get behind the counter.

Milo looked wispy and too thin in her fringed shorts and a shirt that must belong to her brother Rudy, a college student. The sleeves were rolled up and the bottom came nearly to her knees that looked knobby as a little boy's. Not much of her face was left under the big sunglasses and what there was had a peaked look, like somebody just up from an illness.

Luke dropped the can into a paper bag and Milo handed him a five-dollar bill. She stuffed the change into her pocket and smiled at him, her wan smile so rare nowadays. That did it. Without saying a word to his father or old man Thad Wilson, Luke walked right out the door of the store and into the hot, bright street with Milo Tarrant.

"My mother took my dog to the vet this morning," she said, showing no surprise at Luke's coming with her. "I've got to try to get the horrid little things out of the house before poor Gregory gets back or they'll just climb right onto him again."

"I know what you mean," Luke said. "Our old Watch gets them, too. Filthy parasites, they can just about kill a dog. Drink all his blood up. Watch's tongue turned pretty near white, he was so anemic."

It might be a crazy, dumb conversation, but it was something to start with. Luke found himself looking at Milo's neck where only the cross hung from the chain, showing below the open collar of Rudy's shirt. He felt sweat crawling and said, "You can't stay in the house, you know, once that thing's set off."

"I know," Milo said pensively. "I'm kind of scared to start it." Luke offered quickly to do it for her. It made a reason for his latching onto her like this.

"I might go over to Holly's—if she's home," Milo said after thanking Luke. She scuffed her sandals along the pavement, not even bothering to pick her feet up.

38

Luke felt indignation rising, hotter than the weather. It wasn't right for a girl who tried out for cheerleader to be like this—grieving over Forrest MacLane for God and the world to see; she ought to have more spunk. Besides, he wasn't worth it, the creep.

"It's hot, isn't it?" Milo sighed, passing her hand across her forehead. "I could go swimming, I guess—" Luke could feel her looking at him from behind the dark glasses. "Why don't we both go?"

That was nearly four months ago. It still scared Luke silly to think how easily she might have said it to one of the other guys; Chuck Holland was as good-looking as F. MacLane if not quite as smooth. Luke would have laid the odds way out in favor of Charles Holland any old time. But it was him she had said it to, Luke Henry Sawyer!

He had gone into the house with Milo and waited while she got her swim suit. Then he'd turned the air conditioner off and told her to go out on the porch. He started the fogger, lingering just long enough to make sure the fine mist was coming out of the opening, then hurried out to join her.

At the pool Luke rented a pair of trunks. The sidelong looks and whisperings at his being with Milo filled him with pride instead of embarrassment, as they would have a year ago. And from that afternoon his involvement with Milo Tarrant slipped quickly into the boy-girl routine of phone calls and dates. Luke could hardly believe it; he had thought that part of growing up would be so difficult to begin, wasn't sure he would ever consider it worth the trouble. Now, he could not imagine how he had ever got along without Milo. He told her she brought him luck, for that same week he got a job at the Shell Station where Rollo worked and began to stash away a few dollars a week. Maybe he could buy a car so he wouldn't have to ask for the family one. . . .

Forrest MacLane didn't show when school started and Luke heard he was in a private school somewhere in Virginia. Eva Covington did come back, slightly subdued, but her bright, roving glance for boys was unchanged. Luke couldn't help feeling sorry for her, but he avoided her out of embarrassment and because she reminded him of things he didn't want to think about. He didn't even like having to feel sorry for her.

Luke pushed the lighted button of the Tarrants' front door and heard the bell chime as if it were a long way off, muted by the closed doors and windows. The dog began barking and Luke smiled into his turned-up jacket collar; he had a warm spot for Gregory but for whom he might not be here tonight ringing Milo's doorbell.

The door opened and Mr. Tarrant stood under the light, his balding head poked forward like a turtle's.

"Hi, Mr. Tarrant. It's just me. Milo home?"

"Oh hi, Luke. Come in, come right on in." Milo's father had a sort of overeager manner, as if he longed to be friends with everybody but wasn't sure he could bring it off. He called, "Milo honey, Luke's here."

"I can't stay," Luke heard himself saying. "Just dropped by to wish you-all a happy Thanksgiving." The excuse had only just popped into his head and he was rather pleased with it. "What's left of our house is full of kids. If you know what I mean, sir."

"I know what you mean all right. Doesn't take little fellas long to wreck the joint, does it?" His dry laugh always made Luke want to cough. Then Milo was there in one of those long peasant skirts, her bare toes peeking from beneath its ruffle.

"Hi, Milo," Luke said.

Mrs. Tarrant, knitting in a corner of the long sofa, smiled at him. A length of coral-colored wool flowed over her knees to the green carpet. Her hair, a little darker than Milo's, was twisted into a knob on the top of her head. She had a thin, rather too made-up face.

"So you've got company at your house." Mrs. Tarrant twitched at the yarn in her lap. "It *is* a family time, isn't it? But we're taking it easy since Rudolph won't be here." There was a bright sheen over the hurt in her face. Luke remembered Milo had said her brother was going to spend Thanksgiving with a friend. "We're going to eat at Boniface's. No dishes to think about." She smiled again. "Of course, you'll have a much better dinner, but there *will* be dishes!"

And how! Luke thought, seeming to hear already his sisters' chatter all through the doing of them. They would insist on his mother's lying down and would squabble over where things went. . . .

"No, I don't envy you that good dinner," Mrs. Tarrant said. "You pay too high a price for it." She gave him a half-flirtatious look which Luke could see embarrassed Milo. He said, "Well, you haven't got any grandchildren—," tactfully stopping before the "yet." He thought Mrs. Tarrant was a very silly woman and felt sorry for Milo.

He wished now that he had invited her to dine with his family. His mother had suggested it, offered to call and invite Milo, but Luke had got cold feet thinking of her trapped in his overwhelming family. The Tarrants were so different from the Sawyers; Luke thought it was better to take it by stages, sort of ease into it.

Mr. Tarrant urged Luke to take his jacket off, to have a seat. But Luke wouldn't do either.

"I haven't got the car. I was just out for some fresh

air." He looked down at Milo whose head came a little above his shoulder. "Want to take a little walk? We won't go far. I've got to get back, see what they might be saying about me." They all laughed at that, especially Mr. Tarrant, and Milo said something about changing her clothes, that she wouldn't be a minute.

The dog Gregory, a silky, overweight little blond spaniel, fawned for attention at Luke's feet. Mrs. Tarrant looked at the clock on the mantel. It was a glass clock with its internal organs shining golden through it.

"Only half-past eight? Heavens, I thought it was much later than that. It gets late so early, doesn't it?"

Luke wished Milo would hurry. He had the feeling that this kind of idiot talk could go on all night, that he'd escaped the boredom of one family only to get tangled up in another one. He grinned, though, and agreed with everything Mrs. Tarrant said. Mr. T. had returned to his easy chair and his newspaper. Luke saw him reach down absent-mindedly and scoop Milo's gray kitten up and set it on his knee. Luke thought it was the sort of thing his own father would do.

Milo was back now in tight jeans and a heavy turtleneck sweater. Luke said gruffly, to keep his tenderness from showing in front of her parents, "It's cold out. You put your shoes on?" He looked and saw her red sneakers.

The darkness had a sort of wild look and feel now. It excited Luke—or maybe it was only being with Milo that excited him. She had put some perfume on (he remembered Anita and Edith dabbing the lobes of their ears with perfume before dates) and the heady scent made him tighten his fingers around her arm.

They walked the way Luke had come—toward the river. The fog was thicker, the street lights dimmer. Milo's face was a blurred triangle, her hair on her shoulders colorless as the fog. Luke's heart raced and he thought, *This is it. It's got to be Milo or nobody for me.* It was like being a little bit drunk. Like about a year ago when Butch and Chuck had managed between them to bring a lot of beer to a meeting and all of them had got tipsy.

"Why did you come by tonight?" Milo said.

"I wanted to see you."

"Oh." Then she asked, in the half-teasing, half-serious way she had that he never quite understood, and that bugged him, "How do you feel about me, Luke? I mean, really."

"You know, Milo. Don't you know by now?" He stopped and pulled away from her, dropping her arm and turning to look down at her, making his gaze penetrate the mist so he could see her eyes. She sighed.

"I want to know. But I can't."

"On account of MacLane?"

"Well, you see, I believed him and he—"

"I'm not him! Thanks for the compliment. Putting me in the same class with that creep." He backed off from her, furious.

"I'm not," Milo denied. "Nobody thinks you're a creep! Luke Sawyer, all-round good guy—that's what they'll put under your picture in the annual next year when we graduate."

"Aw, cut it out," Luke growled. What was she getting at, anyway?

"Well, it's true. All the kids think that about you, Luke. You know it, too."

"I don't want any crap like that under my picture," he said angrily. He couldn't tell her he wanted something like: Best actor. He couldn't tell anybody that, afraid they'd think him some kind of sissy.

Milo's hair slid forward as she bent her head down.

Luke wanted to touch her but wouldn't, just stood there feeling like a big helpless ox.

"I don't know, Luke. Sometimes I think I don't know anything. How could I be as dumb as I was? I never will get over how dumb I was."

"Everybody's dumb. Lots of times," he said.

"Not that dumb. I thought that guy—that creep as you call him—was absolutely the greatest, I really did. In my mind—not my body, just my mind—I *groveled*. That's what kills me."

"Milo, how come you've got to talk about him tonight?" Luke felt as if his breath was being squeezed by force out of his lungs. "I thought—"

"Thought I'd got over him." She shook her hair back and laughed. "I'm over him all right! I wouldn't go across the street with him, not if he came back here— which he never will, he won't have the guts—and begged me on his knees."

"Hey, take it easy." She was getting dramatic, the way girls were always doing. He shifted his feet, touched her sleeve timidly. She'd never acted like this before; maybe it had something to do with the holidays—old memories or something. His mouth tasted bitter and he swallowed. "Mi, how come you have to talk about the S.O.B. when—"

"When I'm with you? I know. It's not very tactful. Not even nice." She sounded meek all of a sudden. "Maybe it's because I *have* got over it. You know? I can talk about it now." She sounded hoarse. Luke thought, I ought not to have her out here in the damp like this, she might get pneumonia or something. She said, "We've come all this way, nearly to your house, and you haven't kissed me."

"You want me to?"

"Are you kidding? Try and see." She stood on tiptoe.

Luke folded her to him, his mouth moving blindly over her face. But when he found her lips he was suddenly careful not to kiss her with too much ardor because she had wounded his pride, after all. He took her cold hand and they walked on. Past his house that looked quiet enough now, the kids doubtless all bedded down. Past the Mountjoys', the Weavers', the vacant Conway house brooding behind the trees and the For Sale sign glimmering at the edge of the yard. Past the Princes' house where only the dim light burned in the hall to comfort Rollo's mother.

They could hear the river hurrying and burbling over the coppery sand and clean rocks. The mist was very dense on the banks, the cold sharper, more penetrating. Luke rubbed Milo's hands to warm them. He wondered if she was still thinking about old F. MacLane but dared not ask.

He said, "You're cold. I ought to take you home."

"I'm O.K. Your little hut's near here, isn't it?"

"Yeah." Thinking of the dark privacy in the hut made Luke tremble. There was the ruling and he mustn't think about it anyway. . . .

"You never let any girls in, do you?"

"Nope. Against the rules." He was still trembling. If he could take her inside the clubhouse—the key to the padlock was in his pocket and it would be as easy as falling off a greased log. No one would know he'd broken the rule. How did he know some of the others hadn't? Butch—Rollo—Chuck—They could have, it wasn't a crime. They all must have their private lives, their secrets. There wasn't a club rule you had to tell the members everything. . . .

If he could only *know* Milo was over F. MacLane, Luke thought, get her to prove he was the one, not that hovering ghost MacLane. Yet, what if he broke the rule, took her into the dark hut, started to make love to her and she refused? Wouldn't he be worse off?

Luke licked his dry lips, pretended he was cold to account for his shivering. He said hoarsely, "We better go back, Mi, before you freeze." They kissed again and he took her by the shoulders and turned her around and they began to walk briskly up the rise, away from the river.

FOUR

Five days before Christmas Forrest MacLane stopped his mother's Cadillac beside a high-test pump at the Shell Station.

"Fill 'er up and check under the hood, will you?" he said, before he grinned and added, "How you doing, Sawyer? Didn't know you worked here."

It jolted Luke; somehow he had never expected to see Forrest MacLane in Mill Gate again. He could stand to think of him up there in Virginia or West Virginia or wherever it was he was supposed to be in school. Now, without a word of warning, here he was, good-looking as ever, green-striped pants belted round his narrow hips, his long yellow hair perfectly styled.

Luke pulled himself together in a hurry, trying to ignore the butterflies under his brown coveralls with *Jeff's Northside Shell Station* stitched on it.

"I'm doing just fine, MacLane." He put the pump nozzle into the opening of the enormous gas tank. "How you making it?"

"Can't complain," Forrest said, pursing his lips as if he were going to whistle. "Old town doesn't look any different, does it?"

The way he said it prompted Luke to one of his transformations. He loosened his shoulders to slouch, moved his feet in a near-shuffle, made his mouth slack in a vacant smile. From another pump, serving an out-of-state Volkswagen, Rollo turned to watch the performance.

"Well-l," Luke drawled, "I don't reckon it does. Haven't been anywheres myself, so I cain't hardly tell." He shuffled round to the front of the car and raised the hood. He checked the oil, the battery water, and peered conscientiously at the radiator water level, managing meanwhile to slide glances at Forrest to see how he was taking the act.

The guy didn't appear to notice. There was an absent-minded look in his narrowed eyes between the thick, long lashes. Luke closed the hood gently and asked, "You home for Christmas?"

"Right." He gave Luke a smile, showing all his big white square teeth. In fifth or sixth grade, Luke remembered, Forrest had carried a mouthful of hardware around to straighten them. "I won't be here all the holidays, though. Going to New York to visit a friend the day after Christmas."

"That right?" Luke wondered if it was a boy or girl friend.

Forrest handed him a credit card and started the great, beautiful, whispering motor while Luke scribbled in the form, willing his hand not to shake. Giving the card back to MacLane he raised his hand to wave— brush the guy from his sight as he would a pesky gnat— but MacLane leaned out and said jerkily, "I hear you're dating Milo." His face made Luke think of a fellow who broke his wrist one night playing basketball. Luke had been the closest to him when it happened and the guy's face was like F. MacLane's now. Same color, same look in the eyes.

Luke said, "That's right." He wished Forrest didn't look like that; he would have preferred him swaggering or angry. He made his tone very cool, wishing his feelings matched it. "Milo and I have been going together for about five months, now." He wanted to add, "Want to make something out of it?" but didn't.

Forrest ran his tongue over his lips. "Better luck than I had, old man." He pressed the accelerator and the car leapt ahead, making Luke stumble back, the hand that had been on the edge of the door held foolishly in mid-air.

Behind him, Rollo said, "You gonna start that lube job now or you want me to?"

Luke didn't know how much of the exchange between him and MacLane Rollo had heard or why it should matter one way or the other. He only knew that if somebody had to be in on the scene, better it was Rollo.

The Shell Station was at the north edge of town on the Baysboro highway, some distance from the Tarrant house, but Luke knew he was going to go by and see Milo before he went home to supper. If she didn't know Forrest was in town he wanted to be the one to tell her. He had a sickish feeling she'd know before he got there. MacLane might try to see her in spite of what he'd said to Luke. Better luck!—anybody'd know Forrest didn't mean that.

Luke left the station at five o'clock. It was almost dark, due to an overcast sky and a few cold raindrops. They struck meanly against his face as he started out, walking fast toward the Tarrants'. Weird weather for now; it usually came in January and early February. Maybe the weather, like people nowadays, acted up at everything and nothing, full of violence and sullenness, trying to prove something. . . .

Milo and her mother were in the living room. The TV was on but they weren't watching. Mrs. Tarrant was trying to force her thing about knitting onto Milo. A strand of scarlet yarn trickled like a thin stream of blood over Milo's bare knee and she held the lethal-looking needles clumsily, brows puckered and lips set.

"I don't know why they call this soothing to the nerves," she hissed. "Sends me right up the walls. Want I should knit you a muffler, Luke? God knows it's cold enough for one, today."

"Don't swear, darling," Mrs. Tarrant murmured, blinking toward Luke. He wondered if she'd been as playful with F. MacLane as she was always trying to be with him. "Have supper with us, Luke?" she asked, beginning to gather her stuff into a bundle.

Milo scowled at her own ball of yarn. Her hands were brown and square; she never bleached out like most people in winter. Luke guessed she was what you would call a "dark blonde." He started as Mrs. Tarrant repeated her invitation.

"No, ma'am, thanks just the same. Mom's expecting me home. I just wanted to talk to Milo a minute." He looked at the mosslike green of the carpet.

"Well, talk away," Mrs. Tarrant said, yawning and stretching. "I've got to see what's to eat. How I loathe cooking. I hope Milo won't turn out to be like her mother." Me too, Luke thought, but he remembered to rise as Mrs. Tarrant got off the sofa. Milo's kitten jumped into her place and began batting at the yarn in Milo's lap.

Luke eased himself onto the edge of the sofa and stroked the kitten's ear with one finger.

"Milo, you know Forrest MacLane is home." He had meant to ask, but it came out a statement and there was a heaviness like indigestion in his chest. Milo's lashes hid her eyes. She began to wind the yarn very

50

fast, rubbing one foot against the other. "Well? Did you know it?"

She shook her head, her hair sliding like silk over her shoulder, across her breast. Luke saw a little flat brown mole on her neck above the gold chain that used to hold Forrest MacLane's ring. He wondered why he'd never noticed the mole before.

She said, "Who told you?"

"He came by the station. He's home for part of the holidays, said he was going to New York after Christmas."

Still not looking at him, Milo said, "Well. It's nothing to me, I guess—"

"You guess! Don't you know? You have to know, Milo. I have to know, too." He was hot and cold at the same time; he loved and hated her at the same time. "You've got to tell me."

"All right!" She threw the ball of yarn across the room and the kitten darted after it. Tears stood in her gray eyes; Luke saw them, though she still wasn't meeting his eyes. She seemed to be looking intently through her tears at the kitten. "I—I guess I'm just shocked. Can't I be shocked—surprised if you like that better? He could've called—or something."

"But why should he? It's all over between you and him. Been over for half a year. Hasn't it?" He was standing up now, glaring down at her.

"Of course it has." But she had a frantic air. "Oh, Luke. Do you have to be so stupid? There's such a thing as—remembering. And half a year's not so long. Anybody can remember that long, can't they?"

He saw her lips trembling and wished he hadn't come by. He should have let her deal with it in her own way. He'd just put her on the spot with his impatience, acting like a big, dumb bully. The rain was coming down harder now, needling the windowpane behind them. In the pool of light from the rose-shaded lamp Milo's hair had a reddish glow.

"I'm sorry I bothered you," he said stiffly. "I just had a dopey idea I should tell you if you didn't know. Wouldn't it be more of a shock, as you call it, if you— like ran into him in the street? Well, wouldn't it?" He pulled her up from the sofa, holding her arms so tightly she winced a little. He was ashamed. She was so little, nothing to her but softness and littleness. Like the kitten.

"I guess so," she gulped. "It was sweet of you to come. In this lousy rain, too. Oh, I hate this stinking weather. Look—" He could see her pulling herself together, pushing her hair back, blinking the tears out of her eyes. "My brother's coming tonight. I was going with them to pick him up at the airport. You know he wrecked his car and Daddy won't get him another one. But I don't have to. I mean—if I had a date I wouldn't have to go with them to meet Rudy. Do you have to work tonight or go to one of your old club meetings or something?"

Luke shook his head. "If you'd rather go meet your brother—"

"Are you kidding? You know I'd rather be with you." But he didn't know; how could he?

He said, "O.K.," and turned away from her without touching her. She followed him to the door.

"Oh, Lord. Look at that rain! You'll get pneumonia. Let me get the keys, I'll run you home." But he wouldn't let her. He turned his collar up and plunged into the wet dusk, saying in a muffled tone, without turning his head, "See you around seven."

He kept his head down and his collar up against the

rain and felt a self-pitying satisfaction in getting soaked. He knew how his mother would carry on when he got home, about his not calling her to come and get him and goodness knew what-all. Why had he taken it for granted F. MacLane would never show in Mill Gate till Milo Tarrant was Mrs. Luke Henry Sawyer? Why hadn't he figured the guy was sure to turn up sooner or later?

Luke could only guess, miserably, that being Milo's steady these last months had gone to his head. He sneezed mightily and raindrops flew from his hair; he sneezed again and snuffled. Maybe he would get pneumonia, maybe he'd die. Milo would be sorry then. Would she feel bereft?

No matter how Luke tried, those few days before Christmas, to get his mind off Forrest MacLane's return he wasn't successful for long at a time. The date with Milo, riding aimlessly around town in the December rain, didn't make him feel any better. Her bright remarks all sounded phony to Luke and he was inclined to silence, grunting replies to her chatter, glooming like the weather. He knew he was behaving like a sulky brat but couldn't seem to help it. He supposed she thought she was proving something by going out with him instead of with her family to meet her brother. Big deal. She wasn't fooling anybody; any fool could see how tense she was and trying to hide it by carrying on like Esme Holland.

The whole stupid town was stirred up by Forrest's coming home, Luke thought bitterly. He wondered if even the great MacLane himself knew how important he was. It was a wonder they hadn't gone clear to the airport in a body to meet him with the high school band and the Chamber of Commerce to boot. There were even jarring echoes in the homey quiet of the Sawyers' kitchen.

"I do feel sorry for Alice and Elbert MacLane," Martha said without warning as Luke hunched morosely over a snack. "I always have, since that miserable thing. Children never have any idea what they do to their parents, how they hurt them. Not till they have to go through the same things with their own children, then it's too late to do any good." Luke could see how careful she was not to look at him as she meandered on.

"I'm sorry for the Covington girl's mother too, of course, only—" Luke knew what his mother was thinking: that Eva Covington had "got herself talked about" from first year Junior High. All the mothers thought that; it was amazing how much alike their minds worked.

As far as Luke was concerned, poor old Eva wasn't any worse than Esme Holland or Joy Dekle or two or three others he could name if he wanted to. Heck, no. Not as bad, because they had everything and had always been "in" at school, solid as a rock nothing could shake because they were who they were. Eva Covington had nothing but her sex, so maybe there was some excuse for her throwing it at every boy she saw.

Martha was going on sadly, "The Covington child's never had much of a chance. Her mother has to work so hard at that canning plant, I don't suppose she's had much time or energy to spend on her children."

Luke was about to ease out of the kitchen when his mother suddenly looked at him across the ironing board draped with a red-checked curtain. Nobody was coming for Christmas but some compulsion made Martha take the curtains down and do them up anyway.

"I'm so thankful you've got a nice girl, Luke. A good girl." Luke wondered how old-fashioned you could

54

sound in this day and age. Still, he kind of liked his mother being that way; it always bugged him to hear Mrs. Tarrant knocking herself out to sound modern, trying to speak the kids' language and failing. "I believe I'd feel just as bad if you got a girl in that kind of predicament as the girl's mother. Really, I do."

Luke choked with embarrassment and went to the sink for a drink of water. What in the world had got into his mother? He guessed they all worried about that "predicament" as she called it.

"I'm sorry, Luke," Martha went on, giving her attention back to her ironing in an exaggerated way. "These things aren't easy to discuss. I just wanted you to know I feel like that."

"Yes ma'am," Luke said, stony-faced. "Now I know how you feel, could we just not talk about F. MacLane? *Or* Eva Covington? Could we maybe just let it go—or would that be asking too much?"

"No need for you to get impudent with me," Martha said flushing. "I said I was sorry."

"Save your sorrow, Ma. No harm done." But he still felt edgy. It did seem as if she would know he hated the very thought of Forrest MacLane.

One afternoon later that week Craig Simmons climbed the stairs to Luke's room and looked commiserating till Luke broke out, irritably, "Yeh yeh yeh, sonny boy, I know. I've seen his pretty face. The great MacLane himself—the Forrest Primeval." He brayed raucously at his own wit. Sim laughed, too, but his flush made Luke ashamed of having called him sonny boy. Why couldn't they get off his back? All of them.

At the station Jeff Beale rode him good-naturedly, saying he'd have to give Luke half of Christmas Eve off since he had competition to cope with now. Mrs. Beale and the two kids were sitting right there, listening and grinning, and it didn't strike Luke funny at all.

About noon, the day before Christmas, as Luke was about to go home, Clarence Boyle roared into the Shell Station on a motorcycle.

"Fill 'er up, Luke, if you got time and enough gas," he shouted, "an' you can take 'er round the block, after." He took his helmet off and shook out his ragged red mane.

"Can't, Butch, old man," Luke said. "Got to get along home. Where'd you get the Honda? Swipe it or Santy Claus bring it?"

"Belongs to Kenny Holloway," Butch said in disgust. "Can you beat it? That ninny with a beauty like this! Might as well belong to little old Sim. Kenny's scared to death of it, I b'lieve he'd sell it if anybody was to twist his arm, but hell, I got no dough."

"So who has?" Luke shrugged, walking slowly around the Honda, admiring its splendor. "Finished my Christmas shopping, last night. That cleaned me out."

Butch squatted to squint at a tire. "What you get Milo?"

"A white Cadillac," Luke said, thinking of the bracelet in the top drawer under his socks. He had gone to Baysboro yesterday to consult his sister Anita. The more he'd pondered on a gift for Milo, the more desperately at sea he had become.

"I used to love to get jewelry," Anita had told him. "They have such nice costume jewelry now. On the main floor at Kahn's there's a gorgeous display."

But Luke had gone to a jeweler's and blown most of his Christmas money on the bracelet—a fourteen-carat gold circle of tiny doves linked together on a gold chain. He'd fallen for it the minute the salesgirl lifted it from its velvet bed for him to look at. "Something unique in a peace symbol," she'd said, arching her thin eyebrows. He could see it on Milo's wrist and said he'd take it before he even asked the price.

When he showed it to Anita she gave a little scream of delight. Then she saw the jeweler's name on the red velvet box. "Felix Myer! This must have set you back a lot, Luke. You and Milo Tarrant aren't *engaged,* are you?"

Luke hadn't answered that but was pleased she'd thought they might be. He said, apologetically, "It did cost a little more than I figured on, Sis. I hope the rest of you won't mind me skimping on you some this once—"

"Well, of course not." She smiled and hugged him and he knew she'd have Martha Sawyer on the phone, asking if Luke and Milo were engaged, before he got halfway home.

"White Cadillac, huh?" Butch strapped the helmet on, wincing as it pulled his scraggly new beard. "Lucky wench. Know who's back in town, doncha?"

"Yeah."

"You want we should run him out?"

"It's his town same as mine," Luke answered, hardly believing his nonchalant air. If he could only feel that way . . .

Butch spat. "That bastard, I always did hate his guts. So full of hisself and his pretty face. Know who I saw him driving around in that posh car of his old lady's?"

A chill gripped Luke in the pit of his stomach. He held his gaze steadily on Butch's face.

"Esme Holland. Yessiree, old Chuck's kid sister. Pretty Boy MacLane is down to robbing the cradle now, how 'bout that?"

"How about that?" Luke echoed while relief swept over him in wild waves.

"See you round," Butch said, starting the cycle. Over

its noise he yelled, "Come over tonight if you got no-where's else to go. My old lady busted her washing ma-chine and if I don't fix it she's liable to chew at me all Christmas Day."

"I might do that," Luke shouted back. And where the chill had been relief lay, almost as sweet as joy.

FIVE

After supper Luke asked if he could have the car but didn't say where he was going. The whole house was scented by the Christmas tree standing in the living room. It was easy to pick out at a glance Luke's awkwardly-wrapped gifts lying underneath. The front door wore its holly wreath with a white dove for peace added. Henry had put the Christmas carols on the old player; their sound followed Luke out to the garage.

He cruised along Main Street that looked no less shabby under the crossed strings of Christmas lights. The new shopping centers springing up outside town took most of the trade; downtown Mill Gate just didn't bother to try to keep up. Luke turned left into Putney Street, an ugly street with ugly houses. Here and there an unprepossessing place of business stood next to a private dwelling—as if Main Street had spilled over into Putney in an untidy, don't-care sort of way. It looked slightly better in the dark, however, and in most windows there were symbols of Christmas—electric candles, a fat, electrified Santa Claus, a star. Lighted trees graced some of the yards, but not the Boyles'; house and yard were innocent of decoration.

Luke parked in the street in front of the house. Two cars, both incapacitated, stood in the driveway. A high-powered bulb in a black rubber cage over the garage door showed the broken window of one car and the two flat tires of the other. Luke went up the driveway, glad of the harsh light to guide him round the overturned tricycle and a playpen with one side bashed in, past the car corpses and into the garage that served the Boyles as storeroom, workshop, and laundry. Surrounded by a marvel of odds-and-ends that made Luke wonder if they ever threw anything away was Butch, sadly contemplating the dismembered washing machine. He looked up at Luke's "Hiya" and shook his head.

"Lookit this, willya? Ever seen such a helluva mess? I've got it apart and if I get it back together, even if it don't work, it's liable to take me the rest of my natural life."

"Think how nice and heavy and long your beard'll be by then," Luke said, but Butch was not comforted. He kept shaking his red head, murmuring his favorite obscenities in a soft, monotonous tone. He kicked a part out of his way and said, "Pull you up something to sit on."

Luke extracted a backless straight chair from a tangle of furniture in the corner nearest him. There was plenty of strong light inside the garage from another big bulb in the ceiling. It showed cobwebs in the corners, dust, oil stains on the cement floor, and the grease smudges on Butch's face. Cold flowed through the half-open door that didn't slide up and down properly and was propped by a length of lead pipe.

"What seems to be wrong with the washer?" Luke rubbed his chin to hide his smile.

"How the hell should I know? Ma wrecks all her gadgets. I don't know how she does it, but man oh man, has she ever got the hang of it!" He held a mashed pack of cigarettes out and Luke shook his head.

The door leading into the house opened and Mrs.

Boyle edged into the garage. She was a drab little woman with a face shaped like Butch's and hands chapped from constantly being in water. Her flowered shift hung like a sack on her body, but her hair—you have to see it to believe it, Luke thought—was elaborately heaped and twisted upon her head as if in an effort to increase her stature.

"How you coming along, Clarry?" Luke thought, aghast, Clarry. Oh gawd. She jerked her coiffure toward Luke who was getting a little belatedly to his feet. "How are you, Chick dear?"

"Chuck, Ma, not Chick," Butch corrected in a gentle snarl. "And it's Luke anyhow. Damndest thing how you mix people up, I swear. Like busting things. You like go outa your way to screw everything up so can't anybody—" His grumbling trailed off and he began a small whistling between his teeth.

Mrs. Boyle winked at Luke. "Sit down, dear. No need to stand there. Take the load off your feet." She picked her way daintily among the wreckage to the washing machine, looked into the tub as if she half expected something to jump at her.

Luke let himself down onto the broken chair again. Yep, you had to see it to believe it. The mess and clutter and Mrs. B. with her golden wig. It was a fantastic background all right. Luke knew there were four kids younger than Butch in the family, two or three of them preschool age and a middle-sized girl named Penny who had never more than murmured a shy "Hi" to Luke. Clarence Boyle, Senior, was a roofer and made good money when he worked, but his jobs were sporadic and he was a heavy drinker. Butch did a lot of joking about the last, but Luke had long been convinced that Mr. Boyle's weakness was a source of painful embarrassment to his son.

"You boys better come in and get warm," Mrs. Boyle said, ceasing to gaze into the tub of the washer. "It's real chilly out here, I declare."

Through the crack of the door to the kitchen, the overloud voice of the TV ranted and roared. Luke could imagine Mr. B. lying on the couch in his sock feet and the little boys wrestling on the spotty carpet. Penny would be sitting with her eyes glued to the TV screen.

"It's O.K., Mrs. Boyle," he said, smiling at Butch's mother. "I'm not cold."

"Well. You got your jacket on," she conceded, hugging herself with bare arms nearly as red as her hands. "Reckon I'll scoot inside. I hope you can get it fixed, Clarence, I don't want to be doing a wash on Christmas Day."

When his mother had shut the door behind her Butch threw his cigarette into the laundry tub.

"You got the car, why don't we go by Syd's, see if any of the gang's hanging around down there?" He held his hands under the tap, lathered them with gritty, soft soap from a can on the shelf above the tubs. "I'm fed up with this pile o' junk for now. Get a fresh start on it when I'm in the mood." He splashed his face, cold drops shining in his shock of hair.

"You really believe you can fix it?" Luke couldn't help asking.

"Aw, I d'no." Butch wiped his face on a dubious-looking cloth Luke suspected of being part of the laundry Mrs. Boyle had yet to do. "But I'm not about to put in all night on it. You're lucky, man, you know it?"

Luke was startled. "Who, me? How come?"

"Ahhh, I d'no. You got it so nice and quiet at your house. That pad up there all by itself, top of the house, no kids all over the place. None of this crap all over . . ." He looked around as if he were seeing the incredible chaos for the first time. "Your place—it's like private, you know? Nobody on your back all the time."

Embarrassed, Luke said, "I get plenty on my back, don't worry. Family's family. They don't exactly think I'm God at my house. Especially my old man."

"Come on, let's go." As he climbed in beside Luke, Butch said, more sourly than before, "This lousy goddamn weather gets me down, don't it you? Sometimes, I wish I was up north where there's snow. If it's got to be cold might as well have snow, I get to wanting to see some, sometimes."

"Me, too," Luke said, racing the motor to warm it up. "I intend to, one of these days. I'd like to do a lot of traveling."

"Like in the Army?"

"Nope."

None of the crowd was at Syd's. Luke hadn't thought they would be; it was Christmas Eve after all. Matt Webber was sitting tiredly over a cup of coffee at the counter instead of standing behind it. Over in the cosmetics department Miss Letty Thomas was trying to make up her mind between a box of bath powder and a jug of hand-and-body lotion.

Butch looked downcast. Luke thought of the scattered parts of the washing machine and offered to buy him a Coke. Butch shrugged. "Nah. A beer might go good. Coke, forget it."

When they had clowned around a little with Matt, they went back to the car. As Luke stepped on the starter Butch said, very casual and offhand, "Wanta go by and pick up Milo? We might could twist Judy's or Holly's arm into riding around a little."

Luke shook his head. "I'm beat. Guess I ought to go home and wrap some stuff, rather not bother Milo tonight. You know how it is, families and Christmas Eve and all." He wished he hadn't said that, why hadn't he thought? He had an idea that was what was eating Butch —it being a special time for everybody except the Boyles.

Butch said, "Drop me off at your house then. I'll slog on down to Rollo's, see what he's up to."

Luke drove on past his house to the Princes'. "You see if Rollo's home," he said. "I'll wait till you holler."

"Nothin' to do in this dump," Butch exploded. "I don't get a job pretty soon I'm gonna quit school and blow. I mean that, man. I'm gonna shake the sand of little old Mill Gate off my shoes and—"

"What shoes?" Luke said and Butch laughed. It was something, Luke felt, to have got a laugh out of him. Butch was certainly low tonight and Luke couldn't blame him. Not that Christmas was anything to get excited about, more of a drag some ways after you stopped being a kid. But to have a family like Butch's must be kind of rough.

As if he'd read Luke's mind Butch broke out, angrily, "Christmas! It's nothing to me, I mean nothing. You know? The kids'll get some crap and have it tore apart before night and my old lady will cook a hot dinner— turkey and stuff. Hey, I didn't tell you, did I? My old man won a twenty pound turkey in that shoot Wilson's Hardware put on. He's a crack shot."

"Bully for him," Luke said. "My pop didn't get a chance at one, being an employee. We'll be eating a turkey my brother-in-law paid for at the supermarket."

"That's life, ain't it?" Butch laughed. "Don't wait, do me good to walk home. Lookit the fog coming up from the river! Kee-riste. Bet you can't see the club-house till you butt smack into it. See ya, Luke."

Luke waited until the Princes' door showed the hall light, then closed behind Butch. He turned the car around and drove slowly home, thinking about the Boyles and the Princes. Sooner or later, he knew, he was going to have to think about Milo and Forrest Mac-Lane. The relief Butch's news at noon had given him was threatening to wear off. Like a shot of novocaine at the dentist's. MacLane riding around with Esme Holland might not mean anything except that Forrest couldn't stand it not to be with a girl and Esme wasn't exactly one to say no.

In his room, Luke wandered about, feeling lost, too restless to settle himself for sleep, tired as he was. He'd wrapped all his presents except Milo's and he didn't want to wrap it. He didn't want to do anything except stop worrying about those two. It made him ashamed to have so little faith in Milo, but dammit, why couldn't she give him something real to go on? Like if the phone should ring now and he'd dash downstairs and it would be her. She'd say, "Luke?" with a question in her voice and he'd say, "Yeah." Like that. Flat and a little tough maybe. And she'd say, "I just wanted to hear your voice before I went to sleep. I just wanted to say good night, darling." Something like that.

That's all it would take, just something like that. Luke's eyelids stung and the knobs on the chest of drawers blurred suddenly together. He'd thought everything was O.K. after Butch told him about Forrest and Esme. That was why he'd gone to Boyles' tonight, that big warm feeling of gratitude to Butch for telling him. All he'd got out of it in the end was feeling sorry for the guy. How did he know Butch wasn't feeling sorry for *him?* He and Rollo might be sitting down there at Rollo's this minute, both feeling sorry for Luke Sawyer, the poor slob who didn't know when he'd had it. . . .

He could sneak down and call Milo. A little late for that, it might make Mrs. Tarrant sore—or Milo might not be there. Wasn't that really what he was shying at? He had to knock it off, stop this running scared. Without any reason, too. He ought to be ashamed of himself, he was ashamed. Bathed in shame, he threw himself on his bed and stared at the bunk above.

The telephone rang, muffled and far-off sounding in its little nook under the stairs. Luke sprang up, cracking his head against the side of the upper bunk. Swearing, he clawed his door open and started downstairs, stopping on the third step from the top. His mother, still struggling into her dressing gown, was at the door of the phone closet. Luke sat down on the step and waited, head and heart thumping.

He heard Martha's sleepy "Hello," and opened his mouth to call down, "I'm right here, Mom," but the silence in the closet drew out. Luke's heart slowed down and despair settled over him. Milo wouldn't be giving Martha Sawyer a long spiel. . . .

"Was he all right when you put him to bed?" Luke heard his mother asking, her voice not sleepy now, anxious but trying to sound calm. "Oh, I expect it's just a little upset, they're all so excited on Christmas Eve. Have you got baby aspirins?"

Luke tenderly felt the lump rising on his head. So one of Edie's kids had tossed his cookies and she was making a big deal out of it.

"He says his ear hurts?" Martha had stopped faking calm. It would be Steve, then; he was prone to ear infections—as Luke had been at his age. Great. On Christmas Eve and the Sawyers invited to the Donaldsons' for Christmas dinner. Poor old Edie. But he felt his own disappointment so sharply it dulled his pity for his sister and even for Stevie who was only three and stricken with earache for Christmas.

Without letting on he was there, Luke got up and

went back into his room. He got into his pajamas, picked a book from the cascading pile of soft-cover editions beside his bed, put his reading light on but didn't open the book. His mother was still on the phone but he couldn't hear what she was saying. Later, his eyes closed and the book lying on his chest, he could hear the murmur of both his parents' voices in the room below. He felt a warped sort of envy. Maybe it wouldn't be so bad to be old and have nothing to get shook up over than your grandchild's earache.

SIX

The family exchange of gifts was accomplished with less embarrassment than Luke had anticipated. Funny, he thought, how you changed with years; what had been the breath of life as a kid became a self-conscious ordeal with teen age.

Martha had scarcely said "Merry Christmas" to Henry and Luke before she was on the telephone inquiring after little Steve. She came back to tell Henry and Luke that Edith had got hold of Dr. Bob Holland last night and he'd given Steve penicillin for his earache.

Martha hadn't had to knock herself out preparing a special Christmas breakfast. The girls agreed that children ought to have Christmas in their own homes, besides needing a moving van to haul the loot from house to house. Anita called before they left for Edith's and everybody in the Pierce family had to speak to everybody in the Sawyer family.

By that time Luke had worked himself up considerably, wondering when he should take the bracelet over to Milo. He felt a definite unwillingness to see her family and wished there were some way he could see her privately. He wandered about the house, fingering the velvet box in his pocket. What if she didn't like it? He tried to remember whether he had ever seen a bracelet on her wrist. Come to think of it, he'd never seen her wear any jewelry except the tiny gold hoops in her pierced ears and the little cross. And MacLane's ring . . .

To calm his jitters he went out to fool around the car. Crossing the yard he happened to look up at the living room window and saw his father's face. Some trick of the light gave it a weird, disembodied look, floating between the red curtains. It had somehow a very un-Christmas look. Then his father moved away from the window and Luke didn't think about it again for a long time, not till months later.

After he'd fiddled around under the hood of the car for a while Luke went back into the house. A beautiful baritone voice was winging out of the TV, singing *Panis Angelicus,* and Martha was doing the breakfast dishes. Luke went to the telephone and dialed the Tarrants' number. He had made up his mind to say, "Merry Chrismas, darling," but when Milo's voice answered he said gruffly, "Hi, Milo. Merry Christmas." He was furious with himself, certain Forrest MacLane would have said darling and maybe a lot more with no trouble at all.

"You doing anything, Mi? I mean, you know, could I come over for a minute or two? I've got something here belongs to you."

"Luke!" As if she was surprised . . . "Well, I've got something for you, too. Sure, come over, I've been wondering why you didn't call." That helped some, but he still wasn't what you'd call exactly relaxed. At least he'd cleared the way; it was O.K. for him to go over to her house. He'd be seeing her in a few minutes and it seemed as if he'd been waiting a long time for that.

When he came out of the telephone closet his father was standing in the hall by the living room door.

"Could you come in here, son?" he said and Luke immediately began to feel snarled up inside. It was immensely important for him to go at once to Milo's. He pushed his hair off his forehead, frowning with frustration.

"Well, sure, Dad. What for? I mean, will it take long? I was just going to Milo's, but—"

"Oh. All right," Henry Sawyer said too quickly. Luke wasn't sure but thought he saw a flick of that hurt look in his eyes. "If you've got other plans, this can wait." He took off his glasses and held them to the light, squinting at them, getting his handkerchief out. Luke saw it was one of the new monogrammed ones he had given his father along with a shirt and an extra wide, colorful tie. Henry began to polish the glasses.

"My plans can wait," Luke said, martyred. "What did you want, Dad?"

"Nothing of any consequence. You go along to your girl's." The last notes of the *Panis Angelicus* rose, piercingly beautiful.

"But . . . you must've wanted something." A little ashamed, Luke added, "I'm not in that big of a hurry."

"I think you are," Henry said, giving Luke his crooked smile. "I'd as soon wait to talk till you've got plenty of time on your hands." He sat down in the old wing chair by the TV. "Nice song that fellow was singing. Beautiful voice, eh? Only I like to understand what they're saying."

Surprising himself, Luke said, "I know some of the English. The school choir sang it at the Christmas recital. It starts off, 'Oh Lord most merciful, Oh Lord most mighty—' "

"Mm. Nice," Henry said. He settled his glasses, folded and put his handkerchief away. He didn't look at Luke standing awkwardly in the doorway. "Kind of comforting."

"I guess so. Pop—what did you want with me?"

Henry pulled a blank face, comical as Luke's when he clowned. "By gosh now, if I haven't clean forgot. Couldn't've been anything much, could it? You run along, boy. Be sure you get back here with the car, though, so your mother don't get the willies. She's worried about Stevie."

"I know. I'll be back in plenty of time." He was out the door and into the driveway, gulping the morning air that had become milder in the night. The sun was breaking palely through whitish clouds and even down toward the river there was not a shred of mist.

Luke started the car, scowled at the faint-hearted growl of the battery. Tomorrow, he'd take it to the station and charge it up a bit. Tomorrow. F. MacLane would be leaving town—or so he'd said. Luke backed out of the driveway too fast, scattering gravel, making that screeching sound that got on his mother's nerves.

Rudolph Tarrant opened the door to Luke. Thick brown hair curled around his ears and down the back of his neck. His shirt was a gorgeous rose color and bright green trousers hugged his hips. His greeting was almost as hearty as Mr. Tarrant's and he steered Luke into the living room as if they were long-lost pals.

The Christmas tree's angel touched the ceiling, its lights flicked on and off like the sign over a road joint. Soft Christmas music came from the hi-fi set, but nobody seemed to be listening. Wrappings covered half the green carpet and the kitten rolled happily in a tangle of silver ribbon. Mr. and Mrs. Tarrant had bags under their eyes and looked weary; Luke surmised they had overcelebrated Rudy's homecoming.

Milo came from the back of the house somewhere at Mrs. Tarrant's call. She wore a little white leather skirt and a fringed suede shirt and tall white boots. To Luke's dismay her hair had changed from its soft neutral shade to daffodil yellow and hung in a waterfall of curls— *curls* yet—over her slim neck. She had always gone conspicuously light on make-up; now, her eyes were heavily shadowed, her mouth strange with silvery lipstick.

Luke felt like a slob in his jeans and shabby jacket. He would wear his suit to Edith's later, of course, but it hadn't occurred to him to dress up just to give Milo her present. How could he know she'd be dressed out like this? She patted her hair and laughed.

"It's a wig, Luke," she said gaily and Luke thought of Mrs. Boyle in that weird garage last night. "A Christmas present from Rudy. These, too," and she brushed at the skirt, thrust a leg out so he must look at the high-topped boot. "How do you like my outfit? Pretty neat, eh?"

Luke reached into his pocket but didn't take the velvet box out. "Could you—could we ride around a few minutes?" he asked, his throat dry, as if he had stage fright.

"Of course," Mrs. Tarrant said and Luke was sorry for all the times he'd thought her a silly old woman. "Come back, though, and help me clear all this litter up, Milo, you hear? What a mess!" She looked around the room as if it hurt to turn her eyes. Milo went over and took a package from under the tree and Rudolph showed them out the door.

Luke drove out River Street, letting the car glide gently downhill as the street narrowed and the houses gradually petered out. He turned off on the sandy, crooked road under the thin shadows of bare trees laced with wintry sunlight. Milo sat close to him, holding the package that wasn't much bigger than the box in his pocket but wrapped in silver paper with a holly pattern and a green rosette stuck in the middle of it. I should've wrapped hers, he thought. His heart was beating fast and he wondered if she could be feeling the way he was.

At the end of the road where the brown grass was thin from all the night parking he stopped. He put his arms around her, closing his eyes so it wouldn't be like holding a stranger with that crazy yellow hair and all the make-up. He liked the perfume she was wearing, though —it seemed to belong to her—and he drew a deep, dizzying breath of it.

"You love me, Milo?" he whispered onto the top of her strange little head.

"Well, of course, Luke."

Why did she have to say "of course"? He sighed and took his arms from around her and drew out the red velvet box.

"I don't know if you'll like it. I didn't know what to get you."

"Me either," she confessed. "Men are terrible to get things for. Especially if they have no vices. Like, you know, smoking or drinking or something." She pushed her package onto his knee, but he couldn't start unwrapping it till he saw her touch the tiny spring that popped the lid of the box up. Her face seemed to relax, then to light up beautifully in spite of its mask of make-up, and she gave a little cry of joy. Suddenly Luke didn't mind a bit about her changed appearance; the old Milo was shining through it.

"Oh, Luke! How beautiful! It's the prettiest thing I ever saw. Oh, thank you. All the kids'll be wild with envy, they'll *hate* me, you wait and see. And I'll be sorry for all of them. Oh, you're the nicest guy in the world, you know it?"

Luke allowed a long sigh to escape him and began to fumble at the wrappings of Milo's gift. He made clumsy work of it, sliding glances at her, stopping to fasten the tricky catch of the bracelet on her wrist for her.

"Do you really like it, darling?" No trouble at all with the "darling" now. He knew he was acting like a kid, having to be reassured over and over. But he didn't care.

"I love it," she said—without any "of course" tacked onto the end.

Luke's own package, undone at last, revealed a box covered with brown simulated leather. He could feel her anxious eyes on his face as he raised the lid. The cuff links were big and square with bulging green stones. His first thought was that he had never owned a shirt with French cuffs. Well, he could buy one, buy half a dozen whether he had any place to wear them or not. Milo was saying something about their giving each other jewelry.

"I guess cuff links are kind of stupid," she added, looking at her bracelet and biting her lip.

"They are not," Luke denied. "They're great. I never had any before, Mi. These are beauties, no kidding. My dad'll snitch them to wear to church if I don't hide 'em."

Milo looked happier but not entirely convinced her choice had been appropriate. "I thought you might—I thought you might like to wear them to the Prom. I know that's next year, but—"

"Next year? That's a week from today," Luke teased.

"Gosh, that's right. I actually mean year after next, don't I? That's even worse! Well, I mean our Senior Prom anyway. If we ever graduate." She held her wrist up and tipped her gaudy little head to one side, looking at the light glancing from the golden doves.

Luke tenderly closed the brown box, tucked it and its torn wrappings into the junky old glove compartment.

"I like having them now, they'll keep." He wondered if she knew what she had been telling him—that she would still be his girl year after next, a year from next May, and that he would be taking her to the most important social affair of their lives thus far. He had had every intention of doing so, naturally, but it was wonderful to hear from her own lips that she was of the same mind. She had made his Christmas and if old F. MacLane were to drive up in that Cadillac this moment and challenge him to a duel, Luke knew he would have the grace to pity him.

He was about to start the car when Milo said, "Luke, you don't like this dorky wig, do you?"

Luke gave her a long, honest look. "I like your own hair better. Know what color your hair is, Mi? It's beige. And I like it straight, the way you usually wear it."

Milo scooped the wig with its cascading curls right off and there was her neat, smooth, fine hair wound tightly round, the edges tucked up to go under the wig. Luke leaned over and kissed the top of her head. It smelled like the shampoo Anita used—Bright Angel or something like that.

"Sweetheart," Luke murmured. It was as if, having begun, he couldn't get enough of heaping on Milo the endearments he had stored up for so long. What an ass he'd been to get so worked up over Forrest MacLane being in town. And what a creep to doubt Milo. He'd never be caught doubting her again. Never.

They rode back sitting very close together. Luke drove with one hand, an arm about Milo's shoulders.

He didn't know the grin was on his face till she said, "What are you smiling at?"

"My mom," Luke said. "Whenever we come up behind kids riding close together like us Mom says, 'There's one of those two-headed drivers. Pass carefully, Luke.' She's a sketch sometimes."

Milo laughed and said, "She's awfully nice. Your dad, too. You've got nice parents, you know that?"

Luke had never been able to figure out why it always embarrassed him for anyone to say something nice about his father and mother. But it always did and he could feel his neck and ears getting warm now. He conquered the impulse to make a flippant reply, such as "They're still parents" or "They'll do in a pinch." He just squeezed Milo's shoulder a little.

Luke didn't care what happened the rest of the day. He and Milo had agreed to spend Christmas with their families. Tomorrow night they'd go somewhere, just the two of them, Luke had told Milo. Maybe to Baysboro to some nice place like the Glass Palace. He'd buy a pale green shirt with French cuffs and he'd ask Milo to wear that little slippery orange-and-brown flowered dress with the wet look.

He ate outrageously of his sister Edith's good dinner and was patience personified with the children, helping Mike show Steve how to operate mechanical toys—poor Stevie with a wad of cotton in one ear and a mother or grandmother feeling his forehead every time he turned around to see if he was running a temperature. And when the Sawyers left the Donaldsons, Luke thanked Edith and even kissed her.

SEVEN

January was nearly over before the next club meeting. The usual round of flu in Mill Gate at this time of year laid both Sim and Chuck low, then Rollo's mother had it and he couldn't leave her. The next Friday there was a basketball game in which Butch had to play. At last, on a damp but not really cold night they gathered, inclined to be querulous and argumentative.

"Want the heat on?" Luke asked when he and Sim reached the hut. Since his illness little Sim looked more pinched and blue than ever.

"Nah. It stinks up the place," Butch objected. "Hell, it ain't cold. Who needs heat?" He had been twitting Chuck about the new car he'd got for Christmas, a shining, steel-gray sports job that had all the other guys envious. "I'm surprised you didn't drive 'er right on in the clubhouse," Butch declared. "Don't you know somebody's liable to swipe it or slice the tires up outa pure meanness, you don't watch it all the time? If I'd of got that M.G. for Christmas I'd know there was a real Santy Claus, not just an old hippie with a sack fulla crap."

"Rollo, you cold?" Luke demanded.

"Kinda," Rollo admitted, looking at the window where fog had begun to press as if it wanted in.

"You a mouse or a man?" Butch sneered. He was in an arbitrary mood and Luke hoped it wasn't going to

77

turn on poor old Sim who looked even less able to stand up for himself than usual.

"We are all mice," Luke squeaked, nibbling at his big knuckles and twitching his lip. "Only thing is, we have forgotten our little bitty fur coats. I'm colder than a witch's you-know-what. Who will light the heater? Said the little red hen, I will." He waddled across the room in a squatting position, elbows pinioned to ribs, forearms and hands flapping.

"Damn if he don't look just like a hen," Rollo marveled. "One of them fat old buff Orpingtons my granny raises. I don't believe there's a thing in the world old Luke can't mock."

Luke turned the wick up and touched a match to it but nothing happened. "We out of oil?" he muttered, forsaking the role of the little red hen.

"Nah, can't be," Butch said. "We filled 'er up that night we was in here playing rummy, didn't we, Rolly?"

"Yeah, but she always acts up, lately. Put 'er wick down some, Luke."

Luke fiddled with the wick, shook the rusty heater, struck another match. Flame shot up, smoke jetted through the perforations in the top of the heater. "Careful," Sim cried, terror twisting his sharp face.

"You scared?" Butch jeered. "Luke knows that old tin can like a woman. You got to handle her the same way, huh, Luke?"

Luke carefully adjusted the wick. The smoke disappeared, the flame lost its angry red and began to burn blue. Luke got up from his haunches, shook his hair off his forehead. "Reckon I better take that thing apart before next meeting, clean it up some—maybe get a new wick or burner or whatever." He grinned at Butch. "You ever get that washing machine going?"

"Nah." Butch caressed the chin whiskers that were

actually beginning to look like a beard. "Ma got a new one. She'll have it tore up in a month or two, wanta bet?"

"What'd you do with the old one, scoop it up in a basket and give it to the Salvation Army?" Luke was laughing, recalling the chaotic array of parts strewn over the Boyles's garage.

"Kicked it over in the corner," Butch drawled. Luke wondered what corner but said no more. It was none of his business; besides old Butch was probably feeling low enough about his family situation as it was. The boys gathered around the table for a poker game.

The room got too warm and Luke turned the heater off before the game was over. It seemed to him that nobody's heart—except maybe Sim's—was really in what they were doing. Maybe the club was petering out. After all, the time was bound to come, wasn't it, when they would grow out of the need for each other's company, turn to other things. His mind kept straying from the cards and he was glad when they decided to stop playing.

Chuck flung himself onto the sofa and the springs yelped like a live thing. "Why don't we do something different next meeting?"

"Like what?" Rollo said.

"Aw, I don't know. Like have a party maybe. Girls and everything."

"Don't you ever think about anything else?" Butch growled.

"You know anything better to think about?" Chuck said with a smirk. "Man, I mean no place is off limits now I got a car won't break down on me every few yards. Know where I was last night?"

"Home studying for that physics test, I presume." Luke pursed his mouth.

"Nah. That was Sim."

"Old Simmons don't have to bone," Rollo yawned. "It's all up there already in his head. Wisht I had some of it in mine. Sometimes, I feel like dropping the whole damn deal, no kidding. Way it looks now, I'm gonna flunk out anyhow."

"Aw, they'll move you along to get shut of you—like they do me every year," Butch said.

"Hey!" Chuck sat up suddenly. "Sim's not the only brain in our class, you know that? That new girl that showed up after the holidays is in that French class I'm going to drop. Man, is she ever good!"

Butch leered. "You sure you talking about her brain, Chuck?"

"What's her name, Sim? You know who I mean. You all know who I mean. You don't mean you all haven't at least looked her over."

Luke knew which girl Chuck meant—the tall, quiet one with the heavy brown hair tied back and hanging almost to her waist.

"What's that girl's name, Sim?" Chuck asked again.

"Susan," Sim murmured and blushed. "Susan Bently."

Butch guffawed. "Lookit Sim. Red as a beet."

Luke laughed with the others but distaste nudged him. He didn't seem to be in the mood for Butch tonight.

To give Sim's blush time to subside, Luke said, "You never said where you were last night, Chuck."

Chuck looked smug. "Briar Hill. You-all know Leslie Richards?"

Butch whistled. "Heard tell of her—just like you have. What you want us to buy, man? That girl's twenty-five if she's a day."

"I never asked her her age," Chuck said, his handsome face dreamy.

"What *did* you do, park in front of the drugstore and

80

watch Les Richards drink root beer with some Briar Hill *man?*"

"I just talked to her a few minutes," Chuck admitted, lowering his lids modestly. "But I'm taking her out tomorrow night. *Eve's Daughter* is playing at the Camelia over there."

"Oh m'gawd," Butch breathed. "You on the level, Holland? Personally, I b'lieve you're lying like a rug."

"Wall-to-wall," Luke murmured.

"Now, wait a minute," Chuck protested, looking, Luke thought, as if he'd bitten off more than he could chew.

"Aw knock it off, Chuck," Luke said, acting as bored as he suddenly felt. "We going to throw a party here or aren't we? That's what we're supposed to be settling, right?"

"I'm for it," Chuck said quickly, willing to switch the subject now he had them wondering. "Judy'll come, I know."

"How you know?" Butch fingered a beaten cigarette from his flattened pack. "She hears you been tomcattin' round like you claim you have—"

"Why don't we have something special?" Sim put in anxiously, glancing at Luke for approval. "Like a Valentine party."

"Why not?" Luke said, feeling he couldn't care less.

"Yeh. You can hang little hearts and flowers all over the place." Butch blew smoke through his nostrils.

Luke sent a pained look slowly round the room. "We'll have to clean the joint up first. Couldn't invite a mess of pigs here the way it looks now."

"Man, you said it," Rollo sighed. "Them big old cockroaches going to carry it off some night, we don't get get after 'em."

Butch dropped his cigarette butt into a Coke bottle

and rolled it under the table. "Sounds a helluva lot like work."

Sim puckered his brow but his eyes were shining behind his thick glasses. "Nothing's for free—is it?"

Almost in spite of themselves enthusiasm began to mount. They spent another half hour settling a time for the party and decided on next meeting night, two weeks from now. That would put it near enough to St. Valentine's Day to justify the occasion.

It was about ten-thirty when Luke walked into the house. His father was sitting by the TV but it wasn't turned on. Luke stood in the door a moment but his father didn't turn around. His head was bent slightly forward and Luke saw he had fallen asleep. It gave him a little shock—an old man dozing in his chair. His dad wasn't that old for goshsakes! He felt he should wake him, talk to him. Somehow, though they were both here living under the same roof, they didn't seem to see much of each other anymore . . .

"Mom gone to bed?" Luke said loudly and Henry Sawyer's head jerked up. He snatched his glasses off, blinked at Luke.

"Must've dropped off," he said. "Yes, Marty's gone to bed. What time is it?"

"Not eleven yet. You play scrabble?"

Henry began to get up stiffly. "No, my stomach was bothering me a little again and your mother's interested in her book—that one she got from the library, I forget the name of it. Something about the terrible state of the world—food won't go round for exploded population, water giving out, everybody expiring in a pile of garbage. How'd your meeting go?"

"Per usual, I guess." Luke yawned. "Well, reckon I'll sack in. Got to work in the morning."

"That makes two of us." His father turned the lamp off, not waiting for the eleven o'clock news. Luke lingered, watching him make his way out of the living room by the light from the hall.

"Maybe you ought to see Doc Holland about your bellyache, Dad," he said uneasily. He knew how touchy Henry was about the attacks, let alone receiving advice from his son.

"Oh, it's nothing a little soda bicarb won't take care of," Henry said lightly.

Martha's door was open and Luke could see her narrowing her eyes at the print in the thick volume she held at some distance. She needed her glasses changed but kept putting it off. Luke felt irritated. What made them act so childish? You'd think at fifty-five and nearly sixty they'd be grown-up. Unless senility was already setting in.

Martha looked up from her book and wriggled her fingers at Luke. He said, "Night, Mom; night, Pop."

By the time he was in his own room the foolishness of his parents had slid out of Luke's mind. The light shone on Milo's picture. He studied it tenderly, her serious lips, her big eyes behind the silly granny glasses she didn't need, her hair lying long and straight over her shoulders, the chain of her gold cross at the V neck of her sweater.

After he was in bed and the light out, thoughts wound like a slow tune in his head. The word "womanly" came to mind, blooming sweetly, a kind of poetry. Womanly is Milo. Milo is my woman. He liked that much better than "my girl." It was adult, it was good. All his feelings about her since Christmas had been more grown-up and solemn, he thought with satisfaction. They made "girl" and "going steady" sound, as Martha had said, like children playing at something.

Luke began to feel sorry for the others in the club. Scouting around for dates, shooting bull, making something out of nothing. He knew he'd be the same if it wasn't for Milo. I am a lucky guy, he told himself. Luke the lucky. I don't always think that. But look at old Butch and his weird family. And Sim, pulled in two because his mother and father couldn't live together, always having to take off somewhere and visit his father during vacation times. Even Chuck with his new car and a fat allowance seemed somehow groping all the time; it was like he had to ape Butch or somebody, not trusting himself to be just Charles Holland, only son of Dr. Bob Holland whom everybody loved. . . .

Luke's thoughts swung from Chuck back to Milo and he groaned, turning onto his side. Through his squeezed-together lids he could see her at the pool last summer, that first time they went. Two little scraps of material that was her swim suit covering two fragments of her slight body. Drops of water glistening on her tanned skin. Long hair streaming water. . . .

Feverishly, he kicked the covers to the foot of the bed. No way to get to sleep, thinking about Milo in a bikini. He began to feel panicky. Seventeen years old and another whole year of school after this one. Maybe he wasn't so lucky. What did people do about being in love, serious love, not just playing around?

There was the pill, of course. Luke didn't know how they went about it exactly but girls did get hold of that magical little tablet—he'd bet his bottom nickel Esme kept a supply, wouldn't put it past her to swipe them from her father's medicine cupboard! And Joy Dekle was another one. Hell, he'd bet all those smooth little chicks managed.

If he could make love to Milo, Luke thought desperately, he would be a man, not a raw virgin boy, unsure of himself, frightened and inferior. He wouldn't have to be afraid of F. MacLane all the time, wouldn't have to think with envy of his friend Chuck in case he was telling the truth with his boasting.

The thought was hardly formed before shame washed over Luke in a hot, drowning tide. What was with him, thinking of Milo like this, wanting to use her as MacLane had used Eva Covington. . . . It wasn't that, of course it wasn't! He loved Milo. He wanted her for his own, all of her. Most of all, he didn't want the miserable doubting. He wanted Milo completely and forever and no other girl—ever.

But his shame lingered, refusing to be argued away. And no matter how he tried to spread the image of Milo's innocence over her, he still wondered about the other boys—except Sim who had never had a girl. Butch made their hair stand on end with his tales and, cutting down a little for the sake of reason, Luke did not doubt them. Chuck could be making his up out of whole cloth—and then again there could be some truth in them. Rollo you couldn't tell about; he was almost as quiet as Sim when the talk was of girls, but still water ran deep, as they said. What if Luke and Sim were the only ones without experience. . . .

So what. He wanted to marry Milo, have everything right and regular. Another wave of shame welled up in him, even his eyes felt scalded. Then he was cold and pulled the covers back over himself, trembling.

Even if he could persuade Milo to get married—kids did, going across the state line, lying about their ages— they wouldn't be allowed to finish school. Luke could imagine Milo's parents flinging fits all over the place, the shock and disappointment of his own parents. The crying, the floor pacing, like when Edith eloped with Mike Donaldson, only it would be a lot worse because

Mike had been twenty and Edie eighteen. Besides, Milo wouldn't get to be a cheerleader if they got kicked out of school.

Luke put his light on, scratched around under his bed for the book he was reading. The lines ran together at first, but gradually they began to get through to him. The book was *The Red Badge of Courage* and after a while Luke Sawyer faded out of the picture and that other boy, fighting the Civil War, took over. Luke read till his eyes grew too heavy and gritty to stay open.

EIGHT

"I'm worried about your father," Martha said, folding the sewing in her lap. She smoothed the pink material tenderly. As if, Luke thought, it were Sylvy instead of a dress for her.

"How come?" He switched from one channel to another, getting a fuzzy picture every time. Have to have the set repaired again, might be smarter to buy a new one. Be keen if they could get a color set. "How come you're worried about Dad?"

Martha peeked between the folds of material to locate the needle, dropped her thimble into the workbasket.

"Because," she said at last, "he worries about me."

Luke snorted. "That's logical, I must admit. Why does he worry about you? You're O.K., aren't you?"

Martha nodded, a frown seaming her forehead. "I'm all right. That's just it—and it's not like your father to worry. He never was one to worry; that was always my department, according to him. I do wish he'd go see Bob Holland. He seems to feel it would be a disgrace to give in and admit he's not well."

"That's bright, too," Luke muttered. He remembered Friday night, coming in and finding Henry dozing in this very chair, remembered him saying he hadn't felt up to playing scrabble. He hadn't talked with his father since, the week being taken up with one thing and another, and now it was Thursday, almost a week later.

"I told him he ought to see Doc, last week," Luke said. He felt slightly on the defensive, as if someone were blaming him. "What's he working tonight for if he's not feeling good? Ed Baines is a lot younger than Dad, why can't he stay sometimes? Why's it always got to be Henry Sawyer hopping to it when old man Wilson gets a bee in his bonnet? He's nothing but an old skinflint."

"Now Luke," Martha protested, "you ought not to malign Mr. Wilson like that. He thinks the world of Henry."

"Humph. Ought to. Where'd he be without Dad to run the store for him? He thinks the world of Thaddeus Wilson, that's who he thinks the world of."

"Henry loves that business, Luke," Martha said wistfully. "It's like his own, he's been there so long. I think Mr. Thad looks on him as a son, not having any of his own. He hasn't got anybody, you know."

Luke thought of a word he couldn't say in his mother's presence and turned the TV off in disgust. "Mr. Thad looks on him as a handy tool to make more dough for Mr. Thad Wilson," he said.

His mother sighed. "I don't know what makes you young things so bitter and radical-sounding. Especially about everything we older ones do or think. You haven't got that sort of attitude toward Jeff Beale, your boss."

"I haven't worked for him a hundred and one years," Luke growled. "I'm not about to, either."

"What I was thinking," Martha went on carefully, "was that maybe you could talk to your father. Get him to let you take him to the doctor—just for a general checkup, you know. I don't believe he's had one since that time he had pleurisy and that must've been five or six years ago."

Luke looked at his mother as if she had taken leave of her senses.

"Who, me? Me *take* Pop to a *doctor?*"

Martha nodded vigorously. "Yes, you. I've been thinking you and your father aren't—well, you don't have much time together. I don't mean that either of us should monopolize you, Luke. I hope you know that. But you're Henry's only son, the son he'd given up thinking we'd ever have. Well—what I mean is, you're something extra special to your dad. I guess that's what I'm trying to say."

Luke was acutely embarrassed. He wanted to say, "I appreciate the compliment" or "Well for goshsakes, Ma, thanks." But he was silent, wishing he'd gone to Cyd's as he had thought of doing after supper.

"He'd go a lot quicker for you than he would for me," he finally managed when the silence threatened to go on forever. "I can try, if you want me to, but I don't b'lieve he'll budge." The more he said the more uneasy and irritable he felt. "Just don't count on anything," he ended peevishly.

"You'll never know if you don't try," Martha said quietly. She looked at Luke with gratitude. He got up and moved purposefully toward the door.

"I've got a book report to turn in tomorrow. I'd clean forgot about it."

He felt burdened by his mother's suggestion. He was going to sound mighty foolish, trying to lay the law down to his old man. On top of that it would probably irritate Henry Sawyer to one of his rare outbreaks of temper, start up the business over his grades likely as not and Luke sure as heck didn't want that! Well, he was stuck with it now and would have to take a whack at it. He'd do it sometime soon—when it seemed like the psychological moment.

He put a record on and took up *The Red Badge of Courage* to glance through. Once he got going, he forgot he hadn't been in the mood to prepare the report and worked intently, the thump and throb of the music forming the background his parents could never understand was a necessity for homework.

He didn't hear the car come into the driveway. It wasn't till he had put his work away and was in bed that he heard the murmur of voices in the room under him and thought again of the irksome task his mother had set him. Thinking about it made him uncomfortable and he deliberately turned his mind to other things.

On Wednesday before the next club meeting it rained in the night and turned sharply cold by morning. Martha took Henry to work, then came back to drive Luke to school. He was scowling over his oatmeal with grated pecans sprinkled over the top of it and three heaping spoonfuls of sugar on top of that.

"I don't see how you stand it so sweet," his mother said, shuddering. "All that sugar's bad for your skin, not to mention your teeth."

"Only way I can get it down," Luke mumbled, adding another sprinkle of sugar. She knew good and well he didn't like cooked cereal, but this morning he was glad to have something hot under his belt.

He and the other boys had arranged to set everything up at the hut tonight for the party—except the eats—as both Luke and Rollo had to work after school. Luke looked forward to tomorrow night with mixed feelings. You never could tell beforehand how a party was going to turn out—whether it would hum along on its own momentum with everybody having a ball or die on its feet and be a complete drag. Then, there was all that cleaning to do and he wasn't that crazy about housework. On this raw, cold Thursday morning Luke had the feeling he would be glad when the whole stupid thing was over.

It was even colder when, after supper, the boys gathered at the hut. Sim, who had been in a state of high excitement since Esme's acceptance, had to clench his teeth to keep them from chattering, and Rollo had worn two sweat shirts and a sweater. Luke hadn't got around to taking the heater apart as he had intended and had to go through the usual process of dealing with its uncertain temperament to get it started.

They clustered about it with spread hands for a few moments, discussing how and where to begin their house cleaning. Butch made them snigger by comparing the clubhouse to more unsavory buildings, but at last they set to work with a will. Half the floor was wet and sudsy when Rollo let out a yell.

"The heater! Lookit that damn stove, it's gonna blow up."

They froze at their tasks—Butch shoving the sofa against the wall, Rollo sweeping the part of the room Luke hadn't begun to scrub, Sim standing on a chair to tack a paper streamer to the ceiling, Chuck washing the top of the table. Five pairs of eyes were glued to the kerosene heater with red flames and sooty smoke pouring from the perforations in its top. Already its rusty sides and handle glowed red-hot and a low, throbbing roar came out of the oil tank at the base of it.

Sim's chair went over with a crash and he was picking himself up and running toward the heater, still holding an end of paper streamer in his hand. He didn't drop it till it flared up, the flame leaping toward his face. His action broke the spell holding the others. Luke began to pull the cover from the sofa. Rollo seized his discarded sweat shirt, started toward Sim and the heater. Butch, getting there before him, grabbed the handle only to drop it with a yell.

"Get back, you damn fools," he bellowed, pushing Chuck aside while little Sim, mad with terror, flew to the bucket of scrub water, lifting it as if it were a teacup.

"No, Sim," Luke shouted. "Don't! Don't put water on it." But they were all yelling and acting berserk now and Sim half ran, half slid across the soapy floor with the bucket in his skinny arms. Luke saw Chuck clawing at the door as Sim heaved the water onto the flames.

The red-hot metal hissed and white steam mingled with the black smoke rising to the roof. Burning oil ran out of the seam that had cracked as the water struck it and spread a flaming carpet to the door Chuck wrenched open. Luke groaned as he felt the strong draft touch his hot face. Why were they all doing the wrong things? You have to smother fire, keep doors shut. . . .

He beat at the flames with the sofa cover, so big and awkward he couldn't keep a proper grip on it, and stamped his feet at the little tongues of fire licking toward him, closer and closer with unbelievable speed.

"Get out," Chuck was yelling, snatching at Butch, at Rollo. "Sim! get the hell out! Luke! Leave it—Get out—"

Luke ran back to the end of the hut he'd been scrubbing, hoping the wet floor would discourage the flames, but the smoke was rolling like fog now, oil-scented and choking. He seized a chair and smashed the window-pane, heard Rollo cry, "I'm getting outa here, come on, you guys."

Luke dove through the window, scarcely feeling the bits of jagged glass bite into his hands as he pushed himself up. He was stunned by the blow as he landed, headfirst, then scrambled up, looking dizzily around for the others. Surely they'd got out, they had to be out. . . .

He didn't see them and ran around to the door in time to see Chuck stumble through it, slapping at his jeans and shirt that kept breaking out in little smouldering patches. Luke could see the shine of sweat—or tears, he couldn't tell which—on Chuck's smudged face. He tried to ask about the others but nothing would come out of his parched throat.

Then he saw Rollo's dark face against the blue-white face of Sim that looked unconscious. Rollo dumped Sim on the ground, his panting breath coming like sobs. Luke didn't know his own clothing was on fire till Chuck started pounding him. He began to be dimly conscious of pain in his arms and across his back apart from Chuck's blows. His shirt hung in charred tatters and his flesh burned again when mist touched the exposed areas.

"Butch! Where's Butch?" Rollo cried, starting toward the hut, a ghastly bonfire now, lighting the wintry woods. "Butch is in there!"

The door belched a cloud of oily smoke and Rollo leapt back. Luke and Chuck joined him, all screaming like madmen. Luke couldn't believe his scalded eyes when he saw little Sim on all fours, crawling like an animal—or a baby—to the frame of the door outlined in flames.

Their screams changed to "Sim! Come back here, you can't go in. Come back!" The cloud of smoke rolled over Sim's crawling shape, spread and thinned, dissipating in the river mist, and they saw him stand up before he disappeared.

Luke knew what he was seeing couldn't be happening. He'd wake up and find it was a nightmare. In just a minute he'd wake up and find his dad standing over him, shaking him, telling him he'd been yelling in his sleep to beat anything. He tried to go toward the burning doorway, but of course you couldn't move in a nightmare.

Then there was Butch beside him, a devil or an angel right out of hell. Charred bits of hair stuck to his forehead, blackened rags hung on his big body—but how could Butch be here when he was in there burning up with Sim? Even when he heard Butch pant something about coming through a busted window, Luke knew it was just another part of the crazy dream.

They could hear Sim screaming now, screaming Butch's name over and over, choking, screaming, choking again, not screaming anymore.

Luke didn't know Butch had left his side till he saw him plunging into the hut. You couldn't see the door now, just the black, skeletal shape of Butch. Somebody —Luke thought it was Rollo but maybe it was Chuck —was sobbing.

Blubbering and gasping, "Jesus, Ahh-h Jesus," Chuck and Rollo ran toward the fire and though Luke knew he couldn't move, still in the grip of his nightmare, he was running with them, after them. His face and body sizzled in the incredible heat and two figures, Butch's big one and Sim's little one, rolled out of the hut at their feet.

Somehow, they were dragging them, he and Chuck and Rollo. Pulling them over the scorched, ember-strewn ground, away from the burning. A great shushing sound rose with a swirl of sparks and rolling smoke as the roof of the little hut collapsed.

The sirens woke Luke from his nightmare. He could hear them wailing as the two fire trucks roared down River Street. Cars were coming and people spilling out of them, shouting and milling around.

All the starch went out of Luke's knees and he saw

the ground, still red in the glare of the fire, rising toward him. He thought with anguish, I didn't take Dad to the doctor. The ground rose and smacked him in the face but he didn't feel it.

NINE

Luke lay on the hard, flat table under a blanket and shook. The blanket didn't seem to do any good, though it came right up to his chin, scraping his skin that felt tender. He was cold, so cold. He knew he had blacked out just as the fire trucks arrived; maybe the screaming sirens had given him this headache. . . .

Martha Sawyer bent over him. Her face was pale and her chin trembled—as if she were cold, too. "Drink some, Luke," she said holding a paper cup to his lips. "Drink some water." She slipped her arm under his neck and he flinched, shaking harder. Some of the water spilled on his face, running down like tears, and Martha wiped it away.

"You're going to be all right. We're just waiting for Dr. Bob to get to you." She set the paper cup down and turned her face away. So she could cry without him seeing—who did she think she was fooling?

"Where's Dad?" Luke asked, holding his teeth together to keep them from chattering.

"With the doctor."

"The doctor?"

"He wanted to talk to him about you," Martha said. He saw her wipe her eyes on a ragged tissue that had about had it.

"I'm O.K." If that hellish pain would stop pounding

against the back of his skull he would be O.K. He tried to raise his head but gave up, letting it loll back on the skimpy pillow.

"Son?"

Luke opened his eyes and saw his father standing beside him. Henry's face was the color of putty. "How do you feel, Luke?"

"O.K.," Luke said again. "I'm sorry about the hut— and everything—"

"Don't worry about it," his father said. "We're just thankful—" and Martha said on a sob that burst like a bubble, "Oh, dear God yes, Luke. So thankful."

A nurse came in with another blanket and draped it over Luke—he was afraid she was going to cover his face and struggled to raise his chin higher, but she tucked it round his neck. He wondered if they had covered Sim's and Butch's faces, if they were lying down there in the morgue with blankets over them. His shaking became more violent and the nurse said, "You're all right. Doctor's on his way."

Luke swallowed, trying to ask about Butch and Sim but the words wouldn't come. Then the table was being rolled somewhere with him still on it, bundled up like a sack, and Dr. Bob Holland was bending over him, big and homely and very gentle. Even so, Luke had to set his clacking teeth not to yelp like a hound while Dr. Bob worked on his hands with a pair of tweezers.

"You go over there and sit down, Henry," Luke heard him say. "You look worse than Luke does." He heard other things, too—"concussion" and "surface burns" and something about "cuts." He licked his lips and braced himself to ask about the dead boys but still couldn't, asking about Chuck and Rollo instead.

"Chuck and Rollo are home already," Dr. Bob told him. "You'll be home in another half hour."

Several shots and pills later, Luke walked out of the hospital between his father and Mike Donaldson. His hands were bandaged and hung like enormous white sausages at his sides, and his legs felt like rubber, but the pounding in his head was getting fainter.

Every room in the Sawyer house was ablaze with light and Edith had Luke's bed ready, the clean sheets turned down, one of Martha's thermal blankets she'd got for Christmas on the bed instead of the shabby old down comfort he'd clung to for years. It was like the one other time he came home from the hospital, Luke remembered. From having his tonsils out when he was nine.

Edith was pale and looked as if she were scared to get too near Luke. She just whispered his name and put her hand over her mouth as if she'd said a dirty word. The scent of freshly perked coffee drifted from the kitchen, following Luke and his parents and Mike.

"We better leave him so that sedative can start working," Henry said to Martha when they had him settled like a big, gawky baby in bed. Mike had already left; Luke guessed he'd be answering Edie's questions over some of the hot coffee.

"Are you all right, dear? Can I get you anything?" Martha hovered like an anxious mother hen.

"I'm fine, Mom." He tried to smile as she ducked down quickly and kissed him on the cheekbone. She hit a sore spot but he managed not to let on. He let them get as far as the door, then called his father back. "Can I talk to you a minute, Dad?"

Martha, quivering with alarm, turned back, too, but Henry motioned toward the stairs. "Go get some coffee, Marty, it's all right now," and she went, reluctantly, her steps slow.

Henry sat down on the sagging side of Luke's bunk.

His face was not as gray now but he looked sick—as if something had given way inside him. He put his hand carefully on the hump Luke's knee made in the blanket. Someone—Edith, no doubt; she was one to think of everything—had plugged a night light in the outlet just beyond the bed. In its wan light the objects in the room assumed grotesque shapes. Luke took a deep breath, expelled it in a rush of words.

"Dad, I've got to know. They're dead, aren't they— Butch and Sim?" His plunging heart seemed to be right behind his eyes, threatening to burst the sockets, and he could hear the harsh rasp of his breath.

Henry's hand pressed the hump of blanket gently. "No, Luke. They're not dead."

"You . . . you're sure, Dad? You wouldn't be trying to . . . to spare me or something stupid like that—"

"No, I mean yes, I'm sure. I talked with Bob Holland. They didn't get off as light as the rest of you, but—"

"You mean they're going to die. Prob'ly?"

"Probably they're going to be all right. It may be a while before they are but Doc thinks they're going to make it. So do the others, the two doctors they called in from Baysboro. You must rest now, Son. You've had something to make you sleep, mustn't talk it off, you know. There'll be plenty of time to talk later. When you're feeling better."

"O.K. Thanks. Thanks a lot." There was a huge, hard lump in his throat, partly from what his father had told him, partly from the way he'd done it. Understanding that Luke had to know the truth, not treating him like a sick child.

"Good night, Son. I'll leave the door open a crack, O.K.? Sing out if you want anything."

Luke didn't answer. He thought he was falling and tried to catch the side of the bunk. Pain tingled through his hand. He heard his father's steps getting fainter and fainter.

It was a weird week. The more fuss his family made over him, the more out-of-touch and shrunk into himself Luke felt. Chuck and Rollo went back to school in the middle of the week but Dr. Holland said Luke was to take it easy a few more days.

Again and again he tried to reconstruct in his mind all that had happened, but he couldn't quite do it. There were gaps that bothered him. The scene of Butch and Sim rolling like charred stumps out of the burning hut was clear, haunting him when he was awake and returning in dreams when he slept, and he relived his own dive through the broken window with no trouble. He couldn't remember how he'd got to the hospital or whether Milo had been present during any of it.

The morning after the fire he had asked how he got to the hospital and his mother told him Mr. Bently, the new pharmacist, had taken him and Rollo and Chuck. She said it was before she and Henry got to the fire with Mike in his car. Martha shuddered, telling Luke.

"There we were—and couldn't find you. Nobody seemed to know anything. The ambulance, you see, had already gone with the other boys but we didn't know. It was terrible till we got to the hospital and found all five of you there. I hope never to go through anything so horrible again."

"That makes two of us," Luke said.

"Mr. Bently seems a nice kind of person. I'll always be grateful to him, we have so much to be thankful for."

She always ended up like that. "He's Susan Bently's father," Luke said, and when his mother looked at him queerly he knew she was wondering if he'd recovered from his concussion. He guessed it did sound kind of silly; what he really wanted to know was where Milo had been at the time. He hadn't heard a thing from her and it was hours since it had happened, hours that seemed days already.

That afternoon Milo came to see Luke, telephoning first to see if it was all right. "I couldn't say no," Martha told Luke, "even though I know you really aren't up to any excitement. She promised not to stay but a few minutes."

"Aw, heck, Ma," Luke protested. "What'll she think? Did you *tell* her a few minutes?"

"Not exactly. She wouldn't want to do you any harm, Luke."

Luke got up and looked in the mirror over his chest of drawers. Holy Jupiter! He was almost sorry Martha had let Milo come. His face was a mass of red blotches and blisters. And his hair! Enough to make you throw up. A regular pixie cut. He tried to comb the seared bits and points that were all that was left of his long, heavy bang (he guessed it was all right to admit he'd been proud of it, now it was no more).

Milo was awkward and her eyes looked scared behind her glasses. She held a tight little bunch of jonquils toward him, saying timidly, "These were all I could find in the yard; it's early even for them."

"Gee, thanks, Milo." Luke wanted to say something funny, make her laugh so the frightened look would leave her face. He guessed he looked scary all right; he recalled Edith's scared eyes and Anita, driving over just for a couple of hours this morning, had cried and kissed him—very carefully—on the top of his singed head.

"I've never seen your room before," Milo said when

Martha took the flowers downstairs to put them in water. She looked around curiously. "It's much nicer than Rudy's."

"Were you at the fire last night, Milo?" Luke felt he had to know.

Milo shook her head. "I went with my mother to Briar Hill last night to see my aunt. She's sick. Oh, Luke, I'm glad I wasn't here. I'd have died, I think, wondering if you were in the hut." She twisted the ends of her hair. "When we got home and Daddy told us I wanted to call your house but they wouldn't let me. It was late and Mother said I shouldn't bother your folks. But everybody knew by then you were safe. So I could sleep, at least."

Luke felt a little let down; if she'd said she hadn't slept a wink all night . . . oh, well. Wasn't fuss enough being made over him? Martha came up with the jonquils nicely arranged in a blue vase. She set them on the record cabinet and Milo jumped up as if she thought Martha was going to chase her out.

"Sit down, dear," Martha said. "You've only just come. I'll get some Cokes—Luke's supposed to get down all the fluids he can." She went out again and Milo sank again to the edge of her chair.

"You didn't get to see inside the clubhouse," Luke said. He was feeling itchy and restless and his hands throbbed under the bandages. "The old hut's had it."

"Oh, I don't care. I mean, us not getting to see inside. So long as you're all O.K."

They sat looking at each other then, at a loss for words till Martha came with the drinks. She handed Milo a glass and set a sweaty bottle with a straw in it on the table beside Luke. The ends of his fingers sticking out of the bundles of gauze were numb and stiff and he couldn't do much with them.

"I reckon Butch and Sim aren't exactly O.K.," he said.

"The class sent flowers to the hospital today."

Luke could see old Gerry Bishop, the class president, trotting round with pencil and paper getting up the subscriptions to pay for the flowers. He said, "Doc Holland told my dad they're going to be all right, though, only it might take a while."

Milo looked into her glass and didn't say anything. Luke began to feel nervous and sweat broke out in the palms of his hands, stinging the lacerations. Why didn't she say something? Did she know something he didn't about Butch and Sim? When she'd drunk about half her Coke she stood up again. She came hesitantly to the side of the bed where Luke was sitting and his heart started thumping as if he'd been running. He could see tears in her eyes behind the silly glasss.

"I'm glad it didn't wait till tonight to happen," he burst out. "You girls would've been there if it had." He had a brief, awful vision of them—Judy, Esme, Arlene, Joy, and Milo running through the woods with their long hair on fire.

Milo stooped and quickly kissed the bandage of his right hand that was fiddling clumsily with the straw. Then she turned and ran out of the room. Luke eased himself onto his back and stared at the bunk above him. Bunk beds! Of all the stupid kid stuff—time they went to the Salvation Army and he had a man-sized bed in his room. He put both hands up and with the bandages wiped the tears seeping from the corners of his eyes.

Early the next week Chuck and Rollo came to see him. Luke was up and wandering around the house like a lost soul by that time. The headaches had let up and unless he bumped into something—which he was always doing—his burns and cuts didn't hurt too much. Nights

103

weren't so hot, yet; he still took pills to get to sleep, otherwise he was sure to have a nightmare. He had been to the doctor's office once to have the dressings changed and was to go again at the end of the week. Every night he and Milo had a long conversation over the phone.

"Lucky bum," Rollo said. "Still loafing and me and Chuck back at the salt mine."

"Yeah," Chuck grumbled, "and all because you had to jump out that window on your cotton-picking head. How come I couldn't think of that?"

"What we gonna do for a clubhouse?" Rollo asked. No one said anything; Luke thought they must know, as he did, that there wouldn't be a club anymore. How could there, even if Butch and Sim recovered? It seemed to Luke that a time in their lives had gone up in smoke and flames that night.

"Mr. Beale's holding our jobs," Rollo said. "Says he won't hire anybody else. I'll be going back Saturday, I reckon. Would've gone this week but my mama had a fit about it."

Chuck said abruptly after a silence, "Butch's off the critical list now but the No Visitors sign is still on his door. Nobody but his parents can see him."

Luke could just hear Mrs. B. calling him. "Clarry." Poor old Butch.

"Sim is in this cradle thing," Chuck plowed on. "So his skin won't touch anything, you know? First, they had like a tent over it and lights under that. I guess that hurt like hell and they've stopped it, just the cradle's all."

Cradle. Something clicked in Luke's mind: Sim crawling like a baby toward the hut. . . .

"He's had a bunch of debridements," Chuck continued, as if he couldn't stop himself, like somebody making a report.

"What's that?" Rollo asked.

"Like cutting away no-good skin and putting in new."

"You know something?" Luke broke out. "The whole damn thing was my fault."

The other boys stared. Rollo shook his head slowly; it looked small without his Afro. "Nah, Luke. It wasn't anybody's fault. It was just one of those things, right, Chuck?"

"Sure. Could happen to anybody. Does, as a matter of fact. All the time. You're always seeing something awful in the newspapers. Lots of people aren't lucky like we were, either."

"Speaking of newspapers," Rollo said, brightening a little. "You-all read what the *Star* said about us?"

"Yep." Chuck did a fair imitation of Butch's swagger. "Made heroes out of all of us—not just Butch and Sim. It was in the Baysboro paper, too. No pictures, though. Happened too quick for the photographers to get in on it. Bet that put a crimp in their big fat egos."

"It was still my fault," Luke came back doggedly to the subject. "Because I didn't clean that heater like I said I would." He let his tight breath out in a long sigh. "If this don't cure me of putting things off, I don't know what could. I thought sure both those guys had had it. That was all I could think about while I was waiting for Doc to poke needles in me and dig slivers of glass out of my hands. If they had—"

Chuck's voice was thin as a stretched wire. "Well, they haven't. You got to knock it off, Luke, leave it. It's no good mulling over things that could've happened. Far's that goes we could all've been roasted like weenies. But we weren't." Though he was handsome and

Dr. Bob was homely, something in Chuck's face resembled his father's. "You gotta admit we're lucky, even looking like we do." An exaggerated smile showed all his beautiful teeth. He touched one of the blotches on his face with tenderness.

"Yeah," Rollo sighed, passing a hand over his head. A strip of adhesive tape decorated his temple. His burns showed purple on his dark skin. "You gotta knock off those morbid feelings, Luke, you know? Everybody puts thing off. You think you got a priority on it?"

Luke felt better for their attempts to console him but it was Henry Sawyer who helped him most.

It was Thursday, a week after the fire, and Martha had gone to the hospital with Linda Simmons and the Mountjoys to see Sim. Luke and his father were in the living room and Henry asked Luke to tell him exactly what had happened at the hut.

"If you can, son. I know it had something to do with that old heater. I don't expect any trouble. Tandy didn't care about the shack and his woods didn't get burned. I'm sure he'll be glad to forget about the whole thing but we don't want any wild tales going round, you know what I mean? People saying you kids were down there drinking and raising hell. You know how easy it is for something to get started and just go plumb haywire."

So Luke began with the cleaning up and gave Henry as nearly a blow-by-blow account as he could. He was trembling by the time he got to where he had passed out, and he blurted in a cracked voice, "Pa, I don't give a hoot what people say or even about the hut being gone. If Butch and Sim can just get well, if they don't come out of it crippled up or scarred so kids run from 'em in the street—you know?"

Henry nodded, his face looking seamed and old in the light from the brass lamp.

"I know, Luke. D'you think your mother and I don't feel the same way, let alone *their* parents? Your mother says we shouldn't've let you take that old stove over there in the first place and she's right. We should've insisted on having it inspected or reconditioned or whatever. Better still, I could have got one from the store for you. That's what I ought to've done."

"But I was going to take it apart and clean it, fix it up. I could have. I just fiddled around and didn't. Like I'm always doing. So it's my fault it happened. If—"

"Hold on a minute, now. You're heaping the whole load on yourself and that's not fair. I don't say you shouldn't feel regret. Like I say, so do I. That always happens when there's some kind of a tragedy. All of us lock stables after horses are stolen. There just isn't anything you can do about that—except not let your bad feelings go for nothing. Learn, Luke, learn from experience. We all have to. Sim made a mistake, throwing water on burning oil. Smart kid like him ought to've known better, but wouldn't you be the first to feel he'd be wrong to blame himself for the whole unfortunate business?"

Luke didn't answer but the bleakness began to ease out of him. His father's quiet, unexcited tone had a calming effect, his reasonable way of looking at the thing. Luke drew a deep breath.

"There was something else, Dad."

Henry looked startled.

"Before the fire—week or ten days maybe—Mom made me promise to get you to see Dr. Holland. About that stomach trouble that keeps bugging you. I . . . I thought you'd be sore and tell me to mind my own business. I kept stalling and never got around to that, either. I feel lousy about it, even thought about it that night—before I blacked out."

Henry took his glasses off and pulled his handkerchief out to polish them. He made quite a thing out of it, working away with such concentration Luke began to fidget before his father held the glasses to the light, put his handkerchief away.

"You can quit worrying about that. I've been to Bob Holland. Got a prescription from him. I didn't say anything to your mother, she gets so upset these days. Her time of life, I reckon. And you're right, I would like as not have told you to mind your own business or get lost or something. Forget it."

"What did Doc Holland say?"

"Oh, more or less what they always do. You know. Take it easy. Not as young as I used to be. What in the Sam Hill makes people say that? As if anybody was, even the day after they're born." He patted his shirt pocket. "I keep these little pills right with me, like he said to, handy for when I need 'em."

"You ought to tell Mom," Luke said. "She'd feel better."

"Oh, I don't know." Henry began to look vaguely annoyed and Luke secretly resolved to tell her himself. He'd do it, too, not just think about it and then shove it down to the bottom of his mind as he had the other things. He was through procrastinating. . . .

"You better get to bed," his father said. "You look bushed and you've got a doctor's appointment tomorrow. I don't know if you know it, but next to Butch and Craig you were the worst hurt, that lick on your noggin and those cuts on your hands."

Luke tried to shrug his father's words aside, but he was suddenly very tired. He even decided against calling Milo, wanting only to get to bed. He had a feeling he could sleep tonight without a pill.

TEN

The next week Luke went back to school. His hands were still bandaged and he couldn't write but he tried to look, during classes, as if he were taking in everything when, as a matter of fact, his mind was miles away. The respectful attitude of his classmates made him feel self-conscious and uncomfortable.

After school he walked out to the Shell Station to see Jeff Beale.

"You take it easy awhile, Luke," Mr. Beale told him. "No hurry. With Rollo back I can get by." He looked at Luke's swathed hands. "You're not fit for much yet with those mitts."

Dr. Holland told Luke the bandages could come off in another week. "Have to start you on some mild therapy." He smiled. "Got any modeling clay left from your kindergarten days? Or you can squeeze a rubber ball. We don't want any stiffness in your fingers."

Martha wanted him to give up the job at the station. "You've got a whole week's school to make up. It's not necessary for you to have a job now. Plenty of time for that."

Luke didn't argue. But the job *was* necessary. To his self-respect. He was not about to go back to a measly two or three dollar a week allowance doled out by his father.

109

"School is your job now, Luke. It's the important thing," Henry said. Luke was afraid his father would start the old song and dance that could easily turn into a row, but Henry let it go at that. Luke still didn't say anything, knowing that when his hands had healed he would go back to his job.

Since he couldn't drive, he did a lot of walking. Martha, afraid he was overtaxing his strength, offered to drive him anywhere he wanted to go, but he turned the offers down irritably. "Doc says it's good for me to walk." Dr. Holland hadn't said so but Luke was sure he would have if he'd thought of it.

He walked out to where the hut had been and looked at the rubble. He felt nothing at all—just stood there and looked at the black and gray ashes, sodden from rain and fog as well as the fire hose. The rusty, twisted remains of the treacherous heater lay in the pile, its inanimate corpse failing to reproach him. He poked at it with the toe of his sneaker. The metal top of Mrs. Prince's table lay there, too, and the dilapidated springs of the old sofa. Near the heater lay the battered pail that had held the scrub water little Sim had hurled at the flames.

Turning away, Luke wondered if he was really a changed person or if, when the shock had all gone, he'd be the same old procrastinating, aimless Luke Sawyer he'd always been. What was it Milo had said that time, "Luke the good guy" . . . ? Maybe there'd be more to him if he'd been a bad guy. Maybe he just followed the line of least resistance, not wanting to take the trouble to be bad. An uneasy suspicion settled over him that he was a weak character. He could see himself leading a treadmill existence day in and day out like his father, working for somebody else, growing used to it and not minding any more than Henry Sawyer.

Luke went to the hospital to see Sim (he didn't know whether he would be allowed to see Butch, though Martha had told him the night before that the No Visitors sign was no longer on his door). Luke knew he wouldn't be able to banish his anxiety completely till he saw Sim and Butch with his own eyes, no matter what anybody said. Yet he was afraid, too. But he had to go, he couldn't put it off any longer.

Luke walked the length of the block a couple of times, whipping up his courage, before he could bring himself to mount the white-painted steps and push the glass door inward. The sterile, penetrating scent of the lobby was enough to make him jittery and he wanted to turn and rush out again.

Sim, still in the cradle Chuck had talked about, looked like a stranger without his glasses. They had been broken in the fire and their absence was the first thing Luke noticed. Then he went closer and Sim turned. Luke saw the deep, puckered burn extending from Sim's jaw to the corner of his eye, drawing it slightly downward.

"Hi, Sim," Luke said scarcely above a whisper.

"Oh, it's you, Luke." Sim's voice was the same; he sounded pleased. "I can't see very well—without my glasses."

"Yeah. I know." Luke wondered if Sim heard him swallow.

"I'm going to have plastic surgery." He still sounded pleased. "This thing on my face interferes with the functioning of my eyelid, see."

"Plastic surgery," Luke said, making himself sound impressed. "How about that. Like a movie star. Man, you'll send those chicks at school, Sim. The rest of us won't have a prayer."

When Sim smiled his face looked crooked—but not

bad, not really so bad. Luke could only hope Butch wouldn't look any worse.

"I guess you don't have to worry. Your girl wouldn't ever look at anybody else. Not even a movie star. You seen Butch?"

Luke shook his head. "I don't know if they'll let me."

"Is he that bad?"

Luke's heart sank. He'd put his foot in his mouth the very first thing, wouldn't you know? Of course they wouldn't have let on to Sim. He tried to crack his knuckles, forgetting his hands were bound. He cleared his throat, attempted to patch things up.

"He's better now. I—I guess he hasn't suffered any more than you, Simmons. Maybe not as much."

"Those lights were the worst," Sim admitted, turning his head restlessly. "This contraption's not too bad. Those lights made me feel like a chicken being barbecued." He smiled wanly. After a little silence he added, "Luke—my dad was here yesterday. At least, I think it was yesterday. The days all kind of run together—"

"Yeah," Luke said hoarsely. "I bet."

"Well, what I was thinking—that old saw about an ill wind blowing no good, you know? I never liked my father very much. I always thought he never liked me very much. But he came to see me. He was way out in Kansas and he drove day and night getting here and, Luke"—Sim's voice became a whisper—"he cried."

Luke looked at his feet, saying nothing. After a moment Sim said, "He must like me to do that—"

"Well, sure, Sim. I mean, you know. Of course he does."

"He said I wasn't to worry about anything, that he'd take care of everything, the surgery and all—I mean paying the bills so my mother won't have to or my grandfather. That's good, don't you think, Luke?"

"Sure, Sim, that's fine. I—I'm glad."

"You know something?" Sim giggled weakly. "I lie here and think about all your impersonations and it's better than medicine. Makes me forget the pain—when it's not too bad."

"Well, gosh, thanks, Sim. Look, I'm sorry about the hut and everything."

"Don't feel bad, Luke," Sim said earnestly. "Remember what I said about the ill wind. Maybe when I get out of here I can find us a new place to meet."

"I gotta scram now, Sim," Luke said, edging toward the door. "I'll come back. Maybe I can think up a new act or two for you."

"Gee, that'd be great," Sim said. "You do that. My mom reads to me sometimes and I won't be in this thing much longer. Dr. Holland says my burns are healing just fine."

"Well, see ya, Simmons."

As soon as he received permission to see Clarence Boyle—"A few minutes, he tires quickly," the charge nurse told him—Luke knew he'd been hoping he wouldn't be allowed to. It would have been out of his hands then and he'd have the sop to his conscience of having tried. He felt shook up enough over old Sim. Well, he was stuck with it now and would have to do the best he could. Recalling his blunder with Sim, Luke thought maybe he'd better keep his mouth shut, just listen if Butch felt like talking.

Looking for room number 17 Luke thought, queasily, This place is getting to me, this hospital smell. I want out. At least, I can get out, I'm not strung up in some contraption like poor old Sim. . . . The door of number 17 was half-open. Luke hesitated, took a deep breath, and went in.

Butch lay on his stomach, his back grinning through

the opening of the hospital gown. It looked like a bad sunburn between the edges of peeling skin. The arm on the side next to Luke was in a cast and gauze covered the back of Butch's head, a fringe of red hair showing above it. His face, turned away from Luke, had a greasy sheen, his eyes were closed.

Cowardly hope sprang again in Luke. He shouldn't wake Butch; he'd just tiptoe away and let him be. He turned to go, weak with relief, but from the bed came a faint, "Hey, Luke," and he jumped as if he'd been shot at. The voice didn't sound like Butch's, it was much too thin and weak—like a thread that anything could snap. "Sit down, Luke. Take the load off."

There were two chairs in the room, a comfortable-looking one and an uncomfortable-looking one, both covered with blue plastic. Luke took the straight one, farthest from the bed.

"Pull up closer, man," Butch said, carefully settling his head so that he faced Luke. The exertion of turning left him breathing rapidly. "Where's everybody at?"

"Oh, around." Luke made a thing of moving the straight chair closer to the bed. "How you doing, Butch?"

"O.K." His Adam's apple, which seemed to have grown more prominent, traveled up his thin throat and down again. "I'm fine. Never had it so good. Man, am I ever in around here . . ." The thread of his voice trailed off.

Luke searched desperately for something it would be safe to say. "You're in at school, too, Butch," he finally got out. "Hero of the year, no kidding. Whole town says so."

"Shit," Butch sighed. After a brief silence he added, "Sim's the hero. Little punk. Going in that hell after

114

me. How'd he think he was gonna haul me out for Cris-sake?"

"I guess he didn't think, exactly. Just did what he had to." Luke had to lean closer to hear what Butch said next.

"How come he thought he had to? Hard a time as I always gave him—I don't get it."

"I guess . . ." Luke faltered, embarrassed but some-how compelled to come out with it. "I guess he loves you." He waited for Butch to say something typical but Butch said nothing.

In the silence Luke was aware of hospital sounds—the rumble of wheels, a tinkle of glass, a mechanical voice paging somebody. Butch's eyes were closed again. Whatever it was on his face—it looked like vaseline—glistened. Luke stood up.

"I better go now, Butch. Keep your chin up."

Butch smiled without opening his eyes.

Luke walked down the iron stairs. It was only the second floor and he felt he would succumb to claustro-phobia if he took the elevator. In the street he blinked, breathing gulps of the fresh air. The hospital scent eased out of his lungs. He had a sense of escape. He had seen for himself. So now he knew. They were scarred—all five of them were scarred one way and another, weren't they?—but nobody was hideously disfigured, nobody hopelessly maimed.

He began to feel better, a lot better. It would be eas-ier to go back next time to visit them. He wondered how long they would have to stay shut up in that place. He and Chuck and Rollo had been lucky, no getting around that. In a way, Butch and Sim had, too; they'd tumbled out of that inferno alive—and Dr. Bob said they'd be all right. Luke believed it now. He decided to stop at Syd's, have a Coke, see who was there.

ELEVEN

By the middle of March spring had come, not the teasing warmth that sometimes visited Mill Gate for brief intervals in the winter but the real thing. March winds blew but they were warm winds, carrying an elusive scent of greening, growing things.

Martha began to neglect the house for her yard, puttering happily with trowel and packets of flower seeds. Dogwood starred the woods by the river. The town had had the rubbish left from the fire cleared away and violets grew along the edge of the ashes. Chuck Holland and Judy Hayes started going steady. And Butch and Sim came home from the hospital. Out beyond East Mill Gate a clutch of new homes sprang up and Clarence Boyle, Senior, had all the roofing he could do.

Martha said, "Oh, I am glad," when Henry told her. "All that medical expense must have been more than they could manage." Luke thought, but didn't say, I hope old man Boyle won't get stoned out of his mind and fall off the top of one of those houses.

Sim returned to school with new glasses, the scar on his face less disfiguring than when Luke had first seen it. He was to have his plastic surgery in Baysboro in the summer. No one laughed at little Craig Simmons anymore; his status had changed overnight and the change agreed with him. He left off tagging after Luke like a younger brother and began getting crushes on girls. But Butch Boyle did not go back to school.

Sitting in the Boyles's garage doorway (the door was still held up by the lead pipe) in the green-and-gold evening, Luke and Butch talked.

"Aw heck, Butch, you oughta go back to school. A few more weeks of this year, then one more and we're done with it." Luke hardly knew why he was urging Butch like this; maybe it was because nobody else bothered to.

"Nah." Butch lifted his shoulder in the old shrug. "I never was high school material. It's different with old Sim. You and Chuck too, maybe old Rollo even. Not me. I got nothing to prove that way. You know? There's natural dropouts, I reckon, and I'm one. All I needed was a good excuse. Now I got it. I'd never make up the time lost. Tell you the truth, I don't give a damn."

"How will you find a job if you don't? They're not hanging on trees around here, or anywheres else that I know of."

"I might help my old man, my arm toughens up a little. Or I might look around somewheres else."

"You mean you might leave home?" It was strange to think of Butch Boyle not being around. Strange and sad. Luke made a last try. "If you'd come on back to school you'd have it made, man. Look at Simmons. Nobody pokes fun at him anymore. *You'd* be a big shot, no kidding. Everybody's talking about what you did—especially Joy Dekle. She brags her head off about dating you."

"Ah, don't give me that crock o' stuff. No more school for me. I got other ideas, just need to let 'em jell a little bit, get back in shape." He looked sideways at Luke, wanting him to ask questions, but Luke said nothing. He thought, still with the sad feeling, how white

117

Butch's skin looked; even his freckles looked paler. There was a sort of glow over his head where the hair was growing in. Luke had an eerie feeling of Butch slipping away from him somehow.

Luke and Milo walked to the woods on a Sunday afternoon. Nobody parked there anymore. Since the fire the law had been strictly enforced. Milo picked flowers, her tan legs flashing, her tan hair falling forward. She looked like a little girl, running from one patch of wild violets to another—yet she seemed older now. Like him, she would often fall into silence, seem lost in thoughts he did not share. It scared Luke a little, he didn't know why. He wished they were engaged. He was working again at the station, he could buy her a ring. To wear on her finger, not on a chain around her neck.

Suddenly, he came out with it.

"Milo, we're almost seniors now. One more year at Mill Gate High. Why don't we—I mean—you know. Why don't we get engaged?" As soon as it was out he knew he hadn't done it right. Too sudden maybe. Still, he held his breath for her answer.

"Oh, Luke." She didn't look up from the clump of violets she was kneeling among. "Don't be silly."

His face burned. Angrily, he pulled her to her feet. A few violets fell to the ground. Her gray eyes looked scared.

"What do you mean 'silly'?" She twisted but he wouldn't let her go.

"I mean—you know. Well—"

"Well what?"

"It's unrealistic."

"Unrealistic how?" He held her wrists tightly and she whimpered a little.

"You're hurting me, Luke."

"Sorry." He loosened his grip, still angry and con-

118

fused. He said, "It's not unrealistic to me, Milo. Ever since we started going together I've wanted us to be engaged—sometime."

"Well, that's just it. Sometime." She wouldn't look at him.

Luke sighed, releasing her. The river murmured, a breeze set the young leaves fluttering.

"You're different," she burst out, a quaver in her voice. "You didn't use to—"

"Didn't use to what?"

"You never used to be fresh with me—"

"Fresh with you!"

"Well, rough with me, then." Her chin shook. If she cried he couldn't take it, it wasn't fair if she cried.

"I'm sorry, Mi," he said, gentle now, filled with remorse. "I didn't mean to hurt you. I never want to hurt you."

She moved off a little way, fiddling with her hair.

"You're so *serious* about everything."

"I'm serious about us for goshsakes! Aren't you?"

He began to feel afraid, sure he was saying the wrong things but unable to stop. He wanted to go to her and put his arms around her but his pride was hurt; she had moved away from him, she should come to him. Standing there in the spring woods in the soft, sweet air it was as if a chill wind sighed through his spirit. Like the draft in some dank cave.

He stooped and picked up the flowers he had caused her to drop. They looked pathetic in his big, scarred hand. He stared at them, feeling desolate. Milo was right, he was too serious. Chuck and Judy, a dozen couples he could name—he'd bet his bottom dollar they didn't make the production over their feelings that he did. But he couldn't help it, he had to know.

"Aren't you, Milo? Serious about us?"

He sacrificed his pride, going to her, holding out the violets that were already beginning to droop. Milo took the flowers, thrusting them in with the little bunch she still held in her hand.

"Of course I'm serious about us," she said fretfully. "We've got to be practical, that's all. Oh Luke, let's not fight. It's so beautiful out here—the water and the warm weather and everything. Can't we just have fun and be happy being—being boy friend and girl friend? Till we get through school anyway."

She didn't understand. She didn't understand at all. Maybe girls couldn't be expected to understand. Maybe it was only the wild, bursting passage from boyhood to manhood that sent you right up the walls.

He said sullenly, "I didn't say let's get married. I just said engaged."

"I know. But it would be such a long engagement. Our parents would have fits, yours and mine both. You know they would, Luke."

He kicked at a root. "What have our parents got to do with it?"

She looked at him pityingly. "Plenty—if we don't wait till we're a little older."

He put his arms around her and pulled her against him. She was so little and warm, her hair smelled of sunshine. He seemed to feel all the stirring of spring in his veins, the new life everywhere. It was rising in his body. He knew a place near the old mill, before you got to where they'd made the swimming pool, a little glade all shadowy and secret with some kind of lilies growing. If he could take Milo there. . . .

It was like somebody else, a voice outside himself and against his will, saying huskily, "We better go, hadn't we?" as he took his arms from around her so abruptly she stumbled a little. She looked at him questioningly. All he could think was, I want you, I want you, Milo. His hands were shaking and he pushed them into the pockets of his jeans.

They walked a way in silence, Luke not daring even to look at her. He had the feeling of having narrowly escaped something they might both have regretted. It wasn't relief exactly, and he wasn't sure whether he should be ashamed or proud of having pulled himself together. They had come to the edge of the woods when Milo spoke. She still held the bunch of violets and looked at them instead of at Luke.

"Getting engaged wouldn't change anything—that way, you know. We'd still have the problem. Like everybody else."

Luke glanced at her. "You mean you feel like I do?"

"Why not? I'm human, aren't I?"

"I'm glad, Milo," Luke said humbly.

After a moment he took his hands out of his pockets and reached for her hand. They went up the slope and along the sidewalk holding hands. The wild string music in him subsided and he felt almost normal by the time they got to the For Sale sign in front of the old Conway house.

Rollo and Arlene were sitting in the newly-painted lawn swing in the Weavers' yard. They waved and called, "Hi," but Arlene didn't ask them to stop.

"She's so standoffish," Milo complained as she and Luke walked on up River Street. "I've really tried to be friends with Arlene Weaver. So have some of the other girls. Not all, I know, but some of us have. The only white girl she has much to do with is Susan Bently—maybe because she's standoffish, too. I guess they read each other."

"They're both kind of the independent type," Luke said, but he was thinking, Rollo and Arlene are right here close to the woods but they're sitting in the swing in Weavers' yard. Maybe I don't deserve a girl like Milo. Maybe I should be running around like Butch and Chuck pretend they do, playing the field. . . .

When they got to the Sawyers' house Luke said, "Come on in and I'll see if they're going to use the car. Maybe we could ride around a little."

Thoughts of the future began to bear down upon Luke. His future. Its vagueness troubled him in a way he did not understand; it never had till now. He knew Milo was mixed up in it somehow and suspected that, like so many kids, he was putting the cart before the horse, but that kind of thinking didn't help anything either. As the spring advanced he was plagued by a restlessness he had never known before.

He did not really miss the club meetings, though sometimes he felt a fleeting nostalgia for the closeness of the other boys. They were still friends, they still saw each other now and then, but the fire that swept the hut away had somehow made too wide a gap to bridge and there seemed no way they could return to the old companionship. Sim and Chuck dropped in occasionally for music and talk in Luke's room and he had Rollo's companionship at work, but Butch Boyle seemed to have drifted away from them. Luke wondered if it had not been Butch who had drawn them together in the first place.

Luke had never confided to anyone his desire to do some sort of acting, and he was glad he hadn't because now it seemed childish and impossible. Besides, he wasn't sure he really wanted it. Maybe it had been a sort of kicking back at the humdrum, hired-help status of his father. He thought he might like to get into some kind of profession—but what? Certainly he didn't want to be a lawyer like old Euclid Pierce, even if he was smart enough. As for a doctor, forget it; he recalled the suffocation of the hospital atmosphere and wondered how anybody stood it, let alone all those years of school. He felt sorry for old Chuck who seemed to accept without question his parents' expectation that he would carry on the family tradition and wondered what kind of a doctor Chuck would make; somehow he couldn't see him like Doctor Bob, tired and uncomplaining and dealing with all sorts of people and all sorts of suffering.

"Sometimes," Luke said once to Chuck, "I get to feeling like a dumb slob that won't amount to anything. I guess you'll be a doctor, won't you?"

Chuck shrugged. "I guess so. I hate to think of all the preparation, though. If I could get into space medicine now, something keen like that, it might be worth all the studying."

"I know what you mean," Luke said seriously. "School—like it is—is just one big drag."

Luke had never been a good student, had never, as his father was so stuck on reminding him, "applied" himself. He supposed, sourly, that if he had a record like Sim or that girl Sue Bently or Arlene Weaver all sorts of avenues would open up brilliantly to him. As it was, trying to think of the future was like groping his way through the fog off the river.

He didn't really want to be a dropout and didn't think he would even if there were less family pressure. It made him feel bad to think of Butch. When Luke saw him—which wasn't often nowadays—Butch always seemed to be mulling something over, said he had plans but never told what they were. He was not able yet to help his father on the roofing jobs because of periodic headaches and dizziness. Besides, Luke had an idea Butch didn't want to work with his father—which wasn't hard to understand.

Sim's ambition was clear-cut and simple: he wanted to be a teacher. He could get quite shining and eager about it.

"Not a secondary school, Luke. I'm going to aim at instructing college students in English lit."

"That'll suit you, Sim. I can see you lecturing away, happy as a clam. You'll prob'ly write books too, like most college professors. Maybe you'll even be president of a college."

"Aw, knock it off," Sim murmured, but Luke could see he was pleased.

Sooner or later, Luke's thoughts always cycled around to his father. All those years under old Mr. Thad Wilson's thumb, plodding to and from the hardware store, careful to keep a savings account, to put away something out of his small salary against the rainy day that might overtake them. Luke wondered if, at his age, Henry Sawyer had spun bright dreams of making a mark in the world but, having taken the job at the hardware store so he could get married to Martha Clement, had sprung the trap once and for all. It was a scary thought but a common enough occurrence, Luke was convinced. He wondered, too, how Henry Sawyer would have fared if he had been born into Luke's generation. . . .

Martha noticed Luke's preoccupation.

"Are you worried about anything, Luke?"

Luke shook his head. "Why?"

"You seem so serious, lately. You never cut up, mimicking people like you used to. I hope you're not still dwelling on that fire. All of you escaped, thank God. And your father's health seems better. I just feel so thankful. I'm so happy I guess I want everybody else to be, too."

Luke moved restlessly. "I'm not worried, Ma. Forget it."

"Nothing wrong between you and Milo?" Martha got very busy, clearing the table.

"Nothing's wrong, Mom, no kidding. Forget it."

"Anita's found a new school for Sylvy," Martha said, looking at Luke over stacked plates. Her face shone. "A real small group this time, about half a dozen exceptional children. Nita and Euclid feel this one's going to work. They have music and things to do with their hands—craft things."

Luke said, "Sylvy'll be O.K. if she can play and sing."

"That's what I think," Martha said, sounding really happy. She pushed the swing door with her shoulder and disappeared into the kitchen. Luke sat a moment, listening to the clatter of dishes.

He guessed he'd better watch himself, stop glooming around, letting everybody see through him like a clean windshield. First thing you knew, his dad would be at him, trying to find out what was wrong; he was screwed up enough without that. So he had problems. Didn't everybody? He'd muddle through on his own one way or another.

TWELVE

"Never saw such a lasting spring," Henry Sawyer said. "Still wearing a coat to work mornings and it near'bout the first of May. We'll have it to remember when the heat cracks down on us. Can't take away what we've already had, no matter how blasted hot the summer gets."

Luke would never forget those words of his father's. The Sawyers were at breakfast, Martha offering to refill the coffee cups. In her hurry to start the breakfast she had buttoned her housecoat wrong and Henry had been teasing her about it with his crooked smile.

Luke was in English class, so it must have been about ten-thirty when Mr. Mountjoy came for him. He felt the eyes of the other students riveted to his back as he walked out of the room with Sim's grandfather.

"It's your daddy, Luke. He had a heart attack. At the store. He—" The old man didn't get any further, didn't need to. The truth tingled through Luke's body like an electric shock, like something he'd been waiting for without knowing he had.

"Where is he?" Luke asked—as he was to ask himself so many times in the days that followed.

Mr. Mountjoy cleared his throat, fumbled at the ignition. "They called the ambulance, took him to the hospital, but—" He stopped and Luke looked at him with wide, unbelieving eyes, though he knew what the old man had not said. Mr. Mountjoy got the car started and drove out of the school parking lot toward Main Street.

A heart attack. And he'd known. Going to the doctor on his own while Luke was stalling on his promise to Martha. Getting the pills he'd told Luke Dr. Bob gave him for his "stomach trouble." And all the time Henry Sawyer had known about his heart—known and not told anybody. Not wanting to worry Martha or the girls or Luke. It was just like his dad, that consideration that was so stupid—and so fine.

Luke knew he ought to be crying or cursing or something but he couldn't do anything. He could only sit there beside Sim's grandfather, staring straight through the windshield of the Mountjoys' Buick, seeing nothing, feeling nothing, dazed and numb. When the car stopped in front of the Sawyer house Luke went through the motions of getting out, putting one foot before the other, taking care not to stumble on the steps, forcing himself to walk up them instead of running like crazy down the street toward the river.

He couldn't see anybody or hear a sound but the feeling of eyes on him—as when he'd walked out of the classroom—pressed and pierced without breaking through his numbness. He wished darkness would fall and cover him. The front door stood open to the spring warmth but the house was wrapped in silence. Mr. Mountjoy opened the screen door, standing back for Luke to go ahead of him.

The hall looked small and dim, hardly familiar. Nothing seemed familiar. It was the same hall Luke had stood in and said, "I'm home, you lucky people." He wouldn't say that anymore. . . . Nor would he slam out of this hall again, angry, after a row with his father.

"Your mother's in the kitchen, I think," Mr. Mount-joy said. That, too, was strange. What was the sense of Martha being in the kitchen when Henry wouldn't be coming home to midday dinner?

She was in the rocking chair by the window where Luke's father used to sit sometimes and work on the Sunday crossword puzzle. She wasn't crying but her face was creased and furrowed in a struggle for comprehension. Her hands gripped the apron she'd been wearing when the news came and hadn't thought to remove. It was the red-flowered one with the white ruffle. Her fingers, squeezing the cloth, seemed suddenly to be squeezing Luke's heart so that it came to life, cruelly and without any warning.

He stumbled to his knees beside the rocker and put his head in his mother's lap. She let the apron go then and stroked his hair, murmuring, "There, there . . ." It was like years ago when he was little and Luke had for a second a wild, crazy hope that time had actually turned back and there was no now.

"Maybe he can get her to lie down," Luke heard someone say in a low tone. He thought it was Mrs. Mountjoy and was embarrassed at being seen in this childish position. It should be the other way round—him trying to comfort his mother—but it was still a moment before he could bring himself to raise his head. When he could no longer feel Martha's hands on it the whole blasted world might fly apart.

He heard someone sobbing and got to his feet, not knowing what to do with them or his hands. Not knowing what to do, period. He looked dazedly round, shaking his head. A cloud of steam issued from the spout of the kettle and Mrs. Mountjoy was setting the gold-banded cups on a tray. The wrinkles in her face glistened with tears and she was mumbling to herself distractedly. Over near the swing door Edith was sobbing in Mike Donaldson's arms, her straw-colored hair falling across his chest.

All the rest of that weird day was full of people coming and going. Anita and Euclid arrived—Anita's face ugly with crying, even her golden hair seemed dulled by her tears. She is bereft, Luke thought, holding her awkwardly. The neighbors came, bringing food. It filled the kitchen table, the cupboard shelves, and the refrigerator. As if they could chomp their way through grief and thus, reinforced, begin again.

Because they kept at him, Luke urged his mother to lie down. He didn't see why she should if she didn't want to, but the neighbor women and his sisters were insistent. On an inspiration Luke whispered, "You can shut the door, Mother, and be alone in your room." Something flashed in the look Martha turned slowly on him, not a smile but something under the dullness of her dry eyes.

She allowed Luke to lead her out of the kitchen, allowed Edith and Anita to take her outer clothes off and slip the housecoat on—the one, Luke remembered, that had been buttoned wrong this morning. This morning? How impossible that seemed. But it was Luke who closed the door of the room his mother had shared with his father so many years and must now sleep in alone. He saw Mrs. Mountjoy receiving yet another caller at the front door and turned blindly to the stairs leading to his own little room. He hadn't meant to slam his door, but when its noise sounded shockingly through the hushed house he didn't care. He thought, What the hell? What the bloody hell? and flung himself onto his bed, convulsed with weeping.

Luke supposed it was always like this when anyone died.

He tried to think back over his other brief experiences but they hardly counted. His grandparents had died before he was born and he had been spared the two or three funerals that had occurred among his relations because Martha and Henry had not believed in children going to funerals. For that matter, though Luke had not known it, they had not believed in funerals at all.

Martha sat in the living room in Henry's chair—Luke had the thought that she sought his father's presence there as in the kitchen rocker, maybe even imagined a warmth left by his body—and stated her wishes to the minister. Luke's sisters and their husbands were present and Luke himself crouched on the brown ottoman, staring out the window.

"Henry wouldn't have wanted a funeral," Martha told the Reverend Mr. Clayton. "He thought they were vulgar displays, the big ones. I want his to be strictly private. A simple service, just us here."

Later, Edith asked, worried, "Do you think people will talk? About a private service, I mean. Maybe they'll feel hurt at not being allowed to pay their respects."

"I don't know, Edie. I hope not," Anita said, distraught. "Anyway, we can't help it. Mama won't change her mind."

"Why should she?" Luke demanded angrily. "She's right. I—I agree with her about funerals. He'd hate it, lying there helpless, being preached over and people staring at us. You know he would." He bit the blood out of his lip to stop its trembling.

"Anyway," Anita said, looking at Edith with understanding, "lots of people have private services. It's hard in a little town where everybody knows everybody and they all like—liked Daddy. But we can't help it. Don't worry about it, Edith."

Edith wasn't one to give in easily.

"There's . . . Milo Tarrant. Don't you think Milo should be with you, Luke?" she asked hesitantly.

Luke shook his head. He couldn't say what he was thinking: Let's just get it over. Milo had come to the house with her parents that first night—like nearly everybody else in town, Luke thought. Sim and Chuck and Rollo·had come, all miserable and self-conscious. Luke had felt the same way. None of the Boyles came, though, not even Butch. Luke didn't care, he only wanted to be left alone, not to have to say the right things, thank people for doing their duty.

The Weavers came, Mr. Weaver dressed immaculately as always, dignified as always, his fine dark face like a sombre wood carving. Mrs. Prince came, whispering to Anita, "Can't I *do* something, honey? Must be some little thing I can do."

"Your father was a good man," Mr. Weaver said to Luke. "His loss will be sorely felt in the community."

Mr. Thad Wilson and the Baineses came, Mr. Thad with a black arm band, his still-sharp eyes red-rimmed. Luke could not bear to look at him.

In a seemingly never-ending stream they came and went that first day and night, till at last it was late and the house was silent. And in his sore mind Luke ticked off one of the awful three days.

There were no flowers except the day lilies Linda Simmons cut from the bed under the living room window because Henry had liked them best of all Martha's flowers. The paper had suggested donations to the Humane Society instead of floral offerings. "Flowers wither and die so soon," Martha said. "I'd like something to live on in memory of him."

The day lilies stood on the hall table in a blue jug, looking very unfunereal. Luke could imagine Henry Sawyer's little crooked smile if he could see them. Could he? No, of course not. Yet, there was no way to know for sure. . . .

Luke sat beside his mother while the young minister read.

"So teach us to number our days, that we may apply our hearts unto wisdom. . . ." How often had Henry deplored the fact that Luke would not "apply" himself to his schoolwork? "To everything there is a season. . . . A time to be born and a time to die; a time to plant and a time to pluck up that which is planted. . . . A time to weep and a time to laugh; a time to mourn and a time to dance. . . . A time to get and a time to lose. . . . a time to keep silence and a time to speak. . . . And God requireth that which is past."

The minister had a very beautiful voice. In his mind, Luke tried to reproduce it. Why had he attempted only comic impersonations? For laughs, of course. He looked at his sisters' puffed eyelids, his mother's chin that never stopped shaking all through the reading, at his own hands clenched on his knees, the knuckles big, the red ridge of scar on the left one. Would any of them ever laugh again? His father's funny, soundless laughter, his crooked smile, the one lifted eyebrow. Where was his father? How could he be so suddenly gone?

". . . man goeth to his long home and the mourners go about the streets: Or ever the silver cord be loosed, or the golden bowl be broken, or the pitcher be broken at the fountain, or the wheel broken at the cistern.

132

Then shall the dust return to the earth as it was: and the spirit shall return unto God who gave it."

As the first three days passed, so did others.

There were the mornings when the truth jumped at Luke on waking with an ugly jar. His father was dead. It didn't make sense. Henry Sawyer, eating breakfast too fast so he wouldn't be late to work, the man of long patience and sweet reasonableness who could yet lash out at the son whose slovenliness angered and disappointed him. He wasn't the man Ed Baines told about —falling without a gasp to the floor, the unopened plastic bottle of nitroglycerin tablets clutched in his hand. That was a nightmare image, heard of but not accepted till the mind could steady and settle and take. He was Luke's father, the man with the cocked eyebrow, the quiet corny joke, and the boundless love for a brain-damaged grandchild. It couldn't be true. But what was the truth? Surely not the childish mumblings that comforted people; how could they?

There were the practical matters to be attended to. Euclid Pierce went through the papers Henry had kept so meticulously in the old roll-top desk, explaining them to a bewildered Martha. Her struggle to grasp touched Luke; he understood her desire not to lean too heavily on Euclid, for all his willingness. "I've always been stupid about business," she said. "I left it all to Henry. I should have helped, asked about things, but I never thought—"

Luke said, "Don't worry, Ma. I'll take care of you," knowing how like a little boy it sounded. How long would it be before he would be equipped to take care of her and how—the old question—would he go about it? Martha squeezed his hand.

"I've got to learn. I won't saddle you with responsi-

133

bilities beyond your years. There's no need of that."

There was Henry's will, as uncomplicated as Henry Sawyer's life had been. His life insurance that would meet Martha's modest needs; the estate—funny name for the old brown shingle house—that would go to the three offspring at Martha's death; the savings account at the People's Savings Bank of Mill Gate that was to be used for his son Luke Henry Sawyer's education. It amounted to something over five thousand dollars.

Luke turned the bank book in his hands. Was that what his father had wanted to talk to him about on Christmas Day? He saw again the pale face in the window. Why hadn't he humored his father? Milo's present would have kept. If only he could have known . . .

In a way, then, it was settled: he would have to go to college and make something of himself. Maybe by the time he was through high school he would have pulled himself together, be able to think things out. It was hard even to picture himself back at school, passing his exams. In a way, Luke thought, it might have been simpler if he'd had to quit school and peddle his papers anywhere and anyhow he could. It seemed easier than making any sort of decision.

So the days passed. Through them Martha Sawyer was a tower of strength. Luke's sisters and the neighbors said she was "wonderful." The sisters did all they could, hiding their own pain in the effort to help their mother. Martha did not shut them out. Sometimes they brought the children, nervously trying to guard Martha against their questions.

"Let them ask," Martha said. "They have the right and how else can they learn?"

Luke felt his own questions locked in himself, unanswered. When remorse shook him in its teeth he thought of his father's words to him after the fire: "All of us lock stables after the horses are stolen. There just isn't anything you can do about that except not let your bad feelings go for nothing." Well, he hadn't locked any stables—not even after the horses were stolen; he couldn't see that his bad feelings over the fire had gone for anything, either. I must not be any good, he thought despairingly. Every time something awful happens I have to see it was part my fault.

There came a day when Luke saw his mother abandon herself to grief. It was after he'd gone back to school and he'd come home early, cutting his last class, with the feeling he should check on her before going to work at the station.

The car was in the driveway, so he knew she was at home, but the house had a silence that reminded him of the day his father died. Thinking his mother might be asleep, Luke went softly down the hall to her bedroom door. He saw her sprawled across the bed she and his father had shared all those years—he reckoned he and Edith and Anita had all been conceived in that bed— her arms stretched above her head, her hands tearing at the fringed spread. Her hair, blowsed and tangled, showed a blotched and swollen side of her face. Then it happened—the animal howl that was the measure of her desolation, stifled with the pillow but too late. He heard and it froze his blood for a second.

Standing at the door of her room, staring with wide, terrified eyes, Luke didn't know whether to go in or to flee, to speak or to hold his peace. In the end he had tiptoed away, climbed to his own room and crawled onto his bed.

It won't go on like this, he told himself, it can't. It's got to get better or we'll all go nuts. Time passing would make it bearable even for his mother, dull the edge, make it easier till one day it would be forgotten by all except those who'd been closest, and even those it would no longer claw and tear. He knew this not from experience but instinctively. He pulled his knees up against his chest, drawing himself into as tight a knot as he could.

It was perfectly quiet downstairs. Not a sound. Old Watch climbed the steps painfully, thrust a cold, quivering nose against Luke's arm, whimpered softly. Luke stroked the dog's head. After a while he sneaked down and looked in at his mother's door. Her wallowing had pulled her wrinkled housecoat to one side, leaving her heavy, veined legs uncovered. She was still except for one foot moving slowly from side to side as if it kept time. To what? Her thoughts?

Luke crept to the kitchen, the old dog padding sadly after, and put the kettle on. He worked carefully, not allowing his awkwardness to get the upper hand. He remembered the way Anita did it—the linen napkin on the tray, the cup from the china cabinet instead of the cupboard over the counter where the everyday dishes lived. Two slices of toast, buttered, boiling water poured, and the dripping tea bag removed with care so no ugly stain should mar his handiwork.

"Ma?" His hoarse whisper from the door brought Martha upright. She tugged at the housecoat, felt vaguely at her hair. "Want a cup, Mom?" He walked with exquisite care so as not to slosh the tea and set the tray on the night stand.

Afterward, Martha was to say, "It was a kind of turning point somehow, Luke, you fixing the tea so nice and bringing it to me. It made me feel taken care of. I know I had to make room for you in that dark place."

THIRTEEN

To his surprise Luke passed all his exams. He had taken them in a sort of daze, not caring greatly about the results, but when he found he'd scraped through he was relieved that he wouldn't have to make up something in summer school. He could work full time for Mr. Jeff Beale. He'd be like his father—work hard and spend carefully, put something by out of each pay check.

It was just what he had meant not to do. He couldn't see Milo Tarrant getting a charge out of watching the mortgage on an ordinary house slowly dwindle through the years, doing without the little luxuries she'd always had, playing scrabble in the evenings. He couldn't see himself living like that, either—but what did he want?

The heat that had held off so obligingly descended and Mill Gate wilted under its humid assault. For the past three summers Henry and Martha had talked about having the house air-conditioned without doing anything about it.

"Could we, this summer?" Luke asked hesitantly, thinking it might be something to interest his mother. Martha shook her head.

"It's not the money only," she said. "I just don't want it. We got through so many years without it; it seems plain silly to me now. Besides, we—I ought to have the house painted. Your father meant to have it done this summer."

Watching her, Luke thought she had a deflated look —like one of those plastic toys the air was gradually seeping from, leaving it wrinkled and flaccid. It frightened him to see her like that. What if she, too. . . . But he turned the thought off violently. Still, he couldn't help wishing he had really looked at his father more often. Surely, if he had only looked, he could have seen him slipping into the gray mists of death.

Anita tried to get Martha to go to Baysboro for a while. Luke, just outside the window in the wicker porch chair, heard them talking. He had dropped into the chair when he came from work, dreading, as he always did, to go into the house.

"Luke could stay at Edith's," Anita said. But Martha insisted she couldn't go, there were too many things to be done at home.

"I've got to settle into this, Nita," Luke heard her say. "I might as well start getting used to it. It's thoughtful of you, dear, but I'd rather have someone to do for. Luke needs me; he's taking this harder than he lets on."

"I know he is," Anita answered quickly. "I didn't mean—"

"Of course you didn't. It's just that I feel a little worried about him." It was like a slightly changed echo of "I'm worried about your father." So he was the one she'd start worrying about now.

"You and Euclid have done so much already," Martha went on.

"Oh, Mother, we'd do anything to help. Money or anything else—"

"We don't need money. There's the insurance—you know, Nita, I fussed at your father sometimes about that. I told him he was making us insurance poor, that

I'd rather have the money to enjoy life with him than
. . . he was right, of course. Luke makes his own money,
so we're fine that way. You and Euclid have been the
soul of kindness and generosity. Edith and Mike, too.
I'm very fortunate, don't think I don't realize it."

Luke wished she wouldn't talk like that. Maybe it
made Nita feel better but it just made him feel peculiar.
He sat, slumped in the chair, looking at the sky, still
hot, and the sun still high over the massed tops of the
oak trees marching up River Street. He had always
loved summer, never minded it being hot. No school
and swimming and fooling around at Syd's. He felt
older than last summer, though. None of those things
seemed so important now.

Mr. Beale gave Luke a raise in pay; he was making a
dollar seventy-five an hour now instead of a dollar sixty.

"You're the man of your family now, Sawyer," Mr.
Beale said, letting his hand rest on Luke's shoulder.

One day, in front of the drugstore, Luke ran into Dr.
Bob Holland. The doctor was about to get into his car
but he stopped to talk with Luke. After he had asked
after Martha, he said heavily, "You know, I feel re-
sponsible for things happening like they did with your
dad, Luke. I should have made certain your mother
knew his heart was acting up. It never occurred to me
he would keep it from her, but knowing Henry I should
have known. He was so damn considerate of her—of all
of you. I didn't realize and, damn it, I should have. Do
you have any idea how often a doctor has to face up to
things like that, Luke? It takes so little to make such a
difference."

Before Luke could answer, Dr. Holland asked,
"How's the hand coming on?" And when Luke held
the left one out, making and unmaking a fist, flexing the
fingers, Dr. Bob said, "Fine. Hardly any rigidity. You

drop by the office now and then just as a precaution."

Butch Boyle wandered into the station early in June. He and Luke exchanged a few words, then Butch said, awkwardly, "Sorry about your dad. He was a helluva good guy."

"Yeah. Want a Coke, Butch?"

"Sure. I'll get it—one for you, too." He put coins in the machine, made a thing of opening the bottles.

There was something about Butch Luke couldn't put his finger on. He didn't feel at ease around him anymore. It was almost as bad as when he'd gone to see him at the hospital.

"You O.K. now, Butch? Your arm and head and everything?"

For a moment the old Butch flashed out of hiding. "Oh sure, man. My arm's O.K. and I reckon my head's good as it ever was. Never was my strong point, you know?" They laughed together but when the laughter died there was an uneasy silence. When they'd finished the Cokes Butch went away, slogging toward town.

The next time he appeared—a week or so later—he was driving a battered blue Dodge.

"This yours?" Luke asked, removing the cap from the gas tank.

"Partly—when I get it paid for," Butch said, casually. "Other part's my buddy's. I'm goin' into business with Roddy Pitman over at Briar Hill. You know Rod used to live here when we were at Mill Gate Elementary." Luke could not recall anyone of that name. He was going to ask Butch what kind of business, but another car came up and he had to fill and check it and Butch rattled off in the old car before Luke had finished.

"Mr. Wilson left a message for you," Martha told

Luke one evening at supper. "Said for you to stop and see him tomorrow."

"He didn't say at my earliest convenience by any chance," Luke said, beginning to snarl up inside. If there was anybody he didn't want to see, it was old man Thad Wilson.

"Now, Luke," Martha pleaded, "I know you don't like Mr. Wilson, but your father was kind of attached to the poor old fellow."

"Attached is right," Luke growled. So attached he dropped dead on the floor of his lousy store. "Where d'you get that 'poor old fellow' bit, Ma? He's probably been a millionaire for years."

"That doesn't keep him from being old and twisted up with arthritis—and alone." The way she added that "alone" shamed Luke a little. "It doesn't hurt a person to show a drop of compassion, Luke."

Luke helped himself to fried chicken, drowned a mountain of rice in gravy. He glanced at Martha whose plate was empty. Her face looked flushed and glazed with heat.

"You going to starve yourself while you spoil me rotten?" he growled. "You shouldn't cook a supper like this, hot as it is now, Mom. Sandwiches would've been fine."

"I know the kind of lunch you eat at Syd's. Go ahead and eat; I want to cool off before I take anything." But Luke laid his fork down and wouldn't touch his food until he had heaped his mother's plate and watched her begin to pick indifferently at it.

"Just the same, you will go see Mr. Wilson, won't you? It'll look so rude if you don't."

"O.K. Sure."

The dining table, the whole room seemed too big

nowadays. Henry Sawyer hadn't taken up much room, yet it was like that over the whole house. His presence must somehow have commanded much more space than Luke had ever realized. Funny, when he was such a quiet, unobtrusive kind of man.

The familiar smell of the hardware store struck Luke a blow—that mixture of leather and iron and oil. He'd loved it when he was a kid. Used to suck in deep gulps of it when he'd come down here to walk home with Henry. That was before he ever went to school. He didn't know when his taste had changed, only that he hated the scent of the old-fashioned, darkish place now. Mr. Thad had bowed to progress and had air conditioning installed a couple of summers ago, but Luke thought it mainly added yet another ingredient to the hardware aroma as he pulled the scarred double doors to behind him.

"Hi, Luke," Ed Baines greeted him. "How's the boy?"

"O.K., Mr. Baines. How're you?"

"Fine, Luke, just fine. What can I do you for?"

Luke wouldn't let himself look at the floor, tried not to wonder where it was that Henry Sawyer had fallen.

"My mother said Mr. Wilson wanted to see me."

"Oh. Oh sure, that's right. He's back in the office." He turned to a customer with his subservient, "Help you, sir?"

The small office in the back of the store looked like a cage with its barred window. Miss Vanessa Kyle, a sawed-off little old maid who had been "talked about" in her younger days, kept books there. Luke could see her piled dark hair that was beginning to be streaked with gray bent over her work.

"Well, hello there, Luke. How you doing?" Miss Vanessa had this young way of talking that didn't fit her face or shape and she dressed the same way, like a schoolgirl. She made Luke think of a partridge with her rounded bosom. He said, "I think Mr. Wilson is expecting me," pompously, out of pure devilment.

Miss Vanessa said, "Well, sure. He's right here."

As Luke went through the door beside the barred window, he saw the old man's head swivel around and his paper-thin lips get thinner. When he got closer Luke could see red streaks on his eyeballs and remembered him coming to the house the night his father died and how red his eyelids had been. A kind of helpless rage grabbed him. He thought, You old relic, you! Still going strong and my dad six feet under the ground out there in the cemetery. It's not fair!

"Sit down, my boy." So it was *my boy,* was it?

Luke crouched on the edge of the straight metal chair, shaking with belligerence. How had his father stood this old coot, let alone been fond of him as Martha had said?

"Just wanted to talk to you." Mr. Wilson's voice was surprisingly strong and deep. You didn't expect it, looking at his dried-up, papery old face. There was even a certain kindness in it, though Luke hated to admit that to himself with the "my boy" still rankling.

"Might as well come to the point. I'm not one to beat around the bush," old Mr. Thad went on. "Don't mind Van, she knows how to keep things to herself," as Luke glanced toward the bookkeeper. "So did your father, Luke. Henry Sawyer was like my right hand—left one, too, many a time." His face worked, he pawed for his handkerchief and trumpeted into it. "But that's not why I sent for you. What would you say to taking a job here in the store? Your daddy wasn't so much older'n you when I commenced to train him—and look how he went right on up in the hardware business."

Luke gazed, unbelieving. Mr. Wilson couldn't be serious. He had to be senile. Right on up in the business. Lord, you'd think it was Wall Street and Henry Sawyer had been a big executive. Luke cracked his knuckles loudly.

"Well, thanks, Mr. Wilson. I appreciate you thinking about me, but—well, you see I've already got a job at Mr. Jeff Beale's service station out on Slater Street. I—"

Mr. Wilson's brown-spotted hand shot out to stir at a pile of papers on the desk that took up nearly half the office. Vanessa serenely removed them, not even turning her head to look.

"Filling station," the old man snorted. "I'd give you a real job here at the store. When you wasn't in school, that's to say. You must be about done with school, eh?" He looked very cross and upset. Luke hoped he would not have a stroke; that would be rough justice for you. Well, he wasn't that kind of a louse, he didn't want the old man to croak.

"I've got one more year, sir. Then there's college." You didn't know, I guess, that your white-haired boy who was also my dad left me the money to go to college on. Scrimped out of the big money you paid him.

"College?" Mr. Thad blinked, his bony jaw sagged. "Oh. You aiming to go through college. Well, Henry would want that, I can see that. He never said—wasn't one to say much, Henry wasn't."

"No, sir, he wasn't." Luke stood up. The old man's eyes took on a surprising sharpness.

"So you ain't inter-ested in a job here in the store."

Luke felt himself flushing. "I've got a job, sir."

Mr. Wilson made an impatient gesture. "No future in filling gas tanks. Wouldn't quit it for more pay, eh?"

144

"I wouldn't want to do that to Mr. Beale. He's been pretty good to me. I wouldn't want to inconvenience him." Luke hesitated, then added, "He held my job for me while I was hurt and couldn't work, last winter. No, sir, I wouldn't want to put Mr. Beale out."

"Humph. I see." A wintry smile crossed Mr. Wilson's pale, spotted face. "Stubborn squirt, ain't you?"

Luke's face burned.

"Is that all, sir?"

"Reckon you're a chip off the old block some ways." He cackled sourly. "I recollect somebody here trying to hire your daddy away from me once. Fellow over to Baysboro. Henry stuck with me."

Luke had never heard that one. He said once more, "I appreciate you thinking of me." The little office was cramping him; he felt the need of a deep breath.

"That's all then. Give your mama my kind regards."

"Yes, sir. Thanks, Mr. Wilson." As he squeezed past the desk Vanessa Kyle winked at him.

Outside, Luke wondered if he had handled the situation all right. The old buzzard meant well, no doubt about that, but he gave Luke the willies. He began to walk faster, putting distance between him and the hardware store. He couldn't believe his father had been really satisfied to stay on there, he'd just been trapped. Because he'd fallen in love with Martha Clement. If Milo had consented to be engaged that day in the woods would he, Luke, have accepted Mr. Thad Wilson's offer? Maybe he would. The possibility gave him a scared feeling and he walked faster, feeling the sun beat on his head and the sweat seeping down inside his shirt.

The summer days passed. So gradually he hardly realized it, Luke's dread of entering the house dwindled.

Martha kept busy, brushing aside Edith's pleas that she take it easy. Luke knew his mother drove herself so that she would have less time to think and feel; he could understand that. There came the night when he put a record on the player. It was rock music but he turned it low, hoping it wouldn't bother Martha who had gone to bed, exhausted from turning out the kitchen cupboards.

After that, it once again seemed natural to play records when he wanted music. Sometimes, Sim came over to talk in Luke's room. Chuck came a couple of times, too, and Luke had Rollo's companionship at work. He couldn't bring himself to go out at night, though, unless he arranged first with Edith to keep his mother company. The sight of the old scrabble box alongside the dictionary on the bookshelf still gave him a pang that was almost physical.

He began to feel torn between duty toward his mother and letting Milo down. If you had a girl you had to do nice things for her, try to give her a good time at least once in a while, have a little fun. It was a relief in a way when July came and Milo and her mother went to the mountains where Mr. Tarrant would join them for part of August. Luke knew he would miss Milo awfully, but the strain of dividing himself between the two would be eased. Maybe by the time she came home everything would be better, or seem so, and he could make it up to her.

He stopped at the Tarrants' on his way home from work the night before they left and took her for a little ride. It was a long drive to the mountains and Milo said they planned to leave very early in the morning. Beneath her sweet seriousness Luke could sense her excitement at the prospect of the trip and suddenly he longed

146

to be going, too—anywhere, away from Mill Gate that seemed so sad and dull.

"You'll write to me, won't you, Mi?"

"Of course I will." She leaned her head against him and the scent of that shampoo with the silly name drifted sweetly to him, making his heart thump in the old way.

"You won't get carried away by any of those guys up there, will you?"

She giggled obligingly. "Don't be ridiculous. Just think, we'll probably be sleeping under blankets tomorrow night!"

"Lucky you," Luke said, rubbing his chin against her silky hair. At her door he held her tenderly, hating to let her go. "You'll drive carefully—you and your mother?"

"Oh, Luke, of course. We're both very good drivers, you know we are."

"I know, but lots of crazy drivers always on the highway. Well—good-bye, darling. I'll miss you."

"I'll miss you too, Luke." His heart soared when he saw tears shining in her eyes. He kissed her again quickly and hurried away.

Driving home, he thought that a corner had been turned somehow, he didn't quite know how, in his and Milo's relationship. Things would be better when they were together again. They had been going together nearly a year; they were getting older all the time. Maybe this time next year they'd be engaged. . . .

FOURTEEN

The big clock on the wall advertising Goodyear tires told Luke it was nine minutes past ten. Nearly an hour to go. Mr. Beale had said it would be all right to close at eleven. Time dragged here at the Shell Station when Luke was alone; next Saturday Rollo would be the one to work till eleven. Saturday nights weren't any different from other nights, though, with Milo gone.

Business was slow. The last sale must have been around nine-thirty—two couples of teen-agers in an open sports car, the girls' long hair whipped wild and the boys' nearly as long and tangled. They weren't local kids and Luke had never seen them before. Something in their faces and voices made him wonder if they weren't high. He thought about it after they'd gone speeding up the highway toward Baysboro, half hoping they'd get pinched before something worse happened. Getting to be an old granny, he scoffed at himself. Always looking for something awful to happen.

The station was close and hot. He hitched his chair to the door and sat, swatting at a mosquito now and then, his thoughts random and moody. Next week Euclid and Anita were going on a week's vacation, and Martha had begged to keep Sylvy.

"Nita needs to get out from under," she told Luke, "and Sylvy's no trouble. She'll be a comfort to me."

Luke hoped Sylvy wouldn't wander about looking for Henry. She had done that the first time they brought her to see Martha after Henry's death. It was more than two months now, maybe she'd have forgotten.

He took Milo's letter from the breast pocket of his coveralls. It had come in this morning's mail but the daisy-trimmed envelope already had a worn look. He drew the two sheets of orange paper out and read them slowly for about the tenth time. He read all Milo's letters slowly, making them last as long as possible.

Dearest Luke,

I never thought I would be homesick but I am! Will Mill Gate ever look great to me! I must have been out of my mind to think I wanted to get away and stay a long time. The next sentence had been scratched through but Luke had figured it out: *This family togetherness kills me.* She'd evidently thought it was tactless under the circumstances, funny little Milo. Tenderness welled in him and he read on, though he actually knew the letter from memory by now.

The mountains are as grand and beautiful as when I first saw them, of course, but there's no place like home, as they say, and I do miss crummy little old Mill Gate and you (crummy Mill Gate, not crummy you!). There are quite a few kids here, as I told you, from other places like Florida and they are not too bad but I like our crowd much better. Probably I am très provincial and insular and all that.

The last line gave Luke mixed feelings: *I hope you are not feeling so down, though I know from experience that when something terrible happens it takes a long time to recover from it.* Luke thought she must be referring to her experience with Forrest MacLane; he didn't know of anything else that had ever given Milo a really bad time. He sighed and put the envelope back in his pocket.

The lulls in traffic on the highway were becoming more frequent, lasting longer. During them Luke could hear the frantic rasp of insects in the swampy stretch across the little dirt road behind the station. The headlights of a car wheeled, then died in darkness and Luke thought, Guess kids are parking back there since they won't let 'em in the river woods anymore.

At about ten-thirty Luke decided to hose down the area around the pumps. He hadn't been imagining the heat; a thin veil of steam drifted up from the wet concrete, smelling of oil and gasoline. A car pulled up and the man driving it asked Luke if there was a good motel in this town. Luke briskly assured him there was.

"Go right on till you get to the second light. Turn left and go two blocks, then left again and you'll see the sign Gateway Motor Court. It's clean and reasonable."

As the man thanked him and drove on Luke grinned. Who do I think I am, the whole cotton-picking Chamber of Commerce? I never stayed at the Gateway. For all I know it's filthy, got lumps in the mattresses, and is a clip joint besides.

He went inside and began tidying the office for closing. He was about to lock the back door when he saw another car stopping out front, a faded old blue Dodge. He thought it was the car Butch Boyle had been driving the last time he saw him but wasn't sure because the glass was still a bit steamy. He hurried out, pleased at the prospect of seeing Butch.

It was a blue Dodge all right, the same year's model, the same or very similar dent in the left front door. But the driver wasn't anybody Luke remembered ever having seen before. He was young, his face pitted with acne scars, and he wore dark glasses and a soiled T-shirt.

150

"Fillitupandcheckunderthehood," he rattled in a breath.

"Yes, *sir*," Luke said—as if his greatest desire on earth was to serve this character who hadn't a "please" to spare.

When he had taken care of the car the driver thrust a bill at him and started the motor, all in a terrific hurry. Everything about the guy made Luke's hackles rise and he perversely took his time making change. The young man's fingers had scarcely closed on the change before he gunned the old motor without mercy and streaked off up the highway with Luke looking after him.

It was the car Butch had said he partially owned or its identical twin; Luke wished he had looked at the license. If it was the same car, then that must have been the Roddy something-or-other Butch had mentioned, called his "buddy." Luke hoped he wasn't; the fellow didn't seem like a desirable partner, whatever business Butch might have had in mind.

Still looking down the road, Luke had taken two or three steps inside the office before he saw the men. They were standing between the door and the desk, looking like overgrown trick-or-treaters. Masked, black-clad and black-gloved, one of them holding a gun. It had to be some kind of a joke, Luke thought. He said "What the—" and stopped as the shorter of the two, who was holding the gun, jerked his head to the left, saying in a muffled tone, "Over there."

Telling himself the gun wasn't loaded, still believing it a joke, Luke stepped back. He was only a few steps from the door, while the guy with the gun was between him and the telephone. His idea of its being a joke suddenly dissolved and he was scared. Scared green. He heard the door close softly behind him and knew there were three of them. It was a holdup and he was trapped. They'd come in the back door while he was outside, three of them and one of them armed. It happened all the time, of course, all over and to all sorts of people, but he'd never thought it could happen to him. Through the window he could see the car—Henry Sawyer's, now Martha's old car he had driven to work in; it represented at the moment the height of safety. If he could somehow gain its sanctuary this danger would be behind him.

He knew it was fantasy, thinking like this; there was no way he could get to the car or the phone or any kind of help. He was surrounded and if he made a move they'd kill him or batter him to a pulp. He licked his dry lips, said, "Look—" and the guy with the gun took a step toward him. The gun seemed to swell; Luke was looking straight into it, unable to move his eyes from it.

The man with the gun moved his head toward his partner without taking his eyes from Luke. They glinted through the slits in the mask. Luke saw the unarmed one slide around the desk to the cash register and flick the drawer open as if he'd spent a lifetime operating cash registers. The one with the gun said, "Le's have that, you," indicating with a motion of his free hand the change box belted to Luke's coveralls. "Your wallet, too, if you got one."

With a dim, foolish hope of sparing his wallet Luke shook his head, his fingers stiff and clumsy as he took the belt off. Then the man he hadn't seen, the one who'd shut the door behind him, was breathing down his neck. He began to search Luke, brisk and efficient as in the movies, relieving him of the wallet Henry Sawyer had given him the year he was thirteen. Luke felt a queer pang penetrate his fear, followed by a blaze of anger at the sight of the worn but good leather wallet in the gloved hands. At the same time he took in the size of the guy. He was much the biggest of the three, as big as Butch Boyle—and a rush of helpless and furious tears blinded Luke for a second.

Where were all the cars on the highway? Couldn't somebody look in and see what was going on? What about the car he'd heard enter the dirt road behind the station? And then he knew. It was the car the robbers had come in, and it would take them away without Luke's being able to lift a finger.

He saw the black-gloved hands take the bills—there weren't but a couple; he didn't carry much money except when he took Milo somewhere—from his wallet and toss it aside. The wallet looked limp and somehow sad lying on the floor, open. Luke had an almost overpowering impulse to spring at the big one, though he knew he wouldn't stand a chance even without the gun trained on him. There was nothing he could do.

The one who had robbed the cash register was cramming the money into a bag—plastic or something like that—all of them, naturally, in a hurry to get away. Then they seemed undecided about something and hope sprang wildly in Luke. Maybe they would panic, drop the gun, run with the money, and he could get to the phone, call the police before they could get their car going and take off. The hope was so strong he could feel himself tensing all over for the dive toward the telephone. . . .

The one with the bag of money said something to the one with the gun and the one with the gun said, "Yeah, better," and tossed a roll of gold nylon cord— Luke didn't know where it came from, he'd missed that —over to the big one. To his horror Luke felt himself pushed roughly into the chair he had earlier moved to the door to catch the breeze. There was no breeze now, the door was shut and Luke felt the cord going tightly about him, trussing him up like a turkey, binding him fast to the chair.

They're going to gag me, too, he thought, unable to breathe at the prospect. But they did not gag him. Instead, the one with the bag of money raced out the rear door. Soon Luke heard the car in the back road start and a careful, quick beep of the horn. There was a hasty scuffling of feet as the switch beside the door clicked, the lights went off, and the other two hurried out.

Luke didn't know whether to start yelling for help at once or wait till the car pulled away. The sound of the motor barely rose above the drumming of blood against Luke's ears. Who was there to hear if he did shout? Better to save his strength to try and get himself untied. His hands, especially the left one, were beginning to throb from being bound. How should he start trying to get loose? He tried to think how they did it on TV. . . .

The phone rang, piercing in the quiet of the closed, dark office. It rang and rang. Five or six times. Sweat rolled down Luke's face and neck, oozed from his armpits, trickled across his ribs. He tried to see the time, and after looking long enough made it out in the light coming through the window from outside. Not quite eleven-thirty. He stopped struggling with the cord and tried to calm himself. Whoever had called would try again, and all at once he knew it was his mother. She would have got worried at his being late and called to check.

He could see the lights of cars on the highway, not many now, just one now and then. He wouldn't let himself look at the clock again. With the outside lights still on, a car might stop for gas. He opened his mouth to yell and the phone rang. He shut his mouth and held his breath, willing Martha to know something was wrong. It rang six times and stopped. His legs were starting to throb now—he thought he could feel them swelling—and his hands were getting numb. People got gangrene from being bound too tightly. . . .

A car pulled in at the station, stopped on a screech of brakes. Then came agitated steps and a rattling of the doorknob. "Luke, hey Luke! You in there?"

It was Mike, of course, who else? Good old Mike Donaldson. To his shame Luke felt the salty burn of tears he could only blink at, having no hand to wipe his eyes. There was another rattle of the knob and fists pounding. Of course that big bastard had locked it.

"Luke?" Mike's voice was a frenzied note higher.

"The back door," Luke heard his own hoarse voice call. "By the gents', Mike. Round the back."

He had never seen such a beautiful sight as Mike's round face, pasty with fear, as the light flashed on.

"My God, Luke." It was almost a sob and Mike's hands that never came quite clean were at the cord, undoing the knots rapidly in spite of their visible shaking. "You O.K., kid? You sure you're O.K.?"

"Yeah, Mike, I'm O.K. Get the police first or they'll never catch 'em. They've already got a heck of a good start—"

Mike left off working at the cord, stumbled to the desk and began to dial. Luke had never seen him rattled before. "Hello, hello. Reporting a robbery at Jeff's Shell Station." He was back, untying the cord, his hands still shaking like crazy. "You sure you're all right? They didn't try to rough you up any?"

"Didn't but one of 'em touch me," he mumbled, feeling his bonds slide from him. "The big guy that cleaned me out." He moved his hands, his arms that felt as if they'd gone to sleep, and stretched his legs with an effort. He stood up carefully, afraid they would fold under him.

Mike threw the gold nylon cord to the floor. It looked pretty, shining in the light.

"You know how much they took?"

"I don't believe it was more than fifty bucks—including what they got off me personally," Luke said. He added bitterly, "Not so bad at that for like ten minutes' work, even split three ways."

"Three of 'em, huh? Luke, I better call your mom. God, what'll I say to her?"

Luke tried to be flippant. "Tell her I'm sorry about being late but I got tied up here."

"Why don't you talk to her? Then she'll know you're all right. She was in a tizzy because it was late and called me."

Luke was just hanging up when the police car swung in and stopped at the Shell Station. Luke had known Bill Whaley, the older one, all his life but the younger policeman he didn't know. Their questions, simple enough, taxed Luke's mind but he struggled for clear, honest answers. Now that it was over, his brain was in a fog.

At the police station there was more questioning and the same ones over again. Did Luke recognize any of the three? Could he describe them? Were they black or white?

No, he had not recognized any of them, but it would have been hard to, covered as they were. He could only describe their approximate size. He hadn't been able to catch their voices clearly or he'd have remembered, he'd always had a quick ear for voices—

Had he got the license number of the car?

No, he hadn't seen the car at all; it was behind the service station in the little dirt road—

The string of negatives began to sound monotonous. Luke felt uncooperative—and something was nagging, bugging his mind. It had started before Mike's arrival, he thought, but he couldn't run it down. It surfaced with a jolt when Sergeant Whaley asked where he was when the robbers entered the station.

"Taking care of a car out front. They must have gone in through the back door, from the road—"

The pocked face of the driver of the blue Dodge rose sharply through the mist of fatigue and reaction. Luke saw again the faded color of the Dodge, the dented door, remembered the behavior of the driver, how nervous he was and in what a hurry, the running together of his words and the way he had gunned off.

Could he describe the car?

Luke's heart was beating too fast and his throat was dry. "A blue Dodge," he said, trying to swallow. "No, sir, I didn't get the license number. It was a '65 model, I think. Yeah, I'm sure it was. A 1965 Dodge."

Could he describe the driver?

Luke took a sip of the cooling coffee in the paper cup, holding it carefully to hide the shaking of his hand.

"It—it wasn't anybody I know. Never saw him before—that I know of. He kind of put my back up. You know. Not courteous. He was—like I better get on the ball or else."

Was Luke still outside when he drove off?

"Yes, sir. I watched him scratch off. I didn't exactly hurry back inside. When I did go in, they were there." He felt strangely exhausted now, as if he might fall asleep in the middle of a sentence if he had to keep talking.

"Better get him home," he heard Sergeant Whaley say and Luke looked up to see Jeff Beale looking at him in a sort of fatherly way. Mr. Beale said, "So long as you

157

came through all right, Luke—that's what's important. Don't you worry about a thing."

The young police officer took Luke home and Mike said he would pick Martha Sawyer's car up at the Shell Station.

At home, the desire for sleep, almost overpowering at the police station, deserted Luke completely. Keyed-up and wide awake, he rehashed the whole thing for a cringing, shaken Martha—as he knew he'd have to do for his sisters later. Martha kept asking him if he was sure he was all right and talking a little wildly about crime and no place being safe anymore, not even Mill Gate. As she had after the fire, she wound up, "Thank God, you're alive, Luke. If anything happened to you—I don't believe I could stand it."

In bed at last, Luke could hear her padding about, heard water running at the sink. She'd be taking her tranquilizer; he hoped it would do the trick. Poor Ma, he thought. I'm liable to be the death of her yet. Maybe it wasn't such a big deal they had me. Life would've been easier for them with just the girls.

FIFTEEN

There was little sleep for Luke that night.

Even after all was quiet below and he was sure Martha slept, he could not relax. There was something that bothered him more than his concern for his mother. All that night it kept coming into his head. Between confused, half-asleep, half-awake moments it seemed a dream, but it snatched him wide-awake, leaving a question in his mind that burned and tormented. The big guy who had locked the door behind Luke and taken his wallet—*could* he have been Butch Boyle?

The answer was always a violent, protesting no. But it wouldn't stick. Untidy bits and pieces floated in its wake. The blue Dodge about which Luke no longer had a doubt; it was the same car Butch had driven to the station the last time Luke saw him. The way Butch had avoided him practically ever since he got out of the hospital—and not only him, come to think of it, but the other boys, too. His strange way of talking on the few occasions Luke had been with him; those "plans" he'd referred to but not explained. . . .

Luke rolled over against the window, his hunched shoulder pressed against the sill, and stared into the night. The sky was blue-black and a big star hung there, framed by the window. I'm nuts, he told himself. I'm still so shook I can't think straight. Every-

159

thing will straighten out. They'll catch those bastards and ask me if I can identify them, and there won't be one I've ever set eyes on.

The realization that it would be easy enough to find out hit him. If Butch was in town, the whole screwy notion would be blown. And Luke could forget it. Nobody would ever know he'd had such treacherous thoughts about his friend.

Toward morning he sank into a heavy, exhausted sleep. When he woke his head felt thick and achy and he lay for a moment, knowing only that something had happened. Then he remembered and a shiver of unpleasantness ran down his spine, though he was bathed in sweat from another hot day well on its way. He turned over, dreading to face whatever it might offer.

He was in the shower when he decided what he must do. He scrubbed his skin till it burned, as if he could wash last night away, and combed his wet hair carefully. Already, drops of perspiration were gathering again on his face and body. In the shower he had examined his legs for marks, but the nylon cord had left no sign on him.

He was surprised to see it was after ten o'clock. It was a good thing he didn't have to work today. Then he remembered it was Sunday and the station wouldn't be open till twelve. Rollo was due to work this afternoon. Luke grinned a little wanly at his scrubbed face in the mirror over his chest of drawers, wondering what Rollo would have to say about last night. The same as everybody else, he guessed. Probably everybody in town knew by now.

Martha was pale, her face showing the effects of shock and not enough sleep. She brushed her hand lingeringly across his shoulders as she put his breakfast in front of him. "I called Anita," she said, half apologetic. "I know you're not anxious to talk about last night, but they'll want to hear it all straight from you. They're coming over this afternoon—and Edith's asked us to go there for supper. How do you feel, Luke?"

"O.K.," Luke grunted. He shouldn't grudge the family their share of the excitement, but he didn't feel happy about spending the afternoon like that. He thought he would like to go to bed and sleep if he got this thing about Butch squared away. He said, "Guess you haven't heard anything from the police—that they got those punks or anything?"

"No. I haven't spoken to anybody but Anita. Oh, and Rollo Prince. He heard it on the news and came to ask if you were all right."

Luke ate a big breakfast—more to please Martha than because he wanted it. When he had finished he asked her if she wanted the car.

"Luke, you aren't going anywhere!" Her eyes were round with fear and he laughed.

"You didn't plan on locking me up in my room did you, Mom? I had enough of being tied up last night."

"Don't joke about it," Martha said, shuddering. "No, I don't need the car. I'm not going to church, I'm too tired. Think I'll lie down awhile before the children get here."

"You do that," Luke said. "I might, too, later. I want to see Butch about something. I won't be long."

The hot street was wrapped in Sunday quiet. Cars passed, houses either had their windows wide open or were hermetically sealed in air conditioning, sunlight glared between blots of shade cast by the oaks and sycamores. Mill Gate looked just like last Sunday and the one before.

Luke drove slowly, wondering what he would say when he reached Butch's house. He guessed it might look a little strange, making a call on Sunday morning when he was supposed to be recuperating from having been scared out of his mind. He'd have to go easy, not let on what was bugging him. He wouldn't ever have suspected Butch any more than he would have Rollo or Chuck or Craig Simmons if it hadn't been for that old blue car and its driver keeping him out front so the others could get in and be waiting for him.

He turned down Putney Street, going even slower than before. Sweat oozed from his pores, soaking his clean shirt. If only old Butch would be home, he wouldn't have a worry in the world. It would be pure joy to hear his comments and questions. Luke tried to plan what he would say. Ask Butch to ride down by the river, cool off, say he felt like watching the water to calm his nerves. . . . All of a sudden the whole deal seemed silly, part of his jitters. What did he think he was anyhow, some kind of bloody detective?

Butch's sister Penny was sweeping the front porch, her pipestem arms sending the broom in long, lazy strokes across the floor. She shook her hair—a paler red than Butch's—out of her sharp little foxy face and squinted at Luke between pale lashes.

"Hi, Penny," Luke said, striving for nonchalance as he went up the walk.

"Hi." Penny leaned on the broom. If she knew anything about Luke's experience it didn't show. She was so skinny her shorts sagged and she gave them a hitch. Luke judged her to be about eleven or twelve; her thin little chest was flat as a boy's.

"Butch around?" She'd say he was asleep now and Luke would tell her it was O.K., not to bother him, he'd see him later. But Penny shook her head and the straggly hair fell back onto her thin cheeks.

"He went," she said, nudging the broom with a dirty bare foot.

"Oh—" Luke's voice sounded hollow. "You—you know where he went?"

Instead of answering, Penny, without turning her gaze from Luke, screeched, "Mom—c'mere, Mom."

"You didn't need to bother your mom," Luke protested, not wanting to face Mrs. Boyle. "I just thought Butch might be home."

Penny stroked the rough straw of the broom with her toes. The screen door opened and Mrs. Boyle, looking different without her wig, appeared. Her lank hair was pulled tightly back and twisted carelessly on top of her head. She was flushed and cross-looking but when she saw Luke her expression changed to friendliness and surprise.

"Why, it's Chick—I mean Chuck! Hello, dear. I just—"

"It's Luke, Mom, Luke Sawyer," Penny put in. "He's a friend of Butch's."

"Well, I guess I know that, Miss. You get on with your sweeping. Come in, Luke." She had been holding the door open and Luke saw a fly sail triumphantly in. "I heard on the news about you, dear. Lord have mercy, what a horrible experience that must of been! You just don't never know what'll happen next, do you? I would of died from fright if I'd been in your place. Like they say, might as well be killed as scared to death. Come on in."

"I can't stay, thank you ma'am," Luke said. "I just wanted to talk to Butch. I—I haven't seen much of him lately."

Mrs. Boyle's face lengthened. She let the screen door close and came to sit on the top step.

"Clarence is not home, Luke. He left two-three days ago. Him and this feller from Briar Hill. Had some idea of a job up around Claxton—no, I b'lieve it was Mervin. Anyhow, one of them places above Baysboro. I hated to see him go off on a wild goose chase like that. He could of worked for his daddy, only Dr. Holland didn't approve of him being on the roofs in the heat long as he gets those headaches."

Her face became a shade more sombre. "You've had your own troubles, haven't you, Chick, I mean Luke. Your daddy passing away—we was all so sorry about that, a nice man like him—and then last night! My goodness, Ch-Luke, you musta had some shake-up! I just hope they catch those criminals, I sure do."

Luke said, feeling sickish, "Do you know if Butch and this guy from Briar Hill went in their car?" He didn't want Mrs. Boyle to think him overcurious and added, "Last time I saw Butch he was driving a car he said something about owning with a Roddy Pitman." He was doing it badly but Mrs. Boyle didn't seem to notice.

"Yeah, they went in Roddy's car." She laughed. "It wasn't any of Clarence's. You know him. He was just pulling your leg, dear. Maybe he aimed to buy a share in the old wreck after they landed those fine jobs they was so steamed up over, I don't know."

She glanced toward Penny who had begun to push the broom aimlessly about the porch again. "Between you and me, honey, I don't care too much for that Pitman boy. He's not the type I want to have my son friendly with, I'll say that. Not like you and the doctor's boy or even that colored boy that's got such nice manners and all. Mind now, I'm not saying anything against this Pitman kid. I just didn't take to him."

"Yes, ma'am, I know what you mean," Luke murmured. But did he? He didn't know it was Roddy Pitman he'd waited on last night. Couldn't even swear the blue Dodge was the same, though he was convinced it was.

"Anyhow," Mrs. Boyle went on, "to answer your question, yes. They left in that old car. I just hope it didn't break down on them or they didn't get in an accident or something. Times are so evil. Why, look at you, getting held up working an honest job and minding your own business."

To Luke's dismay she began to cry. "I just purely h-hate to have my boy roaming around the country like a—a hobo, me not knowing where he is—" She buried her face in her hands.

Luke didn't know what to say. He scuffed his feet in the sand, embarrassed, wishing he hadn't come. In addition to his own distress over Butch he had upset Mrs. Boyle.

"Don't worry, Mrs. Boyle. I—I didn't mean to make you feel bad, honest." He looked over her bowed head at Penny who stared back with a deadpan face. "Butch will be O.K. I know how it is; my mother's always worrying over nothing. I just thought—I just felt like chewing the rag a little and—well, our old gang's kind of scattered, seems like, since the old hut burnt down and—" He thought despairingly, Why don't I just shut up? I'm only making matters worse.

"Oh, it's not your fault, dear," Mrs. Boyle said, wiping her eyes on her palms. She even managed a teary smile. "Like you say, mothers can't help but worry, times being what they are. You never know—" She pushed at her scalp as if she thought her wig was there.

From inside the house came a sudden loud burst of music—voices of some church choir—quickly turned off.

"There," Mrs. Boyle said as if doom had struck. "He's up and wanting his breakfast. Mr. B., I mean." She scrambled up from the step. "Sure you won't come in and have a cuppa coffee, dear?"

"No thanks," Luke said. "I told Mom I wouldn't be long. You'll be hearing from Butch, Mrs. Boyle, I'm sure you will."

"Well, he said he'd let me know. About the job and where he'll be settled. You come back, Luke. You was always Clarence's favorite, see." As Luke started the car she called piercingly, "I sure hope to God they catch those thugs."

Luke turned the car around and left Putney Street as fast as he dared. Thoughts tumbled in his head and a spot of fear lay, cold and heavy, in his stomach. He didn't blame Butch for leaving home; it must be the most depressing spot in Mill Gate. But his being out of town right now certainly didn't improve Luke's peace-of-mind.

In the midst of his confusion a thought formed, detached itself, and stood clear: He wished he could talk to his father. Then he told himself, bitter and unsparing, If he was there I'd go right past him up to my room and not say a thing, like I always did. I wouldn't think there was anything he could do—and maybe there isn't.

SIXTEEN

All that week Luke went around feeling as if he were somebody else, or outside his skin, as when he impersonated some odd character. It was really weird to think it could have happened to him.

The thieves were not caught and Jeff Beale told Luke not to worry. Luke wondered what Mr. Beale would say if he knew how divided in his own mind Luke was about it. As each day passed he felt mingled relief and shame that they weren't.

"I wish they would catch 'em," Mr. Beale said. "Tough little punks trying to make the world over to suit their convenience. I'd like to see the whole lot meet their comeuppance."

At home, they stopped talking about it; Luke knew his mother wanted to forget it. At the station, at Syd's, in the street, they couldn't get enough of it and Luke found himself obligingly going through the details over and over with that outside himself feeling. It was not bad, seeing himself suddenly special in the eyes of others, but when he was alone depression settled over him. His self-image receded and the image of Butch Boyle took over. The round of questions and answers would begin, Luke both examiner and examinee.

Could that big guy have been Butch? No. I'D HAVE TO BE BLIND AND DEAF FOR BUTCH OR CHUCK OR ROLLO

OR SIM TO GET CLOSE ENOUGH TO TOUCH ME AND ME NOT KNOW THEM.

Why did that character in the old Dodge happen along just when he did, giving them a chance to slip in and be ready for me? IT COULD'VE JUST HAPPENED. A COINCIDENCE.

You don't buy that, you know you don't. It was too smooth. MRS B. SAID BUTCH LEFT TOWN IN PITMAN'S CAR TWO OR THREE DAYS BEFORE THE HOLDUP.

Big deal. If that *was* Roddy Pitman, *he* got back from wherever they went. Did he leave Butch there? HOW DO I KNOW? I DON'T KNOW ANYTHING EXCEPT I GOT HELD UP AND SOME GUYS ROBBED THE TILL. GUYS I NEVER SAW BEFORE.

Sometimes a brief rage washed over Luke and he would hope they'd be caught. If Butch Boyle could do that to him, he didn't deserve Luke's loyalty or even his concern. IF I KNEW IT WAS HIM I'D TELL. I WOULD NOT OBSTRUCT JUSTICE. You wouldn't? Would you turn Butch over to the law, see him go to jail? Could you?

Luke didn't know. Anyway, it wasn't Butch. The car didn't matter, why did his mind have to keep harping on that? Mrs. Boyle said Butch had been putting him on about partly owning it and Luke believed her. It was just the kind of thing old Butch would do. . . .

It got so Luke hated being alone, yet working wasn't that much better. He kept seeing the old car pull up at the pump, kept seeing the scarred face of the driver. He wished Sim was home, coming over to listen to music, to loll around and talk—about something else, anything else.

Anita brought Sylvy to stay with Martha as planned. "Are you sure you still want to keep her, Mother? She won't be too much for you after what happened?"

Martha assured Anita that Sylvy would be good for her, take her mind off her worries. "Luke wasn't harmed, that's the main thing." Not knowing Luke was in the house, she burst out, "Oh, Nita, I wish he'd taken the job at the hardware. It would seem so . . . natural to have him working there. Mr. Wilson did offer, you know. Of course, I know Luke ought to decide for himself and I haven't tried to influence him, but I can't help wishing—"

"He could get held up at the hardware store, too, Mama," Anita said gently. "I think I understand his preference for the station. Mr. Wilson is so old and young people don't have much reason for hanging around the store. The Shell Station's different."

Martha sighed. "I guess you're right. Anyway, don't worry about Sylvy. What little work she makes I'm glad to have. I need her."

Luke felt uncomfortable, listening in the next room. But what could you do for goshsakes? You had to hoe your own row, follow your own road—even when you weren't sure what it was. You couldn't just do what the older ones wanted every time or you'd never grow up.

"You know I do appreciate it, Mother," Anita was saying. "And it will be good to get away for a little while. Euclid needs it as much as I do." Her voice was suddenly vehement. "It's time *somebody* in this family got a decent break! Only it should be you, or Luke. What a summer it's been."

It made Luke feel lonesome to see the Tarrant's house all locked up and not a sign of life anywhere. He got into the habit of going home from work another way. He longed for the sight, the touch of Milo; he was sure everything would fall into place and stop being so warped when he could talk to Milo. Her little scrawl, all exclamation points, after she'd got the news about the holdup from her father wasn't really too much comfort.

Going into Syd's in the middle of the week, Luke saw Forrest MacLane sitting with Esme Holland in a booth near the juke box. His back was to Luke but there was no mistaking the fair hair curling down his neck or the wide shoulders hunched chummily toward Esme across the table. Esme, facing Luke, greeted him with her usual exuberance (if not more so).

"Sit with us, Luke," she urged, patting the space beside her. "Tell Forrest about Saturday night. He didn't get here till Monday, did you, Mac?" So it was Mac, was it? Luke would have thought no girl could bear to give up that fancy first name with its two r's. He and Forrest exchanged nods and Esme babbled on.

"Isn't it funny they haven't been caught? I wonder if they *were* from around here, like Chuck says. He says they must have known exactly the setup at the Shell Station, how you'd be by yourself and everything. Do you think so, Luke?"

Luke said he didn't, he was sure he'd never seen any of them before. He always said that at every opportunity; it had become practically automatic with him. He wouldn't sit with Esme and F. MacLane. He said he was in a hurry and drank a Coke, standing at the counter. Afterwards, carefully examining his feelings, he was gratified to find they were not in an uproar. He had sworn last Christmas never to doubt Milo again. Besides, the uncertainty about Butch was enough to make him feel like a louse without adding to it. He wondered how long MacLane would be around this time and let it go at that.

When Luke got home that evening, he stopped a moment on the shady porch. Through the open door he could hear his mother and Sylvy. First there was his mother's voice questioning, and the little girl's reply-ing. Sylvy hesitated before each word—as if she were feeling of it. Then there was laughter, Martha's and the child's.

The sound gave Luke a shock of pleasure. His mother often smiled and always he was aware of her determina-tion to "keep her spirits up" for his sake, but this wasn't for him or even for Sylvy. It was her own laughter, like something out of the happier past. His mother had been right; she had needed Sylvy.

Ten days after the robbery the police picked Roddy Pitman up on a traffic violation charge and Luke was asked to go to the station and identify him. This is it, Luke thought, his breath coming short. He was sick with dreadful certainty that it was the beginning which would lead to Butch Boyle's arrest in a case of armed rob-bery.

Luke's thoughts scuttled about in his head. What was he going to do? In case Butch was involved, could he shield him without risking charges as an accomplice himself? He didn't know much about the law, had never figured on any entanglement with it, though everyone knew how common it was for teen-agers these days to encounter it one way or another.

All the sickening fear of the night of the holdup came back as he entered the police station. The boy was slumped in a chair, his eyes narrowed in a sullen face. Luke saw at a glance the acne scars on it. He saw, too, the recognition that leaped into the slitted eyes as Roddy Pitman met Luke's frightened look with sullen calm.

"You ever seen this boy before, Sawyer?"

"Yes, sir, once."

"When?"

The night of the robbery."

Roddy Pitman did not look frightened, just faintly insolent, as if he knew nobody could prove anything against him or make him tell anything he had made up his mind not to tell.

The police took Luke around to the back of the building and showed him the car, the battered old blue Dodge. Looking at it, Luke was seeing not Roddy Pitman's slight figure at the wheel but Butch Boyle's.

"Is this the car you served directly preceding the robbery?"

"Yes, sir, it's the one. Like I told you—I didn't look at the license number but it's the same car and the guy inside was driving it."

"Was anybody else with him?"

"No, sir."

"And you never saw this Pitman other than the night of the holdup?"

"No, sir, not to my knowledge. Just then and today."

"O.K., Luke. That's all."

Luke was glad he didn't have to go back inside; he didn't want to see Roddy Pitman's eyes again. It took a while, after he was back at the Shell Station, for him to lose the feeling of things closing in on him.

Jeff Beale said, "They might sneak up on those fellas after all. Stranger things have happened."

Later, and privately to Luke, Rollo said, "I don't believe they'll catch 'em. I believe they're long gone and that money's been spent a while back. What you think, Luke?"

Luke shrugged. He didn't want to talk about it.

For several days he went around feeling uptight and uneasy. When a car stopped near the house he wondered if it was a police car. When the phone rang he tensed up, expecting it to be for him. When the old round of self-examination started up after he'd gone to bed at night, he did his best to turn it off, thinking of anything but the holdup and Butch Boyle.

Martha said sadly, "Luke, I know you're not having any fun this summer. I guess it's got to be like that for a little while, but it hurts me to see you just working and eating and sleeping. Like a settled old man. Milo at the mountains and Sim out in Kansas—maybe you ought to ask Charles Holland to the house sometimes, or go places with him as you used to. I don't want you to feel tied because of me. Nobody can keep me from being lonely, I've just got to learn to live with it."

"Ah, I'm O.K., Ma." Then, to escape the discomfort of her talking to him like this, he said, "Maybe I will slog down to Rollo's, see what he's been doing on his day off. I'll be back in time for supper, O.K.?"

"Take the car if you want to."

"Nah, I need the exercise."

Watch, lying outside the screen door, thumped his tail but made no effort to follow. Luke stooped and stroked his head. "Poor old fellow. Poor old cuss. Getting older than Methuselah, right? Good old Watch." The dog whined in an ecstasy of self-pity, lapping up the sympathy.

River Street had a shabby, tired look after the heat of the day, like people. A sprinkler whirled over the Mountjoys' lawn, chittering foolishly as it turned. At the Weavers' Arlene was practicing her piano lesson, the notes sounding strong and sure in the still, late afternoon. The sun, lancing through the tree branches, was still hot and high; daylight-saving time made the days too long, Luke thought.

Mrs. Prince, home from her job as waitress at the Gateway Cafe, came to the door.

"Rollo's not here," she told Luke, "but I expect him any minute. It's so hot in the house, let's sit out here,

173

maybe catch a breeze." Watching her cross the porch to the swing, Luke saw her shoes were run over at the sides, her legs a little bowed. It made him feel sad. He sat down on the step, listening to the creak of the swing as Mrs. Prince pushed it gently with her foot.

"How's your mama feeling, Luke?"

"She's well, thank you, ma'am."

"It's been a rough summer for you-all hasn't it?" Her voice was soft as velvet.

"Here's Rollo, now," Luke said, glad to see Rollo coming down the street. He hailed Luke before he had the gate unlatched, came jauntily up the walk.

"I reckon I'll leave you-all to yourselves and start supper," Mrs. Prince said. "Time for Rollo's daddy to think about waking up. Stay and eat with us, Luke?"

"No, ma'am, thanks just the same. I told Mom I'd be home for supper. I wouldn't want her to eat by herself."

"Well, I don't blame you. You're like my boy— mighty thoughtful and good to your mother." She closed the screen door softly to keep from waking Rollo's father.

Rollo dragged his arm across his face. "Whew! I'm beat with the heat, Lukey. How 'bout you?"

"Same," Luke said, turning his face to catch the breeze faintly stirring the leaves of the chinaberry tree in the yard.

He was startled when Rollo said, "What I wanta know is, where is Butch?"

The old warning ticked in Luke's mind. He said carefully, "I don't know. Wish I did."

"Well, I'll tell you what I think. I think he just blew everything."

Luke looked sharply at Rollo. "How do you mean 'blew everything'?"

"Like got fed up and ran away from home. I don't blame him, you know? His home, it's not like yours and mine. I don't see much of my dad, but at least he's sober when I do."

Suddenly, Luke wanted to tell Rollo his fear, get it off his chest, share it, ask Rollo what he thought. But he was silent, hanging onto the fear, keeping his secret. The chinaberry leaves whispered and when he had hold of himself Luke said, "Butch's mom—she's kind of nice in a way, you know? Sort of foolish but nice."

"I know what you mean." Rollo chuckled. "I went over to their house to see could I find out anything about Butch—"

"When?" It was out before Luke could stop it, quick and anxious sounding.

"This evening. On my way back from there when you came."

"You find out anything?"

"Nah, not much. I don't b'lieve she knows much herself. Said he went to find a job and showed me a postcard she got from him, mailed from Atlanta. He didn't send any address so she could write back, just said he was working and would get in touch." Rollo's face looked sad. "Anyhow, we sure as hell haven't got a gang anymore."

"Aw, knock it off," Luke said harshly. "You sound like everybody's dead or something."

Rollo attempted another laugh. "Yeh yeh yeh. I know."

They saw the figure then plodding unsteadily down the middle of the street. "The man of God," Rollo whispered, "Reverend Winterbligh himself."

Reverend Winterbligh's black robe flapped about his bony ankles, a ragged beard flowed down his chest, his

175

feet were clad in tattered sandals held together with bits of rope.

"He must of turned hippie for godsakes," Rollo breathed.

The figure lurched, his Bible pitched into the street and the old man made no effort to retrieve it, stumbling on doggedly. He looked like a wounded bird.

"We got to give him a hand," Luke said, getting to his feet. "He's liable to get run over."

Reverend Winterbligh did not appear to see them till Luke touched his shoulder, feeling the sharp, warped bones under the dusty, grease-spotted cloth. The old man turned, his beard jiggling with the trembling of his chin. The yellow skin seemed stretched across his sharp cheekbones. Dirt and age clung to him like an extra garment. Luke wanted to turn away but pale eyes peered into his face, a skeletal hand emerged from the folds of black and palsiedly touched him. Words, jumbled and unrecognizable, spilled from a toothless mouth.

Rollo held the Bible toward him but Reverend Winterbligh babbled on as if he did not see it. "Talking in tongues," Rollo said. Two cars were approaching, one from either direction, slowing to a crawl at the commotion in the middle of the road. Luke took the old man's arm and steered him to the sidewalk, Rollo following with the Bible.

Aletha Prince stood on the porch, a hand shielding her eyes from the ray of late sunlight slanting across it. She told the boys to bring the preacher into the house. He had stopped babbling and was breathing heavily. Luke and Rollo had to help him up the steps. Aletha Prince held the door.

"Just ease him out on the couch," she directed, snatching the cushions up and dropping them to the floor. "Poor old fellow, just look at those feet. No tell-

176

ing how far they've brought him, in all this heat, too. Wonder how come nobody stopped him. . . ." She began to work at the disreputable sandals. "Get me a pan of hot water, Rollo. Soap and a washrag and towel, too. Luke, you help me get his things off."

More than once in bygone summers Luke had seen his mother setting food before Reverend Winterbligh. But Rollo's mother was going to bathe him. Luke thought of his clowning impersonations of the addled old preacher while the boys cheered him on. It didn't seem funny now; he hadn't known about the bunions on the feet Aletha Prince was going to wash. . . .

"Thank the sweet Saviour you-all saw him," she said, taking the washcloth from Rollo and soaping it briskly. "He might've fallen on his face in another minute. I don't know if he's sick or just played out."

"Must be a thousand years old," Rollo whispered in Luke's ear.

"Looks every day of it, too," Luke whispered back.

Aletha said, "I used to go to the camp meetings with my grandmother. She was a great shouter, always got the spirit when the Reverend preached. It used to scare me but I liked it, too, the way little children like scary things."

"Maybe you ought to get the doctor, Mama," Rollo said. "You might be making him worse scrubbing on him like that."

Mrs. Prince snorted, scrubbing harder. "You sound like when *you* were little. Getting him clean can't hurt." She dropped her voice to a murmur. "What bothers me is, they haven't got anything ready for him. No brush arbor, no tent, no nothing. I reckon nobody expected him. Every revival he led looked like it'd be the last."

The old man showed no signs of coming round as Aletha brought her competent washing to an end. Clad in a pair of blue-striped shorts and a T shirt of Rollo's, he resembled a lighter-hued Ghandi. Mrs. Prince brought a flowered housecoat of her own and tossed it to Rollo.

"Get that on him and I'll give this thing an airing on the line." She wrinkled her nose fastidiously at the black robe on her arm.

"Now ain't she the damndest limit!" Rollo exploded when she had gone. "Dressing him out in our clothes." He sucked his breath in and let it out in a soft, "Jesus, just look at him in this kimono." Luke choked on laughter.

"I preach only the Word," Reverend Winterbligh said in a strong voice, making both boys jump guiltily. "Thou shalt not take the name of the Lord thy God in vain." He struggled to sit up, clawing at the upholstery.

"Say something to him," Rollo told Luke. "I've put my foot in it."

"You can't preach your best till you rest some, Reverend," Luke said placatingly. "You came a long ways today and you're beat. You know?"

A tear crept thinly down the old man's face toward the straggling beard. He said shakily, "I admit to some fatigue. The birds have nests, the foxes have holes, but the son of man hath not where to lay his head." He plucked at the sleeves of Aletha Prince's wrapper. "Where am I?"

Luke and Rollo exchanged uneasy looks. Inspired, Rollo said, "With friends, Reverend. Peace be with you."

Mrs. Prince was back then, soothing the old man with her velvety voice. "You'll be all right, Reverend. Everything's all right. You get some food in you and

178

get you a night's sleep and you'll preach the brush right off of that arbor."

"What arbor?" Rollo asked and his mother jabbed him with her elbow.

"He'll have his arbor, or anyway somewheres to preach. Your daddy and me can get some of the folks together. We'll fix something up." She turned a stern eye on Rollo. "You stay right here and see he doesn't stray off while I get him some soup." She hurried to the kitchen, leaving Rollo with a long face.

Luke said, "Rolly, it's getting late. I better be going. Mom'll have supper fixed."

"Yeh yeh yeh, I know. And leave me holding the bag. Everybody's got something real important to do so I can baby-sit the man of God."

Luke made his face as glum as Rollo's.

"No kidding, Rollo, I got to scram. Your dad'll be up any minute, won't he? He can spell you off. I don't mean to run out on you. It's just that Mom'll start worrying. You know how they are."

Rollo whistled through his teeth. "Sure, sure. I ought to, hadn't I? Look at mine, for crying out loud. Fixing to fling up a brush arbor singlehanded if she has to."

SEVENTEEN

"I didn't see him pass here or I'd have tried to stop him," Martha said when Luke told her about Reverend Winterbligh. "Remember the time your father called me to go down to the store and get him? It was a hot summer like this and the poor old soul was in bad shape then. He must be indestructible." A look of sadness came over her face and Luke knew she was thinking of his father, dead at fifty-eight.

"He's something, all right. Rollo's about ready to believe he's like superhuman." Luke piled macaroni-and-cheese on his plate, took a modest portion of green salad. "You know something, Mom? Mrs. Prince is really—" He searched for a word and, failing to find it, finished lamely, "really great."

Martha took a sip of iced tea. "Aletha Prince is a sweet, good little thing."

Luke knew she wasn't being patronizing but the insipid praise irked him. He wished his mother could have seen Mrs. Prince washing old man Winterbligh's dreadful feet.

"She shouldn't have to do it all," Martha went on. "I can give her a hand. I expect Hilda will be willing to go down there with me, too. Why, that old man is almost a legend around Mill Gate. In the whole county, for that matter." Her face saddened again. "I always kind of watched for him. Like looking for certain flowers or rain in its season. This year, I never even thought of him—"

A few hours' rest on Aletha Prince's couch and a hot meal restored the Reverend Winterbligh's body amazingly, but his mind had slipped beyond help. Sometime in the night, with Mr. Prince at work and Rollo and his mother asleep, the old man let himself out of the house and wandered on. It was written up in the Mill Gate *Star* with something of a flair—how he had preached in the street in Briar Hill and afterwards was found sitting in the shade of an oak tree with his Bible in his hands, his head leaning against the huge trunk of the tree.

"Just fell asleep and didn't wake up," Rollo told Luke.

"Was your mama upset about him straying off?"

"No. She said it was the way he wanted to go—reading the Word. I wonder could he read, myself. My dad came home from work and found him gone. We looked all over for him, in the woods down there and all. Dad even wanted to have the river drug, but Mama said not to get the police into it or anything. She was glad he didn't get put in some institution, said it woulda been like jailing him. Best for him to go like he did, under that big ole oak tree.'"

"I reckon she was right," Luke said. "He wasn't like a human exactly. More like a woods animal. Couldn't sleep except under the stars, stuff like that, you know? Crazy old coot. But I guess he was good."

"Yeah. Anyhow, Mama don't have to worry about him anymore."

The hot days crawled along and August had almost had it when Sim came home. At first, Luke thought he had grown taller, then decided it was his improved posture. Just looking at Sim made Luke straighten his own shoulders. It was raining that night—a soft, steady rain that slid in silvery needles down the dark windowpanes. The electric fan on the floor stirred the close air of Luke's room, its busy hum giving the illusion of coolness.

"You have a good summer?" Luke asked.

"So-so," Sim said without much enthusiasm. The light glanced off his glasses as he turned his head to look around the room. "It's great to be back, though. Like they say, home's best."

"You look great," Luke said. "Like just out of military school or something."

"It's from working out in the gym. I'd stay at the Y, see, when my father was on the road. He travels a lot for this Sash and Awning Company. Sometimes I'd go with him but I got sick of so much knocking around, one town the same as another. I got to know this guy and just for something to do I'd go with him to the gym. Gram sent me the clipping out of the *Star* about the holdup. Gosh, it must've been something. Was it awful?"

"Ah, not too bad—looking back. At the time I didn't feel too good, I admit. Just as soon not do it over again."

"They never caught them," Sim marveled. "Funny anybody could get away with something like that."

"Oh, I d'no." Luke shrugged. "They had a pretty good start. I was no help to the law, that's for sure. Tied to a chair and listening to 'em gunning off like crazy."

"Gosh! Tell me all of it, Luke."

Luke started at the beginning and told the whole thing, through his identifying Pitman and the blue Dodge. Naturally he made no reference to Butch

182

Boyle's having any connection with the car or Pitman. It was beginning to seem like a long time ago now and not important—if he could know Butch wasn't involved. Sometimes he wished he could tell his worry to someone just to hear it laughed at as ridiculous, but of course he would never tell anyone, no matter how it came out. Probably he would never know the truth and it would all sink into the past and become like a dream, scarcely remembered. That couldn't happen too soon, either. . . .

When they'd finished with the holdup they talked about school a little. Registration day was less than a week away, after all. Sim admitted he would be glad to get back in harness and Luke smiled. As if they didn't all know Sim's love of school.

"What do you plan to do when you're through school, Luke?"

"I don't know. Wish I did." Luke sighed. "I don't want to work for somebody else for peanuts, I know that." He grinned self-consciously. "I used to think I wanted to be an actor. Remember those old impersonations?"

"Man, you were good at that," Sim said.

"I don't fool around with that stuff anymore. Haven't been in the mood. You know?" Sim nodded. "But I'll have to make up my mind to something. I don't see any use going to college if I don't. It's like taking a road without knowing where it leads to. I'm not like you, go for the love of it." He frowned at the scar on his hand.

There was a little silence, broken by the hum of the fan and the splash of rain running down the gutter. Luke said, leaning to peer closely at where the ugly scar had drawn Sim's face to one side, "That doctor sure did a keen job on your face. You'd never know anything happened to it."

Sim explored the side of his face with his fingers. "Yeah, he was a good surgeon all right."

"Was it painful?"

"Not too bad. Nothing compared to when I was in the hospital here. Now all that seems way back, doesn't it?"

"Yeah, man. Lots of water over the dam since then. This is one summer I'm glad to say good-bye to."

"I know, Luke. Well, I guess I better get on home. Looks like no use waiting for that rain to stop."

Luke woke to find his mother standing beside his bed, shaking him. He had read till late, then had a bad dream—something about the police and Butch and himself—and hadn't got back to sleep till nearly dawn when he had sunk so deep it seemed impossible to come out of it.

"You awake, Luke?"

Luke mumbled, squirming deeper into the tangle of his sheet. "Give me five minutes, Ma—"

"I can't, dear. It's twenty of. I'm going down and start your eggs now."

She went out and Luke lay, still half-drowned in sleep. Then he remembered! It was Tuesday and Milo was coming home. He flung the sheet aside, staggered to the shower. He let the tepid water that passed for cold pour over him and soaped his body, turning under the spray. Milo was coming home at last, just in time to register for school. Would she have changed? Maybe have a crazy new hairdo, talk differently from being up there in Asheville? He would see her tonight—and he hadn't planned anything special, guessed he was out of the habit. She might find him dull after that crowd she'd been with up there.

He got into his clothes, wide-awake now and whistling. He called Milo's image into his mind—tan hair sliding over her shoulders, gray eyes, behind those silly glasses she didn't need. All the girls wore them sometimes—all except Susan Bently. It struck him that Susan, refusing to appear nonconformist, was the only one who was.

Martha set bacon and eggs and a mound of steaming grits in front of him as he drained his glass of juice. Luke looked up and winked at her. She poured herself a cup of coffee and sat down at the end of the table. "Edie's going to Baysboro today, shopping," she said chattily. "I guess I'll go along and have a little visit with Anita. That'll leave the car for you."

"Good. If it's not busy at the station maybe I can clean the plugs." He had neglected the car through the summer, having little need for it. He should, of course, have done it for his mother. Well, he would today—but it was Milo he was thinking of.

When he got off work he drove by the Tarrants' house. The car was standing in the driveway but he didn't stop. He went home to the empty house, showered and dressed carefully. He looked at his clothes hanging in the closet—all cleaned and repaired. Martha never missed a button or a tear now that she had no such little tasks to perform for Henry.

Luke selected a bright green shirt, beautifully ironed, and a pair of russet-colored slacks with a knife crease. Tie or open shirt? The decision weighed on him for a moment, then he grinned and shut the closet door. Milo would think he was nuts if he showed up with a necktie. He went down and dialed her number, his fingers fumbling. Mrs. Tarrant answered and he felt a letdown; somehow he'd hoped Milo would be hovering at the telephone.

"Mrs. Tarrant? Luke. W-welcome home."

"Luke, honey! How nice to hear you again." She sounded as silly as ever. "Milo just took the dog out. I'll have her call you the minute she gets back."

Luke wanted to hang up but remembered his manners and asked about the summer, Milo's parents' health, the dog, the kitten that had become a cat. (He completely forgot Rudolph's existence.) Mrs. Tarrant rattled along as if it was all she had to do, and Luke fidgeted in the hot little hole under the stairs. Finally, she interrupted herself to say, "Oh, here's Milo now, dear. Hang on." Luke hung on, the phone slippery in his sweating hand.

He was totally unnerved at Milo's "Hi, Luke," forgetting what he'd meant to say to her—something to make her laugh right away in case she dreaded to see the old sombre Luke she had left.

"You too tired to see me, Milo?"

"Don't be silly. Of course not."

"Could I come over now?" He was annoyed at the dampness spreading under his arms. What was the use of a shower if he was going to arrive at the Tarrants' sweaty as a mule?

"Well, sure, Luke. Why not?"

"O.K. I'll be right over."

He had washed the car in his spare moments at the station and cleaned the plugs. It was running smooth as could be. He drove slowly, though his heart was racing.

Milo took him into the living room where the furniture stood, ghostly in dust covers. There wasn't a sign of her family, not even the dog Gregory or the cat that wasn't a kitten anymore. He was surprised and pleased to see she looked just the same: faded shorts and her tan hair hanging smooth on either side of her pointed face, no glasses and barefooted. Yet, almost at once, he saw she wasn't the same. He couldn't say what it was

186

that was different, nothing you could see right off—unless maybe her eyes that avoided him. He folded her to him, trying to calm his breathing.

"Milo—gee, Milo, I didn't know I missed you so much." Her hair tickled his bare throat. "You still love me, Milo?"

She laughed nervously, pulling back a little. Luke said, "Where is everybody?"

"Somewhere—I don't know. Mama's in the kitchen, I think."

Luke let his arms fall reluctantly to his sides. He sat down pulling her beside him on the muslin-swathed sofa.

Luke, that robbery, was it terrible?" She edged away the tiniest bit, smoothing her hair, her eyebrows. "It gives me the creeps to think about it."

"They didn't hurt me." The room felt chilly, the air conditioning too cold. "It wasn't me they were after."

"Just the same, people do get—hurt in those things. I would have felt terrible if anything had happened to you."

"Would you, Milo?"

"Of course!"

Luke heard Mrs. Tarrant's footsteps and sprang up as she appeared in the doorway. Her trim pants suit showed how good her figure was for forty-odd. "My, but it's good to see you looking so well," she said and kissed Luke. He wasn't expecting it and blushed, saying the first thing that came into his head.

"It must have been great up there in the Smokies."

Mrs. Tarrant began to rave and when she got a chance Milo said, making a face, "It wasn't *that* great —except maybe the size of the mountains. I got homesick." Mrs. Tarrant winked at Luke. At last she said she must get back to work, there were a million things to do, they'd stayed away so long. Luke asked Milo if she could go out with him later and Milo said, "Sure, why not?"

He went home and tried to take a little nap on the living room couch but he couldn't sleep. Martha hadn't got home from Baysboro, and Luke fed Watch and ate one of the ham sandwiches she had left in the refrigerator for him and drank two glasses of milk. He couldn't put his mind to reading or watching TV. He could only mark time till he and Milo could be alone.

They rode out the old Briar Hill road, abandoned by traffic since the completion of the new highway. It was a pleasant road with strips of woodland and farmhouses bordering it. Pale flashes of distant lightning streaked the star-scattered sky, and the air was pleasantly cool for a change. Luke's right arm lay loosely about Milo's shoulders.

"Tired, darling?" Saying the word made his heart beat faster.

"Not so very. Why?"

"You're so quiet." His fingertips touched the ends of her hair. "I don't mind you being quiet. Not if you're thinking about us." He thought her shoulder moved slightly. "Were you?"

"Yes," Milo said. "I was thinking about you and your dad, rather. Oh, Luke, I wish he was still here."

"God, Milo. So do I. I never had the sense to know I needed him when he was here. You know? He was just there, that's all. Nobody should ever take anybody for granted, you know that? Afterwards, you feel like such a heel."

Milo sighed. "I know what you mean. I take my parents for granted—when I'm not fighting with them like crazy. If it happened to my father, I'd have lots more to regret than you have, that's for sure. And if it happened to my *mother* I know I'd never be able to think of anything except how rotten I'd been to her—"

"You're not rotten to anybody, Milo. You couldn't be," Luke said, thickly. "You know something else? I've thought about it a lot since my dad died. People are a lot kinder to the dead than to the living. You say only nice things about them, you even think only nice things. All the stuff you should have said and done before it was too late. That can really bug you, you know?"

He pulled off the road into a little clearing in a pine grove and took her into his arms. As he kissed her an immense hunger for her rose in him, making him forget his father and the anxiety about Butch Boyle that had tormented him since the robbery. He knew the hunger had been swelling and building up in him all this crazy, aching summer and he forgot to be gentle.

"Luke, don't." She twisted her face from under his, pushing at him. "We aren't supposed to park. It's dangerous! You know that."

"I know. But you've been away such a long time. We'll go in just a minute. Just let me—"

"If a police car came along I'd feel so humiliated," she cried, pushing at his chest.

"Mi, look. Just let me . . . just tell me you love me. You do, don't you—still?"

"I—Yes. I mean, I . . . I don't know—"

He was suddenly still. "What do you mean, you don't know?"

"Luke, please, let's get out of here. I don't want to park. It's—"

"Dangerous. I know. But you've got to tell me, Milo. I thought it was all settled between us long ago. And now you say you don't know."

"I'll tell you if you'll just drive on," she said in a kind of wail.

His fingers felt numb starting the car. There was a dull pain under his breastbone. He backed, turned, and drove out into the old road again, headed toward town. "O.K.," he said when they'd gone a little way and she was silent. "You said you'd tell me," thinking, Tell me what?

He heard a forlorn sniffle but he wouldn't look aside, keeping his eyes on the narrow road with the potholes and breaks in its hard surface. "Tell me, Milo."

"I saw Forrest tonight, Luke. He came to the house after you'd gone. He said he wanted to be friends, just friends. He told my mother he wanted to beg her pardon for what happened. He didn't expect me to date him or anything—" She was fumbling at her silly tote bag—plastic with the picture of a donkey on it—for a tissue. "My mother said all right and he asked if he could s-see me and we talked. I never thought I could bear to talk about it, but we did. Luke—" Her voice rose shrilly. "Say something—you're *supposed* to f-forgive people, aren't you?"

Luke said nothing.

"Well, aren't you?"

Luke's mouth was dry and bitter as he said, "Yeh yeh yeh, sure. So you forgive F. MacLane."

Anger touched her voice, making it stronger. "There wasn't anything to forgive Forrest, really, because I never blamed him for it. I blamed her, not him."

"Well now. That's real big of you, Milo. That's a heart of gold you've got there if I do say so myself."

"Luke, please—"

"Please what, Milo?"

"Please try to understand. I'm all mixed up. Don't you ever feel like that?"

"Not about you. It's about the only thing I'm *not* mixed up about."

"Well, I am! I'm mixed up about you and Forrest and everything, myself most of all. If you just wouldn't push me so, Luke. It confuses me and I—"

"I won't push you anymore. You can count on that." He could hardly believe it was his voice—cold and furious and strange to him. "Just don't worry, my girl, I won't push you one little bit."

"Oh, Luke," Milo wailed. "Now you're angry."

"Too bad about that, huh, Milo? I suppose I should be tickled to death about you and F. MacLane burying the hatchet." His eyeballs had the scalded feeling that comes before crying. Weep before her after what she'd told him? Forget it.

"I want to love you, Luke—"

"But you can't make it. Well, I wouldn't want you to strain yourself. I sure wouldn't want you to do that."

"No, no, no. That's *not* it. I do love you, only—"

"Only you love F. MacLane better. MacLane the great lover. I reckon it figures."

Milo beat her little fists against the tote bag with the donkey, shaking her head so the silky ends of her hair flew against Luke's bare arm. She said, "I didn't say that, you did. I said I didn't know. Luke, can't you just give me a little time?"

"To choose between MacLane and me? Well, I don't need time, see? I know. I've known since we started going together more than a year ago. So it's kind of hard for me to see how come you need so much time."

She was crying now, too hard to talk, breathing in choked gulps. Luke wanted to touch her but it was too much, the summer had been too much. He had a wild feeling that fate or God or whatever had it in for him and wouldn't let up till he was ground to a pulp.

Mill Gate looked sleepy and deserted, the hour seemed later than it was. Some windows showed lights, some the eerie blue of television screens. Milo had stopped crying. Luke slid an oblique look at her delicate profile, the sweep of her hair along her cheek and down to her breasts. He wanted to forget pride or self-respect and cry out to her, "Don't let me lose you, too." He ground his teeth and kept silent.

In the Tarrants' living room shadows moved against the curtains, the muted throb of music sounded, and someone laughed. Milo groaned softly, "I forgot. Rudy's got friends in. They're dancing."

Luke got out of the car and stalked round to Milo's side. He opened the door and took her arm, holding it formally as they went up the walk and across the porch. He asked coldly, "Is MacLane going to school here this year?"

Milo flinched, drawing her breath in a quick gasp as if he had said something shocking.

"Oh, no. He'll be going back to Danville. In just a day or two—I think." She suddenly wilted against him, her head down. He could smell that Angel-or-whatever-it-was shampoo she used. "Luke, please, *please*—"

He turned and stalked back to the car and drove off in a shriek of tires.

EIGHTEEN

Luke had to fumble around for his house key. He hadn't got used to carrying it; when his father was alive the door had never been locked while Luke was out. He located it at last and let himself in quietly.

Upstairs he fell into bed without brushing his teeth. He and Milo had quarreled. Damn Forrest MacLane. Damn him. He had forfeited his claim on Milo long ago, but he couldn't take it that she was Luke's girl— ordinary old Luke Sawyer who hadn't any money or any prestige, whose ordinary parents hadn't any money or prestige.

Luke thought with disgust that he could have done more about himself. He could have gone in for athletics —he'd have been good at track—if he had seen any point in it. Or if he'd stuck with band instead of selling that stupid cornet he'd let his father buy for him. He recalled his father's anger, quiet but deep, when he found Luke had sold it at half price to that guy in the music store in Baysboro. He couldn't even remember now what he'd done with the money he'd got for it. . . .

Luke lay on his back and stared through the dark at the bunk above him. He'd meant all summer to give the bunks to Edith for her boys and buy himself a man-sized bed. He whispered Milo's name, and his heart and his loins ached. His hands remembered the smoothness of her skin and hair. She was his, he wasn't about to let anybody else date her—certainly not that slimy F. MacLane. But if she wanted MacLane—

He was bone-tired, every inch of him saturated with weariness. He might as well have been pulling stumps all day, the way his muscles ached; it must be what they called emotional fatigue. He felt afraid, too. How had Luke the lucky so quickly become Luke the loser? Well, he didn't have to be! There must be some way to prove he wasn't a big fat zero. He'd get Milo back. MacLane would go back to his fine school and Milo Tarrant wasn't one to go through her senior year without a steady. . . .

Luke groaned and rolled over. What was with him? He wasn't about to play second fiddle to anybody. If he couldn't be first with Milo, forget it. Let her have her cheerleader bit and her pick of a half-dozen guys. Luke Sawyer would simply withdraw—with dignity. He didn't have to have a girl at all—but her name seemed to echo in his head, Milo Milo Milo. . . . Why couldn't things have stayed as they were?

Expecting to pass a sleepless night, Luke suddenly fell into deep and dreamless sleep. The next thing he knew sunlight was pouring through his window across his legs; the curtains moved in a breeze that had for the first time the briskness of early autumn, and his mother was calling from the foot of the stairs.

On his lunch break Luke called Milo. The noise of the juke box faintly penetrated the booth in front of Syd's. He had felt most reluctant to call her, but he was sure he'd go out of his mind if he had to sweat out the hours between now and four without hearing her voice.

All morning he had grappled with what she'd told him. Should he do nothing and wait for her to take the initiative? Should he lay the blame on himself? Should he attempt to woo her away from Forrest MacLane with a "let the best man win" attitude? And now, without having reached any decision, here he was dialing the Tarrants' number.

"Milo? I'm sorry about last night."

"Oh—that's O.K." Her voice sounded forlorn. "I'm sorry, too. It was my fault—"

"No. I guess I was kind of a b-boor." He swallowed. "You want to see me again, or should I get lost?"

After a pause Milo said, "I'd never want you to get lost. You know that, Luke."

All the feelings of the last twenty-four hours seemed to gather and burst in Luke's chest.

"I don't know anything except how crazy about you I am," he said.

"Luke, I told you I wasn't going to date Forrest." Her voice got shrill, the way it always did when she was tense. "Anyhow, he's going away." Luke wondered if she really sounded that sad or if he imagined it. "Why don't you stop by on your way home from work? I'm supposed to go over to Holly's but I can fix it with her."

Luke's spirits lifted, then he remembered. "I can't. Not this afternoon. I've got an appointment with Dr. Holland. To look at my hand. What about tonight?"

"I don't think so, Luke. Gee, I'm sorry but Rudy's leaving first thing in the morning and scads of relatives are coming to dinner. I've been helping my mother get the house cleaned up today. You know what family parties are."

"Yeah. Yeah, I know, Milo." He widened the crack of the door to let some air into the stifling booth, the freshness of early morning having long since given in to early September heat. "How about I call you tomorrow, same time?"

"O.K. That'll be fine. There's a cheerleader practice tomorrow morning, but I'll be through by lunch time."

Luke hung up and stepped out of the booth, wiping his damp palms on the legs of his coveralls. He didn't know whether to be glad or sorry he had called her. He hated knuckling under like this but at least he would see her again. It gave him a sort of "where there's life there's hope" feeling and on the strength of it he drove the Shell pickup truck back to the station.

The doctor's waiting room was full, as always. Luke decided to stand rather than squeeze himself in between the stout lady and the oldish man on the shiny bench under the double window. He picked a dated magazine from the rack and leafed through it without interest. Kind of silly, his being here anyway. He made a fist of his left hand, then moved his fingers, one at a time. If there was any stiffness he couldn't tell it. Inconsiderate to take a busy doctor's time, but he hadn't kept his promise to come in during the summer; he'd been careless about the exercises, too. He guessed it would serve him right if he did wind up with a bum left hand.

Luke's was the last name called and the waiting room was empty except for Mrs. Ed Baines who was trying to calm her twin boys after their booster shots for school. The hands of the clock on the waiting room wall pointed to five minutes past five, but Martha Sawyer knew what doctors' waiting rooms were like these days and would have held off starting supper.

Dr. Holland was sitting behind his big desk, looking more tired than Luke had ever seen him. He looked older, too, Luke thought, than the day he'd stopped him in front of the drugstore less than four months ago. A doctor's life must be one hell of a rat race. It must take a strong man to choose such a profession, though of course not many were like Dr. Bob. He still made house calls and his office had no mean little sign, "Bills payable at time of office call" or whatever it was they said, for the patients to look at while they waited their turn.

Luke tried to picture Chuck in Dr. Holland's swivel chair and couldn't. Just for kicks he tried to imagine himself there. Dr. Luke. A remembered phrase slid through his idle imaginings: Luke, the beloved physician.

"Well, Luke. How's the boy?"

"O.K., sir." He was glad Dr. Holland wasn't a head-shrinker, trying to see into his mind.

"Hand bothering you any?"

"No, sir, just some little twinges sometimes. You know. Like my fingers going to sleep. I yell at 'em and it wakes 'em up." He laid his hand on the desk, blushing at the rim of grease under his nails. He should have scrubbed harder but he hadn't thought about it. Dirty fingernails were all right for Mike Donaldson, suited his mechanic's hands somehow, but here in the doctor's office with everything so clean they seemed almost an insult.

Dr. Bob worked Luke's fingers gently back and forth. "Been pretty faithful with the exercises?"

"Not too, I guess," Luke admitted. "I forget sometimes—" The truth was, he forgot most of the time and he was pretty sure Doc knew it.

"Guess you've had other things on your mind. How's it going, anyway?"

"O.K. I mean fine, Dr. Holland."

"Your mother keeping pretty well?"

"Yes, sir, she's fine. Far as I can tell, that is."

"Martha Sawyer's not one to crumple under adversity." The doctor could have been talking to himself.

He gave Luke's hand back to him. "You want to keep those fingers limbered up, you know. They'll come out of it if you make up your mind to it."

"Yes, sir."

"You'll be back at school in a few days. Last chance you'll have at Mill Gate High, right? Seems like yesterday you and Chuck started, makes me feel like an old codger to think about it. What do you think you'll do with yourself when you get out?"

Luke studied his hands.

"I don't know, Dr. Bob. I thought about it a lot before things happened like they did—" He had a sudden, unaccountable impulse to confide in Chuck's father, tell him how the future looked—like River Street in the fog. "I never came up with any answers. You know?" Dr. Holland nodded and Luke felt sure he would understand all the screwy things a guy would be ashamed to say to his own father. "I guess I'll go to college—somewhere. Baysboro Junior College, I guess. I wouldn't want to go too far away. My mother would be kind of lost if she didn't have somebody to fuss over."

"Don't underrate your mother, Luke. She'd want the best for you, you know." His voice was a little dry but his face retained the kind, understanding look.

"Yes, sir, I know. Dad left some money for me to go on. If I worked, too, I could make it see me through." He moved restlessly on the slippery chair. "It's just not knowing what to aim at, I guess, that bugs me." And wanting to marry Milo Tarrant, he thought.

"I believe most men have been through the stage you're going through now," Dr. Holland said, reasonably. Luke liked the way he said "men," not boys. "It's nothing to worry about. What you want to do with your life might hit you like that." He snapped his clean, blunt fingers. "Or you may have to dredge it up bit by

198

bit from all around you, whether it's college or Jeff's Shell Station. Both ought to help."

"How did it—I mean, how did you make up your mind to be a doctor?" Luke asked, not giving himself a chance to back down, though he felt embarrassed and pushy.

"The hard way." Dr. Bob's big, crooked teeth flashed in a smile that put Luke at ease. "I was a doctor's son and determined not to follow in my father's steps—the way Chuck's probably feeling right now without knowing how to tell me. I tore up the patch all right. Quit school—premed that was—and took some piddling little jobs, even had a stab at running away. Mind you, I'm not recommending any of this, just trying to show you things come in their own way and in their own time to some of us. Finally, my self caught up to me and I had to quit running scared and do a little soul searching. I faced the fact that there wasn't any satisfaction in the way I'd been living. The truth was," his eyes, dark and alert above the tired pouches, twinkled at Luke, "I wanted to do something about pain—all pain, everywhere. And that was it. Very simple and extremely complicated. Like most things." He pushed his swivel chair back and Luke found his own feet. He was both bemused and excited.

He was in the street before he remembered the unsmooth course of his love. What if he, Luke Henry Sawyer, should decide to go to medical school. That was a crock, now wasn't it! A middling student (when not downright poor), low on ambition, probably not over stable (look at how he went into a tailspin of guilt over everything, look how he worried). He remembered the smell of the hospital the day he went to see Sim and Butch, how he'd felt he'd smother if he didn't get out of the place. Hospitals and sick people, people in pain, people dying. All in the day's work for a doctor. He could never stand it, not he. Still, he felt better for the little talk with Dr. Bob Holland.

With the beginning of school, order seemed to return to Luke's days.

By mid-September the oppressive heat gave way to cool, bright mornings and almost chilly evenings, and by October Luke and Sim were wearing jackets to school, though they often discarded them before noon. Forrest MacLane's return to his school was not the least of Luke's blessings; he tried to tell himself Milo was more like her old self but he didn't quite believe it.

He had made up his mind to ask her for dates only on weekends. If he was going to make anything of himself he would have to buckle down and take his homework seriously. When he told Milo, trying to be funny about it to cover his embarrassment, she nodded, her gray eyes solemn and understanding.

"I'll have to keep my grades up, too, or I'll get kicked out of cheerleading."

Though he could never quite understand the girls' passion for this particular status symbol, Luke couldn't help being proud of Milo out there in front of the bleachers at the games. She looked great in her white top and maroon shorts, her golden legs flashing and her tan hair flying.

He treated her very carefully these autumn days while the leaves fell slowly from the sycamores and the colors of autumn appeared in the wood by the river. He was careful to be gentle, not to "push" her, as she called it. Neither of them ever referred to their quarrel the night she came home and Luke never suggested parking except in the Tarrants' driveway. He handled her as if she were made of glass.

Sometimes, climbing the stairs to his room after a date with her, Luke's whole body ached with restraint and he would wonder if being in love was worth the price. It had been so much easier back in the days when he had only to string along with the gang, enjoying in turn his clowning and theirs, both admiring and being annoyed by Butch Boyle, being idolized by Craig Simmons.

Luke agreed to keep on working for Jeff Beale after school and on Saturdays but not at night. Mr. Beale was willing to go along with him. "Sure, Luke. You got your education and your mama to think of, I understand that. You and Rollo both. Jake Munson from down in the Hollow—he graduated last year—came looking for a job. Guess I'll try him for helping out. Prob'ly slow as the seven-year itch. I can tell by looking at him he hasn't got yours and Rollo's get-up-and-get."

"You've been mighty good to me, Mr. Beale," Luke said. "I appreciate it."

"Forget it, kid. It's a two-way road." He grinned slyly. "We might could start us a partnership one of these days, you keep on as sharp as you started."

A year ago, Luke thought, such a hint would really have turned him on; now, somehow, it didn't. He thanked Jeff Beale and hurried away from the station, thinking of other things.

NINETEEN

Now that fall had come, the fogs rolled up from the river, dripping from the trees, veiling the street lights, shrouding the houses at the lower end of River Street.

Luke searched for signs of change in his mother, some indication that the burden of her sorrow had eased, or at least grown lighter. Martha never pined—not where he could see—but he could sense her loneliness. The way she brightened when he came into the house made him wonder if she cried a lot when he wasn't there. Her life, on the surface, appeared as orderly and busy, as when Henry Sawyer was alive, but her interest in her daughters and their husbands and children gave Luke a vague uneasiness.

One October evening, coming from the telephone, Luke stopped to stand in the kitchen door, watching his mother. She was ironing—something she never used to do at night; it upset Henry to see her working at anything that required being on her feet because she'd begun to suffer from varicose veins. Luke thought her shoulders looked rounder than they had last spring, and he was sure he could see new strands of gray in her hair. A lock hung across her cheek, lank and tired-looking.

She guided the point of the steam iron round the collar of Luke's shirt. "Anita is so pleased with this new school Sylvy's in. She can sing little songs now. Sing the words of them, not just hum or make the words up like she used to. She can sing two or three little songs straight through without forgetting a single word."

"That's great, Ma," Luke said, thinking. That's great all right. Real great. Kid going on eleven years old and can sing two or three little songs without forgetting the words!

"Your father would have been so pleased."

It seemed dreadful to Luke that his mother should count so much on what would have pleased his father.

"Are you going to Milo's dear?"

"Not tonight. I'm kinda beat."

Martha eyed him sharply. "Are you taking those vitamins regularly? I think you're working too hard—"

"That's the laugh of the year. I'm liable to kill myself working. However I go, it's not going to be from overwork, Ma. We both know that."

Martha smiled. "You sound like your father, running yourself down. There's no need to do that with me. I know what you are, just like I know what he was."

It bothered Luke that Martha kept the little boys so much for Edith. Once, coming home to find her giving them supper (with the inevitable tipped-over glass of milk to mop up after Steve) he lashed out at her.

"You're the one should be going out and seeing your friends. If you ask me, Edie's getting to be an old gadabout."

"I don't believe I asked you," Martha said. "Edith's too young to be tied down all the time. I enjoy the children, Luke. You know that."

"They tire you out," Luke grumbled, stalking off toward the bathroom. He shouldn't have jumped on her like that, it was none of his cotton-picking business. Besides, it was a reproach to him to think maybe old Edie knew better than he what their mother needed. Still, she ought to realize that Martha would let herself be imposed upon, and without Henry it was up to Luke to protect her, wasn't it?

Then there was the thing about old Mr. Thad Wilson.

Martha had been downtown in the afternoon. She had already started making a thing of her Christmas shopping, and Hallowe'en not here yet! In other years Luke could not remember her ever having got through much before Christmas Eve; she'd always laughed at early shoppers, saying she couldn't work up any proper spirit till it was in the air. Luke suspected she was trying to show them she could face holidays with the same courage she had shown all along. He wished she didn't feel she had to be brave. Why couldn't she sit back and let the girls handle the holidays as they were planning to do?

Luke had dried the supper dishes for her and she was idly turning the pages of the paper, too tired to read it, he suspected.

"Mr. Thad's showing his age," she said, sliding her feet out of her slippers, rubbing one gingerly against the other.

"Been showing it ever since I can remember," Luke commented.

"He doesn't keep his eye on things like he used to."

"I bet that breaks Mr. Ed and Miss Vanessa all up. I hear 'em crying in the night sometimes when I can't sleep. Thought it was that little old screech owl used to roost in Princes' chinaberry tree."

Martha ignored him rather grandly.

"He just sits out in front of the store in his straight chair—you know, the kind I call country chairs. Makes me think of our old Watch, sunning himself. He looked kind of cold, nice and bright as it was this afternoon.

I wasn't right sure he recognized me when I spoke. Then he kind of blinked and said, 'Oh, it's Marty Sawyer.' He started talking about your father then. I thought he was going to cry. Say what you will, it won't be the same when all the old ones have gone on."

Luke covered his groan with a cough. "It's time some of 'em cashed in. Mr. Thad's older than God by about—"

"I don't care for that expression," Martha interrupted sharply. She looked at Luke in perplexity. "Why you can't live and let live where that old man is concerned I cannot understand. What's he ever done to you, Luke, except put bread in your mouth?"

Luke groaned again. "Maybe that's it. I don't know. He just makes me mad—trying to get me to take a job in his precious store. You think he'd offer Rollo Prince or Butch Boyle a job? Not if they were hungry he wouldn't! Every time I look at him—" Luke's voice rose, thin and agitated—"I think about Dad lying on that old oily floor. Mr. Thad makes poor weak-minded Link Jackson oil it because he's too stingy to lay rubber tiles he could get for about a penny apiece wholesale. You know Dad tried to get him to refloor and remodel the smelly old place. It looks like about World War I or something. I just can't stand him *or* his crappy old store, that's all."

Martha looked at him steadily, her hands folded in her lap. They had a pink, innocent look, but her face had paled at Luke's reference to his father lying on the floor.

"I don't think that *is* all, son. Are you sure you weren't maybe a little bit ashamed of your father's job? A clerk in a store you despise, employed by a man you despise."

A painful blush flamed up in Luke's face.

"Ashamed! Why would I be ashamed for goshsakes? A job's a job, I don't care what, long as it's honest. You calling me a snob or something?"

"I hope you're not," Martha said quietly. "Your father wasn't in a position to be choosy when he started working for Mr. Thad. We wanted to get married, you see, and Henry intended to support me and our children. He didn't do too bad a job of it when you stop to think. He always wanted your sisters and you—especially you—to do better than him, have a better education, get better jobs. That was his real ambition. If you turn out to be the man Henry Sawyer was I'll have no complaints. Neither will the girl lucky enough to marry you if she's worth her salt."

Luke sat like a stone as his mother walked out of the room, carrying her slippers. Could it be possible that in some screwy way she was right? That he was ashamed of his father's job, ashamed of his father? He couldn't be that kind of a creep, he couldn't. . . .

He didn't know how long he sat there in his father's old chair by the blank and silent TV set. He could hear his mother puttering about in her room—and singing! She never bothered to learn all the words of a song and would jump from one to another without warning. It was only lately she'd begun to sing again. Now, she sounded like someone who'd got a load off her chest and was obliged to give expression to her lightness of heart.

Maybe he was wrong, Luke thought, to worry about her. Maybe all he needed to do was get himself squared away and let the chips fall. . . . Dr. Holland's voice echoed in his confused mind: "Don't underestimate your mother." Luke rubbed his eyes, trying to get rid of the gritty feeling in them. One thing was for sure: she'd given him something to think about.

Although Luke had determined to make better grades this year, he had no intention of becoming a grind. He wasn't *that* dumb, he told himself. He had one subject that stumped him; he couldn't seem to get the hang of chemistry. He guessed he must have started on the wrong foot, and his teacher wasn't exactly inspiring. He thought seriously of dropping it, but he needed the credits. Besides, chemistry might come in handy someday. Probably not, but you never could tell—especially as muddled as he was over things in general.

Martha suggested he get Sim to help him but Luke didn't cotton to that idea. He could just see old Sim looking teacherish while Luke wrestled with what was a snap to Craig Simmons. He was in study hall one bright November day when he got the new idea.

Through the high windows he could see a strip of blue sky that looked as if it had got left over from October. It made him wish, as he had years ago in elementary school, that he could flee the confines of the building and be off to woods and river, free as a bird. With an undisguised yawn, Luke brought his gaze back from the slice of blue and found himself looking straight into the long, serious eyes of Susan Bently.

Caught staring at him, Susan blushed and looked down, beginning to write in the strange, awkward way of the left-handed. Luke had never noticed that she was left-handed—but then he'd never noticed her particularly. Like the others, he considered her a rather unfriendly girl. "Standoffish," Milo had called her.

Now, seeing her flushed face bent over her notebook and her left hand scribbling so rapidly, it occurred to Luke she might only be shy. Sometimes that made a person appear unfriendly. She was still relatively new at Mill Gate High; most of the students had started school together and would graduate together. Look what a rough time Sim had had his first year or two.

Thinking along this line, Luke began to feel a little sorry for Susan Bently. He couldn't imagine what it was like not to have plenty of friends and didn't want to find out. It wouldn't hurt those stuck-up, silly girls to make some real effort to include her, go more than halfway if it took that. She wasn't bad-looking. In fact, now that he really looked at her, Luke had to admit she was rather good-looking—in a different sort of way. She wasn't like Milo, naturally, nobody was. She wasn't even pretty in the way Judy and Holly were, and not being loud-mouthed like Esme and Joy, she sort of got overlooked.

The buzzer went for the end of study period and Luke scrabbled his papers together, stuffing them into his chemistry book. Without giving himself a chance to back down, he caught up to Susan in the corridor. After a "Hi Susan," he went straight to the point, which was his new idea. "This chemistry's sending me up the walls. Could you—would you—I mean like straighten me out on some of it?" He gave her what he hoped was an engaging grin.

Susan smiled back uncertainly. "Well—sure. If I can."

"I know you can," Luke said earnestly. "You're such a whiz at it."

Her smile disappeared and she said, "Oh, stop it." There was nothing silly or flirtatious about her. It was almost as if her seriousness was an affliction she would have been glad to do away with but didn't know how.

Luke saw Milo farther down the hall with Chuck and Judy and Holly. Chuck was clowning around and the girls were giggling. Luke stole a glance at Susan, but if she saw them she didn't let on.

He said, feeling hurried and a little nervous now he'd seen Milo, "If you'd be willing to give me a little time one night—I work afternoons, see—I could come over to your place or, if it's easier for you, I could bring you to my house. There's only my mother and me, and it would be quiet. I wouldn't want to take too much of your time—"

Susan nodded. "Whichever you'd rather, Luke. It's pretty quiet at my house, too. I—we'd be glad to have you." Saying that, she blushed again, faintly. And again Luke thought she wasn't bad-looking at all. Something about her looks grew on you. . . .

"Well, gee, thanks, Sue." He tried the "Sue" for size, wondering if anybody ever called her that. She appeared not to notice it. "Which night would be like convenient? And what time?"

Susan hitched at her books, frowning a little in thought.

"Tomorrow? That's Wednesday. Would that be O.K., about seven?"

"Tomorrow'll be fine," Luke assured her, already a step or two ahead of her, hurrying to catch up with Milo before she went to class. "And thanks a million. I'll try to make it up to you somehow or other." He was afraid he was blushing now and her smile didn't help any.

He loped ahead of her and grabbed Milo's shoulder, laughing at her small yelp. She spun around and dropped her notebook—a fat one with mushrooms all over the plastic cover.

"Oh, Luke Sawyer," she cried. "Look what you made me do." She bent to pick it up but Luke had the notebook in his hands, grabbing at the papers sliding from between its covers. He stopped the papers in mid-air but a thin air mail envelope escaped and drifted to the floor. Milo swooped, her hair hiding her face. Luke saw the return address on the corner of the envelope as she picked it up and reached, flushed and angry-looking, for the notebook he still held.

Stunned, Luke handed it to her. He felt like a goon; it hadn't occurred to him that Milo and Forrest might be writing to each other. The others had gone on ahead and Luke asked, trying to sound as if nothing had happened, "Want to stop at Syd's after school? I don't mind having a Coke on company time."

"Sure," Milo said, pushing the envelope into her notebook. "I'll meet you at the bus circle." And she began to run down the hall, calling to Holly to wait for her.

TWENTY

Luke walked in a daze, kids pushing past and chattering. Somebody said, "Hi, Sawyer" and he didn't know whether or not he replied. He had meant to tell Milo about asking Susan Bently to help him with chemistry—but why bother? She probably couldn't care less. Then he tried to gather himself together. It was stupid to push the panic button over every little thing. So MacLane wrote Milo letters, probably she didn't even answer them. But Luke couldn't make the bluff work. He felt sick and hollow—like last year when MacLane had showed up at Christmas time.

Luke had two classes to get through and Milo was in one of them. The class had barely begun when the scrap of paper, folded to about the size of a postage stamp, reached him by the usual circuitous route of passed notes. He read it under cover of his history book. Even her squiggly handwriting had a scared look.

"I was going to tell you when I got a chance. You don't have to get all uptight about nothing. See you at the circle. Mi."

He fastened his steely gaze on the history teacher and tore the bit of paper into infinitesimal shreds and pushed them into the pocket of his jeans. He remembered a hot summer day just after he'd learned to swim. Overconfident, he'd tried to cross the pool and couldn't make it. The life guard had to dive in and rescue him. He'd felt terribly humiliated and the other boys had kidded him about it. Well, he was going to make it now; one way or another he was going to prove he was a better man than Forrest MacLane.

Milo was waiting for Luke at the circular drive where the school buses turned around. She was alone and there was scarcely a trace of her nervousness left. Her face looked as if she'd just washed it and her hair as if she'd just brushed it—but she was wearing her glasses, as if their phony, transparent lenses could shield her. Luke had decided to act as if nothing had happened, to let her call the turns. The muscles of his face felt strained by his forced smile but a sort of hopeful look came into Milo's face at the sight of it.

They started across the schoolyard and, forcing himself again, Luke reached for her hand. It was slightly clammy but her fingers curled in the way he loved inside his palm, causing his heart to lift in spite of himself. He'd probably made a mountain out of a molehill; after all, he had no right to act as if he owned her— had he? Outside the low brick wall that enclosed the school grounds he felt a small tremor in her hand and squeezed, hardly thinking what he was doing.

"Luke, you got my note?"

"Yeah, I got it."

"Well, I meant what it said. No kidding, Luke."

"I'm not your—keeper, Milo. It's not for me to say who you can write to or talk to or—be friends with." He liked the bitter way the last phrase sounded.

"I know, but it must have seemed kind of sneaky, me carrying that letter around and not saying anything. It only came yesterday and I haven't talked to you till now. Well . . . have I?"

"That's right, Milo. You don't have to explain everything to me."

"Oh, for heaven's sake! You say that but you don't mean it. Otherwise you wouldn't get sore every time I turn around." Luke didn't answer and Milo added, humbly, "That wasn't fair. You're not like that, but—"

"I'm not sore at you," Luke said, careful to keep his tone even.

"It's not like I was *dating* him—"

"That would be kind of difficult, wouldn't it, under the circumstances?"

Milo snatched her hand away. "You know what I mean. Even if he was here—"

"Even if he *were* here," Luke corrected her in the accent of their English teacher. Milo giggled and he took her hand again. Under their feet the dry sycamore leaves rattled and over them the sky shouted its glorious blue. They were in sight of Syd's and could see boys and girls going in, a knot of boys waiting outside on the sidewalk to eye unescorted girls, if any, and maybe mutter a few cracks. Luke drew Milo back.

"Since it's like a truth session, Mi, I better make a confession myself." She looked up, startled, and he said, scowling because he felt a little silly now he was about to tell her, "I asked Susan Bently to help me with some chemistry. I'm supposed to go over to her house tomorrow night. Yeh yeh yeh, to do homework."

Milo shrugged. "Susan's O.K.," she said, looking like her mother. "I thought you were going to say you took Eva Covington out."

Luke dropped her hand as if it burnt him. Looking down at her he saw her face go crimson. She lowered her eyes. "I'm sorry. That was a really lousy thing to say. I meant to be funny, but I—"

Luke muttered, "Forget it," and steered her ahead of him through Syd's door.

When Luke reached the Shell Station half an hour later, Jeff Beale handed him the Baysboro evening paper.

"Take a look at that, kid," he said, puffing excitedly on his just-lighted cigar. "Only wish it had been our local police that nabbed 'em."

The headlines jumped at Luke: *Robbers of Jeff's Shell Station in Mill Gate confess.* He read on. The three boys—all under twenty years of age—had been apprehended in a supermarket holdup in Whitfield, the fourth in a series of similar crimes. Under questioning the delinquents had confessed to the holding up of Jeff's Shell Station in Mill Gate on July fourteenth. The boys were: Alton Burgess, Paul Adamson, and Milton Hines. Their pictures, looking from the page at Luke, were very young, strangely innocent. They were all of Baysboro, all of highly respected families. Rodney Pitman, nineteen, of Briar Hill had been named as an accomplice. . . .

Luke skimmed the details of the story but gazed long at the faces. Roddy Pitman's was not there but Luke could see the defiant eyes staring at him out of the acne-pitted face. He laid the paper on Mr. Beale's desk.

"You're white as cotton, Luke," Mr. Beale said. "Didn't mean to give you a shock. Boy, am I glad they got 'em. Time all this hoodlumism was stopped. I'll even go so far as to say I hope they don't get off too light." Mr. Beale was inclined to be gabby, but Luke murmured something and escaped as soon as he could to work outside.

Jake, the new boy, was full of it. He stopped repairing a tire to talk. "They'll try 'em over at the county seat, them being from Baysboro. You'll have to be at the trial, won't you, Luke? Wisht I was in your shoes. Musta been spooky, you coulda been shot up like that guy over in Long County last year, you know?"

"Thanks for reminding me," Luke said out of the side of his mouth. He was beginning to think now, his thoughts making sense. It wasn't Butch, I should've known. I did know, didn't I? Butch wouldn't have done a thing like that to me. Not to anybody, Butch wouldn't. I was a bastard to think he could. I wasn't thinking straight, never have since Dad died.

He guessed Jake Munson was right and he'd have to go to court, but it didn't matter. He could meet Roddy Pitman's eyes now and stare him down. He wished he knew where Butch was. How was it nobody cared enough to have found out? Thank God he'd never breathed his suspicion to a living soul. Now he would never have to. And it wasn't too late; he could write to Butch. There had to be some way he could get hold of an address.

Suddenly, Luke felt lighter all over, inside and out. He wouldn't have to worry anymore about Butch's guilt or innocence. He was free of it, could chalk it off into the past. He thought of the young minster's beautiful voice reading his father's funeral service, "And God requireth that which is past . . ."

They didn't take the evening paper at home, but Mike or Edith or Anita or all of them would have seen it. Martha would know about the arrests by the time he got home. Good. He wouldn't have to tell her. Luke found he could actually smile at his and Milo's problems that had seemed so overwhelming an hour ago. He could think of Butch as he used to, with admiration and pity, with exasperation and love. It took a crushing load off him, one he had thought he would never get out from under. For the moment he felt able to handle anything.

When Luke got home the letter was there, just as if it were planned, a part of the whole deal. Its impact was as startling as if Butch Boyle's voice had spoken to him. He lifted the grayish envelope from the hall table, staring at his name in Butch's childish, sprawling handwriting. He heard his mother talking over the telephone and knew one of his sisters was at the other end of the line. If he tried to sneak past the phone closet Martha would see him, maybe stop him. He went into the living room.

The lamp was on beside the wing chair and Luke sat down, slowly opened the letter. There was a kind of mist in front of his eyes and he shook his head, blinked a time or two before he could see properly.

Dear Luke,

Wonder how you are making out in old M.G. How are the other guys making out? Reckon the town hasn't fell apart with me gone ha ha. I am O.K. and found enough work to keep me from wasting away to a barrel and even get a little fun on the side (there's women up here too).

I'm on a construction job in this crappy place not too far from Chicago. Man, that is a town but is it cold!!! I guess I am what you would call mostly a drifter but I'm studying on taking a coarse in heavy equipment operating come summer and saving up for it. This guy I work with sold me on the idea. If you get around to writing someday I will be at this address a while, don't know how long tho.

Give old Rollo a punch in the arm for me and tell Chuck to watch out he don't get a dose of something from all those women he sleeps around with ha ha. Ma wrote me you came to see her. That was nice as she likes you. One of these days I'm going to write old Sim—he won't have any better sense than to answer, will he? Guess I've got a soft spot in my head for the little towheaded punk.

Wish you could join me but I know how it is you have to stand by since your dad passed on and besides you've got Milo. How is she? Well I got to sack in and hope to hear from you when you got nothing better to do. That Rod Pitman I was going to team up with turned out to be a genuwine jerk and we split up before we even got out of Georgia. I told him to shove his car and I don't mean into a telephone pole ha ha. I should of known my real friends were the guys from Mice or Men but what it comes to is you have to live your own life. Right? After I get some dough stashed away I might come back to see how you all are making out.

Yrs.
Butch

Luke pulled his sleeve angrily across his stinging eyes and tucked the folded pages back into the envelope. He would write to Butch tonight—not tomorrow or to-morrow night. If he kept in touch with him he might someday be able to make it up to him for his secret doubts. It sure was the damndest thing, the letter coming now after all this time. . . .

He heard his mother going from the telephone to the kitchen. She hadn't heard him come in, then. He went softly up the stairs and put Butch's letter in the top drawer of the chest, thinking how little it had said and

217

how much it had told him. He went to the stair landing and called, "I'm home, Ma," and quickly, before she could get going on the story, "I saw the paper."

Martha's voice came quavery from below, "Oh, Luke, I'm *glad* they got them at last," and Luke called back, "Yeah, so'm I."

She started something about feeling sorry for all those poor parents but Luke didn't listen. He lay down on his bed and thought about Butch—without dread or fear or guilt.

TWENTY-ONE

The Bentlys lived in the old Kirch house on Ingle Street. Luke remembered riding his bike out there to play with the Kirch boys, years ago. It had been on the edge of town then, but Mill Gate had grown beyond it so that it was now between the old part of town and East Mill Gate where new houses and a modest shopping center had gone up. It was a sprawling, old-fashioned house that had been painted and repaired before Mr. Bently, the new pharmacist, bought it.

That Wednesday night, parking the car in the driveway, Luke was a bit nervous. Everybody knew Mr. Bently, of course, but Luke had never seen Susan's mother. Martha Sawyer had met her at church or somewhere when the Bentlys first came to Mill Gate, and Luke remembered hearing her tell Edith that she seemed a nice little person but was in poor health and didn't get out much.

Luke tried to master his nervousness as he crossed the wide porch. He admired the bright blue of the door and the gleaming white of the house, and took pains to rap lightly with the brass knocker that shone in the glare of the porch light in case Mrs. Bently's poor health might have become worse.

Susan opened the door—a Susan in blue jeans and plaid shirt, looking like the other girls. Her trim, neat school clothes had always set her apart in a time of studiedly careless attire. The shy, reserved manner of the day before had entirely disappeared and she greeted Luke as if his coming here were a perfectly ordinary occurrence.

"Come and meet my mother," Susan said.

Luke saw the piano first, for it seemed to dominate the room. Then he saw Susan's mother. She sat in a weird position in a swivel armchair. A little fringed shawl hugged her shoulders, though the big room seemed very warm to Luke. The hand she held toward him as Susan led him forward was twisted, its fingers lumped with arthritis.

Luke shifted his books and took the hand carefully, not daring to exert any pressure, so that it was rather a dead-fish handshake. Susan said, "This is Luke Sawyer, Mother—probably the most talked-of boy in school today. You read about them arresting the thugs who held up the Shell Station this summer."

Oh, dear me, yes! I'm glad to meet you, Luke." Her smile was very like Susan's except for a slight crookedness. Luke learned later that in addition to the torment of arthritis Mrs. Bently had suffered an attack of Bell's palsy. "You don't look as if you'd be too easy to deal with—even where there were three against one."

"Oh, I wasn't much of a handful," Luke admitted, feeling foolish. "Not when one of them had a gun on me."

"I should think not," Mrs. Bently said, shivering in her little shawl. "It must have been an awful thing."

"Daddy's still at the store," Susan said. "It's open till ten, Wednesday nights." She hesitated, then went on. "Mother suggested we work in the dining room where it's nice and quiet."

Luke was accustomed to doing his homework against a background of very unquiet music as were all the kids he knew, but apparently Susan Bently was not. He murmured, "Nice to have met you" to her mother and followed Susan into the dining room that was almost as large as the living room. She switched on the chandelier and folded the lace cloth back from one end of the oval table. Luke laid his books down and moved two chairs up, feeling self-conscious as he placed them side by side. They were like Anita's chairs with needle-point seats. He thought of commenting on the needle point as a preliminary, but Susan did not appear to require preliminaries.

She sat down and pushed at her rolled shirt sleeves and smiled at Luke. "What bothers you about chemistry?"

Luke folded his long legs, put his elbows on the table and his face in his hands.

"Everything," he said. "I guess, mainly, it just doesn't interest me. Half the time I don't know what's going on. Guess I got off on the wrong foot like I usually do, to tell you the truth."

"I don't like it either," Susan admitted to Luke's astonishment. "I'm only taking it because my dad's so keen on it. He thinks nobody's got an education if they don't know some chemistry. You see, I thought I might study pharmacy myself but I've given that idea up. Now I want to go for either medicine or nursing. So the chemistry won't hurt either way."

A tingle of excitement raced along Luke's nerves. He raised his head out of his hands and stared at her.

"You're going to study medicine?" The light from the ornate chandelier with its dangling prisms gave Susan's smooth brown hair glints of gold, and for the first time

221

Luke noticed that her dark eyebrows were very beautiful—shaped like little wings and clearly arched. She nodded.

"If I get a scholarship. All that college is terribly expensive. I can get a nurse's degree in four years, three if I go to Baysboro J.C., but I don't think Daddy would settle for that. I'd rather be a doctor, naturally. But nursing would be second best." She looked a little defiantly at Luke—as if she thought he might laugh or tease her. "It would be in the field of healing—and that's what I want."

Luke had never felt less like laughing or teasing.

He said, "Gee, that's great. I mean—you know. I think that's really great, Sue."

Susan glanced toward the living room and said in a low voice, "It's not only my father, you see, and wanting to please him. He wanted to study medicine but it didn't work out. There wasn't enough money and he settled for being a pharmacist. It's my mother." There was real pain in her low voice and her long dark eyes. "When you see someone you love suffer—it makes you want to do something more than just stand around and watch." She ended simply, "That's why I've boned so all through high school, not because I like to."

"But you don't have to bone, you're so smart."

"Not that smart. I've worked for every A I've scored, don't forget."

"Well, I don't care. I still think you're great," Luke said firmly.

Susan opened her fat notebook, bent her smooth head over it. "I don't know why I got into all that. I never told but one other person in Mill Gate about it—"

"Arlene?"

Susan nodded, glanced shyly at Luke and back at the notebook. "Her boy friend's a friend of yours, isn't he?"

Luke thought he must remember to pass this bit on to Rollo.

"Right. I don't know how much she thinks of Rollo, but he thinks a lot of her."

"I don't believe Arlene has much time for boy friends."

Luke wanted to say, "And you don't either?" but stopped himself. It was none of his business. Besides, time was passing and he had to call Milo when he got home, so he mustn't be too late. Lying awake last night he had hatched out a plan for Friday—a private celebration of Butch Boyle's proven innocence and a peace offering to Milo at the same time.

"Well!" Susan was suddenly brisk and businesslike. "This isn't getting any chemistry into our heads, is it?"

"Speak for yourself, girl. Mine's the head we've got to cram. Yours is O.K., that's for sure." Luke began to think, half angrily, half enviously, that he'd master this lousy stuff if it killed him. If Susan could, he could, too.

"We'd better get started then," she said, hitching her chair a little closer to the table. From the living room came the first soft strains of recorded music; Luke wasn't sure but he thought it was Beethoven. Without looking up from the set of old test questions in front of her, Susan said, "That's been the worst of my mother's illness. She had to give up playing the piano because of her hands being so crippled."

Luke started to say, "Did you know it was your dad took me to the hospital the night the old hut burned down?" But it didn't seem relevant so he was silent, and Susan immediately applied herself to the work at hand.

Fog had begun to gather—but thinly—when Luke went out to the car. He dug the old towel out of the glove compartment and wiped the rear window. His mind was a curious mixture of what he had learned in the last couple of hours. He was not sure which was the most important—the chemistry or what Susan had told him about herself. He was a little flattered by her confidence and he had a sort of warm feeling about her. She wasn't the "new girl" anymore. Actually, he felt very well acquainted with her.

Martha was half-asleep in front of the TV when Luke got home.

"How'd it go?" she asked, bleary-eyed and covering a yawn.

"Fine. I learned more than I have so far, that's for sure. Susan Bently's a darned sight better teacher than old Bassett any day."

"Well, that's wonderful, Luke. I'm so glad you thought of asking her to help you."

"Ma?" He put his books on the mantel, nudging Watch gently with the toe of his shoe. "Is it O.K. if she comes over here next Wednesday?" He grinned. "I already asked her, matter of fact. I thought I should, since I was there this time."

"Why, of course, dear." Luke could see she was about to say more, get steamed up as she did now over little things, but Luke shut her off by saying he had to call Milo.

It wasn't nine-thirty yet, not too late to call. Even if he hadn't made the plan he thought he'd have felt a need to talk to Milo. . . .

Mr. Tarrant answered and Luke hung onto his patience while the old guy carried on in his usual manner: "Luke. How's the boy? How's the world treating you? See they got those juvenile delinquents. After all this time. Good thing, right? Reckon you'll be having your day in court eventually. Ha." Finally he got around to calling his daughter to the phone.

224

Milo made no reference to Luke's evening. He thought he ought to tell her he and Susan had arranged —tentatively—to meet every Wednesday for the coaching, but there was plenty of time for that, better get on with his plan now.

"Mi, I've got this yen to go out on the town. You and me. I haven't taken you anywhere or done anything nice for you in so long I'm liable to forget how if I don't."

She made a little sound of denial and he rushed on, beginning to feel excited about it as he had last night. "How about going to Boniface's for dinner, Friday night? Dancing and everything, the works. We could dress out. My cuff links and your blue job with the shiny trimming. You know the dress I mean."

"Oh, Luke. That old thing!" But he was sure he caught an edge of excitement in her giggle.

"Yeh yeh yeh. That old thing." He mimicked her, affectionately. "I've been wanting to do something special ever since you got home from North Carolina. There's no game Friday, is there?"

"No. Friday will be great."

"O.K. then. I think my suit's out of moth balls. Might even trim my sideburns." It was a joke; his sideburns were a bit skimpy but his long bang and the thickly waving sandy hair on his neck made up, he hoped. Milo giggled again and Luke said softly, "Good night, darling." He could never say the word without a surge of tenderness. It was still with him when he came out of the cubbyhole under the stairs.

Martha called, "Want a glass of milk, dear?"

Luke was about to refuse but some wistfulness in her tone changed his mind. How lonely her evenings must be. . . . "If you'll have one with me," he said.

TWENTY-TWO

Luke and Milo, coming out of the restaurant, confronted a shifting wall of fog. Luke held her hand tightly as they groped their way to the parking lot. Milo wore her mother's blue velvet evening cape over the sequin-trimmed dress Luke had asked her to wear and she pulled it tightly about her, shivering in the damp cold.

"Sometimes I think November's the worst month for fog," Luke said, starting the motor. "Unless it's January. Rollo always blames the river and I guess he's right. Used to be so thick when we'd come out of the clubhouse we'd have to feel our way out of the woods."

"I used to be kind of jealous of your club," Milo admitted. "But I'm sorry you haven't got it anymore." Luke kissed her temple.

"I don't need anything but you," he said.

The headlights did little to cut the fog and Luke drove at a careful crawl, feeling the old, odd excitement of blurred street lights and dim yellow rectangles of house windows.

"Must be like London," he said. "Proper oald pea-soupah."

At the Tarrants' house he said, hopefully, "You don't have to go in yet, do you? It's not eleven yet."

Milo snuggled deeper into the folds of the cape. "I

guess not. It was a marvelous evening, Luke. You were sweet to think of it."

"Ah, forget it, Mi. You and me—you and I were overdue a good time."

"But I know you don't like to dance—you're really not that bad, you know. It's all in your mind."

Luke guided the car into the driveway. "Somebody's liable to slam into us out here."

He pulled Milo against him, bending to kiss her lips. Maybe it was an accident that he kept missing them, kissing her cheek instead. She said, ducking her head and laughing in a queer, breathless way, "I had a beautiful time, Luke. I love going to Boniface's. It's the only elegant eating place around here, you know?"

He knew she was evading him now, trying to change the subject.

"Forget the restaurant, Milo. Can't I even kiss you?"

"Well, you have! About a million times already."

"And you don't like it." A kind of stillness came into him.

"I didn't say that," she cried. "Oh, Luke, I don't understand you. You're so—complicated."

"You mean you do understand MacLane? He's not complicated, I guess. He's just a sweet, unsophisticated guy you can read loud and clear." He was sorry he'd said it; he hadn't meant to. If there was one subject he'd intended to steer clear of tonight it was that. He moved over, trying to pull himself together, trying not to be sulky.

"Yes," Milo flared, turning her face to him. In the foggy darkness he could but dimly trace its delicate shape. "I mean, I don't know, but—yes, I understand him better than you."

With a trembling hand Luke stroked her hair.

"I'm not complicated, Mi."

"Yes you are. I never know what you're thinking about."

"You, mostly."

"You're just saying that. You've changed, Luke, you've changed a lot. I know you can't help it. It's things that have happened—like about your father. And nothing being like it used to be—"

"What do you mean, nothing like it used to be?" But he knew. He knew it was not only he who had changed; Milo had, everything had—and it could not be put back. He cautiously drew her into his arms again and went on stroking her hair as if he hadn't been interrupted. He didn't know he was going to and was startled when he asked, "Are you still in love with him?"

The silence stretched and spread. He imagined it stealing out into the darkness with the fog. He waited for her to pull away from him but she did not. She buried her face against his arm.

"You are, aren't you? You tried to love me—I know. You told me that one time. On account of me being an all-round guy who never got a girl in trouble or any of that stuff. But it's always been him. Right, Milo?" He felt her shoulders shake and knew she was weeping. He said gently, "Don't cry, darling."

He didn't know why he should be gentle with her—unless it was the still, deadly knowledge beneath her words and his that it was all over between them. After he'd held her and let her cry for what seemed a long time, he kissed the top of her head. Her hair was as fine and silky as Sylvy's. He had always loved Milo's hair that seemed to move across her thin shoulders with a life of its own.

At last she pulled away from him and pawed around in her little velvet bag for a tissue. She wiped her eyes and blew her nose softly. She said on a sad little hiccup,

"Luke, let me go. Don't be mad—don't hate me. Just let me go. . . ."

Even though he had known—it seemed a long time, now—that it was coming, the shock of hearing her say it went through him like flame. He had to try a couple of times even to breathe. He could hear her little motions at putting herself to rights, smoothing her hair, patting her cheeks and eyelids with the ragged tissue. From his breast pocket he took the cologne-scented, bluc-bordered handkerchief Martha had folded for him, and pressed it into her hand.

After a while, when he could trust his voice not to crack, he said, "I can't hold you, Milo. If you have to hold onto a person, it's no good. You know that, don't you? You're free to go or stay."

She cried a little more, then said in a quavering voice, "Thank you, Luke. You—you'll find a girl who's right for you, I know you will. I never was—"

"You let me be the judge of that," Luke said, suddenly fierce, his gentleness run dry at last. It had served too long a hitch and could survive no more.

He was able to turn his thoughts off quite neatly when the Tarrants' door closed behind Milo. He didn't linger on the porch but went down the steps and to the car, his mind a vacuum. The fog had lifted a little in this higher part of town, but as he turned into River Street it rose to meet him in shifting, bumbly clouds. It was capricious, thinning and thickening, but as the street sloped toward the river it was like a silent, weightless, gray-white sea.

He managed to get the car into the garage without bumping into the hedge bordering the driveway. Still in the weird but welcome vacuous state he let himself into the house without a sound. Watch no longer shared Luke's room; the stairs were too much for his rheumatic joints and he slept on the rug in the living room, merely thumping his tail in welcome. Luke took his shoes off and crept up the stairs.

There was no sound from below; his mother must for once be fast asleep. It was a wonder she hadn't sat up for him, afraid he'd have an accident because of the heavy fog. Probably she'd sacked in without knowing it was so dense.

Luke hung his suit carefully in the closet, removed the cuff links Milo had given him last Christmas from the pale green shirt that had cost six dollars and laid them on the chest of drawers. Funny to think he and Milo wouldn't be giving each other anything this Christmas. There was a constricted feeling in his throat; outside of that he didn't feel much of anything.

He started to open the small drawer to put the links in their box and it stuck. He gave it a savage yank and Milo's picture fell, face down, on top of the cuff links. He picked it up, set it back carefully, the roughness gone out of him. He stood gazing at it, drinking in every delicate feature of the small, pointed face, and feeling began to come back. Like novocaine wearing off and exposing the throb where a tooth had been, pain flowed into him, incredible and outrageous.

He jerked his tie off—the beautiful, wide, dark-green one Anita had given him to go with the shirt—and threw it on the floor, tears scalding his eyes. It was impossible to tell whether he felt more grief or rage. What had he done, quietly handing the girl he loved over to another guy? A guy hundreds of miles away at that! He hadn't even put up a fight—just let him have her like he'd let the big punk at the Shell Station have his wallet. Choked with humiliation, he thought of school—all the kids yacking their heads off. Maybe they knew already and had just been waiting for it to happen. Girls were

230

always confiding in each other; maybe Milo had told Holly Mason. . . . No! Milo wasn't that sort. She wouldn't . . .

Who had he thought he was, for Crissake, some fat-headed Galahad, bowing out because his lady wept over another knight, a creep like F. MacLane at that? He hadn't given himself a chance. The crazy summer had dulled such wits as he had. That must be it. Milo was probably thinking how easy he'd been, despising him because of it—Luke Sawyer, the all-round guy, the good guy. Well, he'd give her something else to think about. He wasn't about to "let her sleep on it," congratulate herself on getting off with a few tears and talk of him being "complicated." He'd really get complicated and see how she liked that.

Luke gripped the sides of the picture frame, putting his face so close his agitated breath clouded the glass. Her face still looked back at him. He would call her now, tonight, late as it was, and if her old man answered and gave him any guff he'd tell him what he could do with it. It came dully through to him that the room was chilly; that must be why he was shaking so.

He pulled on the pair of jeans he had left draped across the back of a chair, opened the door—just enough to let him squeeze through without the damn yelp he'd meant to oil it against—and went quickly and noiselessly down the stairs. Without turning the light on over the telephone he sat, willing his trembling to stop. Rather to his surprise it did—or slowed down so as to be scarcely noticeable. Motionless, his hands clenched on his knees, he tried to think out what he was going to say.

He would tell her what a big, dumb dope he'd been not to let her realize how much he loved her or that she loved him—whether she knew it or not! He'd say she had got confused and thought she was still in the clutches of that silly old romance with a guy she'd never be able to trust out of her sight. He'd tell her they were going to get engaged, Luke Sawyer and Milo Tarrant, as of this minute. Or, better still, they'd get married just as soon as possible. . . .

It made all kinds of sense. Luke grew almost calm thinking about it. It would be like his mother and father, marrying young and poor because they loved each other. His mother would give her consent and so would Milo's parents—when they saw he and she were in earnest and might do something desperate like eloping across the state line if they didn't. They'd get kicked out of school. So what. They could go to night school in Baysboro. He'd get a job that paid more than the one at the Shell Station and they could live here with his mother. She'd be glad to have them, tickled to death to have them. He'd even go to old Mr. Thad Wilson, humble himself, and ask for another chance at the job in the store. . . .

A muscle began to jerk in his leg and Luke shifted cautiously. Then it started in the other leg. He reached for the little chain to pull the light on, but the strength seemed to have gone out of him and he let his hand drop back to his knee. His grand thoughts were slipping away, others crowding in. Even if it wasn't so late, how could he say these things over the phone? She might simply hang up on him. . . . Who ever heard of spilling your life's blood out over a damn telephone? She'd think he'd gone off his rocker or got drunk. He put his hands over his face and whispered into his clammy palms, "Oh, God, I can't do it this way."

Luke eased himself up out of the chair and out of the dark cubbyhole. He stood outside the door of his mother's room, listening. When he heard the little snuffle that was the nearest thing to a snore she ever produced, he sighed and opened the door of the coat closet. He felt around the floor till he located a pair of old rubber boots and slipped his feet into them. He took his jacket from the hook and, putting the lock off, let himself out the front door.

He had forgotten the fog. More dense than ever, it folded itself about the street, wrapped the night in mystery. It looked solid at first, then nebulous, moving, lifting a second to reveal the dark shape of a shrub, the trunk of a dripping tree, then settling again, gray-white and impenetrable. All his life Luke had known and, in a way, loved the river fogs. But there was something strange in this one. Strange and menacing. He leaned against the house wall, straining his eyes to see through it.

He shook his head, muttered, "Nuts to you, Luke Henry," and went down the steps, feeling the flagstones through the flabby rubber soles of the boots. He walked toward the river, his shoulders hunched, his eyes straining but guided mainly by his feet—as he used to be, coming from the hut in the old days. The old, old days —hardly a year ago. . . .

Sometimes Luke could see for several yards with little difficulty, then he would strike a pocket and mist would enfold him, woolly and wet. The Princes' house was completely hidden and Luke had to feel his way by with the help of the saggy wire fence. He began to have an eerie feeling—as if he were a lost soul struggling through a purgatory of winding clouds. He knew it could hardly be midnight but the silence of the street suggested the early morning hours. He began to go over again in his mind what he planned to say to Milo. Tomorrow? Sunday? It didn't matter, just so it was soon.

They would live with Martha and she would be happy

233

to see Luke happy. She was very fond of Milo. They'd get along, anybody could get along with Martha. And Milo was sweet, Milo was. And it wouldn't kill him to crawl on his belly to old Mr. Thad; be good for him, probably. He'd likely exaggerated his dislike of the old goat. As a matter-of fact, Luke hadn't felt nearly so violent about him since Martha had told him off about it that night. And he could still get his diploma; he didn't have to do it on a stage in a long blue robe and a tasseled cap on his head. It was what was inside his head that mattered. What was inside his head . . .

Luke was near the river now. A few steps more and he would be where the road petered out into the path with all the roots waiting to trip him. He walked very slowly and carefully, "seeing" with his feet in the old rubber boots. He heard the burble of water, then the soft rushing farther up toward the mill race. He figured he was passing where the hut had been, back in the wild plum thicket.

The mist lifted suddenly—or dropped—for his head was in the clear. He shook his hair away from his face and drops flew as if he had been under water. He tipped his head back and saw the sky with one star visible, large and brilliant. His heart began to hammer. It was like a little miracle—the one brilliant star far above all the fog. He looked down, held his hands out at waist level and could barely make out the shapes of them. Something like fear brushed him and he said angrily, "Nuts."

In the grass to the side of him there was a panic skittering as some little woods creature—a rabbit maybe—fled in terror toward the thicket where the hut had been. The unseen creature's terror filled Luke with sadness—a tiny, pitiful part of all the fear and misery in the world. Some of it had shone in Susan Bently's eyes when she spoke of her mother. It was why she wanted to be a doctor or a nurse: to lessen the world's misery. It had been in Dr. Bob's tired face when he'd told Luke he had wanted to do something about the pain in the world.

If I worked for Mr. Thad Wilson, Luke thought, I could never be a doctor. I'd be trapped for the rest of my life in that store. Like Dad. So what? Who'd ever said he wanted to be a doctor? But as if he had no control over them, his thoughts persisted. Even if I managed to go to college and then to medical school, Milō wouldn't think much of that. It wouldn't be right to ask her to go through all those rough years. Even if I could make her see I'm the one for her she wouldn't, it would just be one long drag to her.

The root caught his foot then. Stumbling, flinging his arms out, he struck the trunk of a tree, caught at it, kept himself from falling. He leaned against it, panting, and out of nowhere those idiot words floated once more through his mind: Luke, the beloved physician. If he were a doctor, if such a crazy fool thing could ever happen, would people call him "Dr. Luke"? He liked it almost as well as "Dr. Bob."

The mist parted and, leaning against the tree, looking toward the sound of the river, Luke saw a dark gleam of water beyond the sandy bank. Then the mist drifted between him and the river again, thin as gauze. For some time he stood there, slumped against the wet tree trunk. He was dimly conscious of cold and of weariness, too tired to pull his jacket closer about him. He lifted his face, searching for the star—bright as the shiny trimming on Milo's blue dress—but the dripping branches of the tree, not quite bare of leaves, came between. He said in a whisper, feeling sentimental and not ashamed of it, "Milo, dear love."

Well, he guessed he had better be done with sentimentality for a while. He didn't have to get married. He couldn't in any case imagine himself ever getting married to anybody but Milo. Shivering against the tree, Luke felt as if he were saying good-bye to more than romantic love, much more. The days of the club and its members—to Butch already gone and the others who, even if they stayed, would not be the boys who had made the club but men, each with his own life to live. The time when Henry Sawyer was alive, the good and the bad of it, long gone it now seemed to Luke. What had Henry left his son besides a few thousand dollars to start him on a long, unknown road? A great deal, Luke knew, but his mind staggered under the effort of assessing any of it. He guessed the years ahead would have to do that, make sense out of what seemed senselessness now.

Luke rubbed his cold hand against the rough bark of the tree, trying to think. They weren't merely endings, not empty, stupid loss. He couldn't buy that. They must be—somehow—ways to beginnings. . . .

He started back, his feet feeling for the roots. The path sloped upward to River Street. He could see the blurred, distorted globes of the street lamps, see the fog swirling slowly, thinning gradually—or so it seemed. He pushed his hands into his pockets. The left one went through the torn lining he'd forgotten to tell his mother about and he flexed the fingers that were stiff with cold. It made him think again of Dr. Bob. He thought, Dr. Luke—and laughed aloud, the hoarse sound startling him in the silent, fog-walled night.

At the gate of Rollo's house Luke paused a moment, seeing now the weak eye of Aletha Prince's hall light. He thought of the times they'd told each other good night in the silly, swaggering way they all affected—

Rollo, Chuck, even little Sim, Butch and himself. He walked on. Fog draped the lower part of the Weavers' house but the roof showed dark against the sky. Luke turned his head, trying to gauge the level of the fog and saw that, here, it was about to his shoulders. It was weird, like wading with his head just above water.

Watch hobbled from the living room, whining, and Luke bent to touch his head. "Sh, boy, quiet," he whispered. The old dog padded stiffly back and after the three ritual turns lay down with a soft moan in front of Henry Sawyer's wing chair.

Luke followed the dog into the living room and stood beside his father's chair, dimly outlined by the veiled light from the street. His eyes still burned from the fog and he closed them. At once, the remembered image of his father sitting there etched itself sharply against his eyelids. It was so clear and perfect Luke trembled, expecting the remembered voice to come from the chair, call him "Son," say something that would in simple wisdom guide him.

The silence of the room, broken only by the old dog's asthmatic breathing, wrapped about Luke. He did not know whether he whispered or only thought, I'm going to study medicine, Dad—and envisioned Henry Sawyer's crooked smile, his blue eyes pleased and proud. Luke put a cold hand out and touched a wing of the worn chair, clutched it tightly, straining toward the comfort of something known and solid. He thought in a sort of sweet anguish, Whatever I am I hope I can be as good a man as my dad was.

Luke hung his jacket on the hook, put the boots in the closet, and crept upstairs. He hadn't turned out the light in his room; lucky his mother hadn't wakened and come up to see if he was sick or something. He was shaking pretty hard and now he knew it was from cold.

On the chest of drawers the big green stones in the cuff links looked like a cat's eyes reflecting the light from the lamp. The balky drawer gaped crookedly open as he had left it. Luke put the cuff links in their simulated leather box and tucked them into a corner of the drawer. He lifted Milo's picture and laid it beside them and closed the drawer, carefully and with patience.

"Simply one of the best novels written for any age group this year."—*Newsweek*

I AM THE CHEESE

BY ROBERT CORMIER
AUTHOR OF THE CHOCOLATE WAR

Adam Farmer is a teenager on a suspenseful quest, at once an arduous journey by bicycle to find his father and a desperate investigation into the mysteries of the mind. What exactly is Adam looking for? Where is his father? Why does he have two birth certificates? What is the meaning of his parents' whispered conferences? Of their sudden move to a new town? Of his mother's secret Thursday afternoon phone calls? Of the strange man who appears and reappears in their lives? And why are Adam's thoughts constantly interrupted by an unidentified interrogator who prods him to recall some recent, devastating catastrophe? "The secret, revealed at the end, explodes like an H-bomb."—*Publishers Weekly*

Laurel-Leaf Library $1.50

At your local bookstore or use this handy coupon for ordering:

Dell **DELL BOOKS**   I Am The Cheese $1.50 (94060-5)
P.O. BOX 1000, PINEBROOK, N.J. 07058

Please send me the above title. I am enclosing $_____
(please add 35¢ per copy to cover postage and handling). Send check or money order—no cash or C.O.D.'s. Please allow up to 8 weeks for shipment.

Mr/Mrs/Miss_____

Address_____

City_____State/Zip_____

"Unique in its uncompromising portrait
of human cruelty and conformity."
—*School Library Journal*

THE
CHOCOLATE
WAR

by Robert Cormier

A compelling combination of
Lord Of The Flies and *A Separate Peace*

Jerry Renault, a New England high school student,
is stunned by his mother's recent death and appalled
by the way his father sleepwalks through life. At
school, he resists the leader of a secret society by
refusing to sell candies for the chocolate sale, wondering: Do I dare disturb the universe?

"**Masterfully structured and rich in theme. . . .
The action is well crafted, well timed, suspenseful;
complex ideas develop and unfold with clarity.**"
—*The New York Times*

"**Readers will respect the uncompromising ending.**"
—*Kirkus Reviews*

"**Close enough to the reality of the tribal world of
adolescence to make one squirm.**"—*Best Sellers*

Laurel-Leaf Fiction $1.25

At your local bookstore or use this handy coupon for ordering:

Dell **DELL BOOKS** The Chocolate War $1.25 (94459-7)
P.O. BOX 1000, PINEBROOK, N.J. 07058

Please send me the above title. I am enclosing $_____
(please add 35¢ per copy to cover postage and handling). Send check or money
order—no cash or C.O.D.'s. Please allow up to 8 weeks for shipment.

Mr/Mrs/Miss_____

Address_____

City_____State/Zip_____